SHUNNED

A reverse harem bully romance

STEFFANIE HOLMES

Cover design: Amanda Rose

ISBN: 978-0-9951222-4-6

✿ Created with Vellum

JOIN THE NEWSLETTER FOR UPDATES

Get bonus scenes and additional material in *Cabinet of Curiosities*, a Steffanie Holmes compendium of short stories and bonus scenes. To get this collection, all you need to do is sign up for updates with the Steffanie Holmes newsletter.

www.steffanieholmes.com/newsletter

Every week in my newsletter I talk about the true-life hauntings, strange happenings, crumbling ruins, and creepy facts that inspire my stories. You'll also get newsletter-exclusive bonus scenes and updates. I love to talk to my readers, so come join me for some spooky fun :)

A NOTE ON DARK CONTENT

This series goes to some dark places.

I'm writing this note because I want you a heads up about some of the content in this book. Reading should be fun, so I want to make sure you don't get any nasty surprises. If you're cool with anything and you don't want spoilers, then skip this note and dive in.

Keep reading if you like a bit of warning about what to expect in a dark series.

- There is some bullying in the first couple of books, but our heroine holds her own. Our heroes have been born into cruelty and they'll need to redeem themselves.

- This series deals with themes of inequality and cycles of violence – there may be times where this is tough to read, especially if it hits too close to your lived reality.

- This is a reverse harem series, which means that in the end our heroine, Hazel, will have at least three heroes. She does not have to choose, and sometimes her heroes like to share. Although this book is set in high school, I'd call it R18 for sexual content.

- Subsequent books contain violence, threat of sexual violence (that doesn't succeed), and cruel and capricious cosmic deities.

Hazel and her friends are deep in a cruel, bloodthirsty world. It's not pretty, but I promise there will be suspense, hot sex, occult mysteries, and beautiful retribution. If that's not your jam, that's totally cool. I suggest you pick up my Nevermore Bookshop Mysteries series — all of the mystery without the gore and trauma and violence.

Enjoy, you beautiful depraved human, you :) Steff

To James,
Who didn't just stand up for me,
but taught me how to stand up for myself

"The most merciful thing in the world, I think, is the inability of the human mind to correlate all its contents. We live on a placid island of ignorance in the midst of black seas of infinity, and it was not meant that we should voyage far."

– HP Lovecraft, *The Call of Cthulhu* (1926)

CHAPTER ONE

Who the hell builds a school on top of an inaccessible cliff?

Whoever built Derleth Academy, my new school. I answered my own question as the car's wheel skidded over the rough gravel on the way up the steep peninsula. A scream escaped my lips as the car lurched toward the edge of the cliff, one wheel spinning completely free.

Muttering under his breath, the driver for the school slammed the car into reverse and backed us onto the road before slamming on the gas again. We continued our wary climb along the narrow gravel path.

Surely the Academy can't be completely *cut-off.* The school had to bring up food and supplies. Parents must visit on the weekends. My driver was certainly giving it his all, tearing around the corners like he was on a Formula 1 racetrack and not a goat path hugging the side of a mountain. I gritted my teeth and gripped the back of the seat as rocks rolled from beneath the wheels and clattered over the sheer drop into the raging waters below. One wrong move, and we'd tumble down a two-hundred-foot cliff and be dashed against the cliffs so hard and fast that boats would mistake our remains for rock paintings.

Not the way I ever imagined I'd go.

We passed into thick vegetation, the cliff and ocean on one side giving way to looming trees that blocked out the grey sky. I let out the breath I'd been holding. Branches scraped the sides of the car, and my phone beeped with protest as we moved out of cell range. *No contact with the outside world,* the school brochure read. *At Derleth Academy, we foster a competitive academic program requiring the full attention of our students. Distracting technology or personal items will not be tolerated.*

In other words, I couldn't call for help. It was the opening sequence to every horror film, ever.

Not that I had anyone to call. Not anymore.

"Almost there," the driver said, swinging the car around a hairpin corner and launching my stomach into my throat. It was the most words he'd spoken to me the entire trip. "You can see the school through the trees."

I squinted into the forest, trying to make out some kind of building that might pass as a school. But I couldn't see a thing. We rounded another corner and—

Well, that's terrifying.

We rolled between two towering stone pillars obscured by creeping vines, past an ornate sign that read DERLETH ACADEMY. A wide, pristine concrete drive flanked by an avenue of towering trees and wide, manicured lawns led up to an imposing stone building, stretching in all directions with narrow arched windows, spiky towers, and a row of leering gargoyles along the roof.

What is this place? It looked more like Dracula's castle than a prestigious preparatory school.

I couldn't believe the wealthiest people in the country sent their children up that winding road to get educated. *Who's the headmistress, Morticia Addams?* But according to the brochure, that was exactly what they did. In droves. Derleth Academy had a waiting list a mile long, and you couldn't even pay to get in. You had to be *invited*.

Somehow, I, Hazel Waite – an overachieving orphan from the wrong side of Philly – ended up on their radar.

I flashed back to the day two weeks ago, when a banging on the door of my dingy apartment dragged me from a deep slumber. A woman with coiffed hair and a designer suit that cost more than a car staggered backward in surprise when I glared at her through the chain wearing only my pajamas and what must have been a terrifying scowl. Well, *she* wasn't the one being dragged from a pleasant Jason Momoa sex dream during the four-hour reprieve between night shift at the diner and cleaning rooms at a retirement home.

"Are you Hazel Waite?" she asked, her brown eyes wide and curious.

"No. Piss off." I glowered, slamming the door in her face. She was probably from CPS, trying to force me into foster care. Fuck that. I only had seven more months to survive before I turned eighteen. No way was I going to spend it in the hell that had destroyed Dante.

The woman didn't go away. She sat out on the road in her sports car and waited me out. I had to leave for work or I'd lose my job, and it wasn't easy to find work when you were underage and using an obviously fake ID. As soon as I left the house, she ambushed me.

"I'm not here to hand you over to the authorities," she said hurriedly, shoving a thick envelope into your hands. "I'm a scholarship administrator from Derleth Academy in Arkham, Massachusetts. Your current school put you forward for one of our four senior scholarship positions – a fully funded year at a first-class prep school, where our students go on to attend the top colleges in the world. I know the first quarter has already started, but it's taken me this long to track you down. You've only missed a week so far."

I stared at the envelope in my hands, at the red, black and gold school crest – a crooked five-pointed star inside a shield with some kind of Latin phrase beneath it. *This has got to be a joke.*

"I know what you're thinking," the woman said. "It's not a joke or a trick. I promise you that it's not. If you come to Derleth, we will assume guardianship duties until you turn eighteen. You'll be housed, clothed, and have all your schoolbooks and other needs met, as well as receiving a first-class education. You're a promising student, Hazel, and I know you've been dealt a cruel lot in life. This could be where you turn everything around. Don't answer me now. Read over the paperwork, and I'll return tomorrow for your decision."

And now, just ten days after I signed my soul over to this school in exchange for paid tuition, room, and board, I stared up at the imposing facade and wondered if I'd made a terrible mistake.

Sure, my life was miserable. I was drowning in grief, and even working two jobs I could barely pull in enough money to survive. College was out of the question, because I couldn't finish high school without going into foster care. But at least all that was familiar territory. That was the world I'd grown up in – the world of pain and struggle and loss. Derleth Academy was the exact opposite. Every element of this building screamed wealth and privilege and *you don't belong here.*

The driver pulled to a stop on the wide circular drive beside a towering stone fountain. A woman with big doe eyes wearing a drab grey smock darted out of the shadows of the porch and approached the car. I held my hand out to her. "Hello, I'm Hazel Waite—"

The woman ducked her head, avoiding me. She popped open the trunk, hauled out my heavy suitcase and bookbag, and hurried off to the house with them before I could offer to help.

Weird much? I swiped a dreadlock off my face. My friend Dante's foster sister had done them for me last year, back when things were perfect and the most I had to worry about was whether my mom would ground me for getting dreadlocks.

An awful feeling twisted in my gut. I wished Mom was here, hating my loss, right now. But she was gone, gone, gone, and so was Dante, and it was just me and this terrifying school and no other options.

Three figures descended the grand stone steps toward me: A woman with translucent skin and a flowing black dress, flanked on either side by two students wearing the Derleth uniform. Fallen leaves skittered away from the woman's hem, and she moved with such poise that she appeared to float over the steps. With her severe features and a gauzy black ribbon pinned in her hair, she looked more like she was attending a funeral. Behind her, the two students – a guy and a girl – glared at me, distrust emanating from their every pore.

The woman stopped on the second-to-last step, peering down her nose at me as if I were a bug that wasn't even worth squashing. "You'll have to do something about that hair. We enforce a strict dress code in my school, Ms. Waite. I'll not have you flouting it on your very first day."

This must be the principal, Hermia West. My Morticia Addams guess wasn't far off. This woman looked like she drank the blood of students to sustain her beauty. The way her grey eyes stabbed right through me sent a cold shiver through my body.

There was nothing in the student handbook about dreadlocks. Although, of course, I'd only skim-read the thing on the bus from Philly. The handbook was boring. And *long.* "I'm sorry, Ms. West. I didn't know—"

"Ignorance is no excuse. That's 3 demerit points for you. And you're to refer to me as Headmistress."

Beside her, the boy sniggered. I turned my gaze to look at him, and my heart nearly stopped. *Wow, he's beautiful.* I had no idea boys that hot existed outside of magazines and Hollywood movies. He stood practically the same height as Ms. West, his broad shoulders accentuated by the tailored cut of his red-trimmed blazer. Prefect and merit badges decorated both lapels. Dark brown curls caught the grey light filtering through the clouds, throwing back beautiful shades of russet and silver. His clean-shaven face and high, majestic cheekbones appeared angelic, but his ice-blue eyes were cold and cruel.

The girl moved closer to him, touching his arm and shooting me a possessive glare, like a cat in heat. She had the appearance of a cat, too — slanted green eyes accentuated with heavy makeup, pointed chin, and the lithe body and long legs of a panther. Beautiful but deadly.

"This is Trey Bloomberg and Courtney Haynes," Headmistress West said. "I've appointed them as your student guides. They will show you the dorm, library, and dining hall, go over your schedule and classrooms, and ensure you understand *all* our rules. You will dine with the student body in two hours' time, and tomorrow you begin classes. I've had a copy of your schedule and the school handbook placed in your room. Memorize them, for failure to comply will result in further demerits. Here's your dorm room key."

In my pocket, my phone gave another defiant chirp. *Great.* I'd practically worn down the battery looking for a signal on the death road.

Headmistress West descended the last step to drop an ancient-looking metal key into my hand. Her pointy black boots lined up with my scuffed Docs. She loomed over me, her disapproval seeping into my bones. "You have a phone in your pocket." It wasn't a question.

"Yes."

Behind her, the boy smirked. I felt naked, exposed. My legs itched to make a run for the woods. Headmistress West held out her hand, unfurling long fingers topped with red-painted nails, the tips pointed like talons. "Hand it over. We don't allow outside technology on campus."

Instinctively, my hand flew to my pocket. "I won't use it to call or text. It doesn't work here, anyway, so what's the—"

"Ms. Waite, failure to obey a teacher's command is an automatic loss of 10 points. You seem most anxious to find out what punishments await the students at the bottom of the class list."

A lump rose in my throat. My phone contained photographs – snaps of my mom smiling demurely or brushing her hair in the mirror before she went out to work at the strip club. Of Dante and I hanging out around the neighborhood, smoking on the rusted playground behind my house, tagging the concrete wall of the boxing gym on the corner. Every other one of my possessions had been destroyed in the fire. Those photographs were practically all I had left of them.

Trey and Courtney covered their mouths with their hands, barely disguising their laughter. Courtney leaned over and whispered something to Trey. They both cracked up. Despite myself, my cheeks flushed. *Better get used to this.*

Headmistress West, of course, ignored them. She wasn't backing down on this phone thing. My fingers closed around it, the comfortable weight of it in my hand reminding me that it was one of the last connections to my old life.

What does it matter? They're gone. Looking at their photos won't bring them back. But this school could be the only chance I have at a real future.

My hand trembling, I dropped my phone into her talons. As soon as it left my hand, I itched to get it back. Headmistress West slipped the phone into a fold of her dress, where it disappeared from sight.

"Follow me." The headmistress swirled on her heel and floated up the stairs. Numb, I fell in step behind her. Trey came up beside me. His arm brushed mine, and a jolt of warmth rocketed through my body. I dared a look up at his face. As we moved into the shadow of the porch, the colors in his hair changed, becoming a deep brown and blood red. A curl flopped over his eye, and I noticed flecks of silver on the edges of those arresting blue irises. My fingers itched to reach up and swipe that curl off his face, to touch his smooth skin, feel his cheek move beneath my fingers, to cut myself on his cheekbones. A familiar longing pooled in my stomach, an ache that I'd never been able to sate before, and now never would.

I'd never seen a boy that *perfect*.

Trey's fingers brushed me again. My breath froze in my mouth as his hand lingered on my elbow. To anyone looking at us from a distance, it would appear as though he was helping me, steadying me up the steep steps. The touch on my skin was white-hot, lighting up parts of my body that hadn't felt anything since Dante... since before the fire. *How can this boy with such cruel eyes have this effect on me?*

When he caught me looking, Trey's perfect lips curled back into a sneer. His fingers tightened on my arm, squeezing my skin. Tighter, tighter, until he was cutting off circulation. I yelped in protest.

"You don't belong here," he murmured, his perfect lips forming hateful words. "You should leave now."

He said it so casually, like he was chatting about the weather, and that self-satisfied smirk never left his face. My stomach twisted, the air driving from my lungs as though he'd punched me.

"No thanks," I said brightly, pretending that I misunderstood him. "I'm good."

"We don't want you, and we're used to getting what we want. We're going to eat you alive, new meat." Trey flashed me a smile that was all teeth and violence. The venom in his eyes frightened me. *This is not a guy to mess with.*

Too bad he seemed to already have it out for me, and I hadn't even got inside the school yet. My plan to keep my head down and stay invisible fizzled before my eyes. Already I could see how the school year was going to play out. *We don't want you here.* Trey spoke for the entire student body. He was a King in this school.

It was written in his smile, dripping from the menace in his words.

I'd pissed him off. Just by existing. Just by setting foot on the hallowed grounds of his kingdom. *Well, fuck you, Trey Bloomberg.* I could handle a year of insults and loneliness if I got my diploma at the end of it. My life was already hell on earth – if Trey Bloomberg thought he could break me, he'd have to try a lot harder.

I wrenched my arm away from us. "Don't touch me." Behind us, Courtney giggled.

"Yeah, Trey. You should know not to handle garbage. She's a gutter-trash whore who's probably fucked so many guys that your dick wouldn't even touch the sides."

The comment stung. I thought of my sweet mother, all candy smiles and sticky skin as she stripped off her sweat-soaked lace g-string and six-inch heels after her shift and pulled on the cloud-pink pajamas I found for her in a thrift store. A hard lump rose in my throat. I shoved the image aside. *Not now.*

Wait until you get to your room, until you're alone, then you can break down.

"I guess we're not going to be braiding each other's hair," I muttered to Courtney.

"I wouldn't touch that rat's nest on your head if someone hid a *Faberge* egg inside," Courtney sneered. "I bet it's got real eggs in it, though. Insect eggs, laid by the gross things crawling around in there."

Instinctively, my hand flew up to my face, to touch the dread-lock that always fell over my eye, to tuck it behind my ear – a gesture that Dante would so often do when he noticed my locs in my eyes, which was all the time because I liked them unruly. Ever since the fire, I'd been touching my own hair more and more, seeking the comfort of the familiar weight of a hand moving the dreadlocks. But it wasn't the same. It would never be the same.

Courtney wrinkled her face in disgust, while Trey continued to smirk at me. The force of his loathing sank my stomach to my knees. He didn't even know me, but it didn't matter.

At the top of the stairs, the headmistress turned and frowned at me. "Don't dawdle," she snapped. "The school doesn't bite."

"She's wrong," Trey whispered. "Are you ready to find out just how bad we bite?"

The lump of hard, bitterness burned at the back of my throat. They were right. I didn't belong here. I was the poor gutter-trash girl from the wrong side of the tracks, and they were *royalty*. They were the monarchs. *They're going to make my life miserable, and there's nothing I can do.*

CHAPTER TWO

I followed Headmistress West beneath a pair of towering wooden doors into an enormous atrium. You could fit my entire Philly apartment building into this one room. Diffused light poured from a stained-glass dome in the roof, projecting prisms of colors across the marble floor. I noticed the red glass in the dome formed the school's star-shaped crest. Hallways snaked off in both directions, and two sweeping staircases led to the second story. Glass French doors at the back of the atrium led into an enclosed courtyard at the center of the academic buildings and dormitories – open now, letting a cool breeze and a few stray fall leaves blow in. Class must've been in session, because apart from a man in academic dress crossing the upper landing and two women in grey smocks polishing a gilt frame, the space was empty.

Headmistress West's shoes clopped across the marble floor, echoing through the cavernous space. She stopped in front of three enormous electronic boards in gilt frames that hung above the staircase. They flashed a list of names with numbers, some of which flicked up or down a few points. Trey Bloomberg was at the top with 1163 points. Two below him, after someone named Ayaz Demir with 1102 points, was Courtney Haynes, with 1051 points.

"These are the class lists," Headmistress West explained. "Every student is listed in their year, along with their current points total. Points are awarded based on academic excellence, distinction in extracurricular activities, and service to the school. Tardiness, rudeness, and behavior unbecoming of Derleth's reputation will result in a loss of points. Teachers can give or deduct merit points at any time, for any reason. Your ranking will not only determine your place in the final end-of-year list, but throughout the year your ranking will determine rewards you receive, as well as punishments or privileges withheld for falling below certain thresholds. Here, we teach our students that all actions have consequences, and that their hard work offers tangible rewards."

Oooo-kay. At my old school, we also had a class list. I was always the top. Only, students didn't see that list until the end of the year, and it couldn't be affected by how well you played sports or your phone usage or how you styled your hair. Our faculty was too busy worrying about kids bringing knives to school and gangs selling drugs in the cafeteria. At Derleth, I'd get a reminder every day as I walked past the boards exactly where I fell in the hierarchy.

Also, how can Trey have over eleven-hundred points already? It's only three weeks into the quarter, and he doesn't exactly look like a teacher's pet.

Succeeding at Derleth already felt impossible, and I'd only been here twenty minutes. I scanned the list for my name, but before I got halfway down, the headmistress nodded to Trey. Without saying another word to me, she whipped around and hurried away, disappearing into a small door beneath the staircase labeled Faculty Only. I winced as the slamming door shattered the vast and silent space.

A hand grabbed my shoulder. "You're ours now," Trey whispered against my ear, his voice soft, menacing.

I hated the way my body reacted as his touch, to the tickle of his breath against my skin. My pulse quickened. A hot flush dropped through my stomach, scorching me between my legs. I chewed on my lip, forcing myself to remember that this guy hated me just because I existed, that his touch was meant to unnerve me, not excite me. "I told you not to touch me."

Trey whirled me around, pressing my back against the carved balustrade. His gaze swept over my body, his lips curling into a sneer as he took in every inch of me. *Cut a girl some slack, man.* I'd been traveling for twelve hours, first on a smelly bus from Philly, and then the final three with the school's driver on that wild road. My dreadlocks were plastered to the back of my neck. My rumpled clothes – Dante's old basketball tank and my cuffed red pants – hung off my narrow frame in an unflattering way. My scuffed black Docs looked ridiculous next to his and Courtney's impossibly shiny dress shoes. Judging by the way Courtney sniffed the air and wrinkled her nose, I guessed that I smelled like a truck stop.

I sure do know how to make an excellent first impression.

"You need to understand a few things about your new school, Meat," Trey said, his casual tone making his words even more sinister. *Lovely, I've already got a nickname.* "Number one – my parents donate the money that pays for your place at this school. If it weren't for them, you'd be back in the gutter where you belong. You owe my family, and you owe me – don't ever forget that. Number two – no one wants you here. The adults might think it's a good idea to pretend to be good samaritans and lift some hopeless alley cat out of the gutter, but we know better. Trash like you is just going to screw up the curve and punish everyone. When standards slip, we all suffer, and since you're at the bottom, you'll suffer more than anyone. Number three, and this is the most important – I *am* this school. Courtney and I and our friends are the royalty. We're your Kings and your Queens, and you and the rest of the scholarship students lick our boots.

You'll be good at that – I bet your mother taught you the best ways to pay reverence to your betters." He grabbed his crotch, his cruel laugh like shattered glass against my already battered defenses.

"And don't think about hiding from us or reporting to the teachers, because we have spies everywhere, don't we, Trey?" Courtney beamed, tossing her golden blonde hair over her shoulder. "We can see your every move, Meat. Hell, we can see into your darkest dreams and innermost thoughts. So be very, very careful."

"If you're trying to scare me with your horror film introduction, you've failed dismally," I retorted, yanking myself from Trey's grasp. "This is a school, not some fucking cult."

"Is that so?" Trey's lips curled back into a twisted smile.

"Yeah, it is so. You don't like me? Fine. I've known you for a couple of minutes and already you're off my Christmas card list. I'm not here to make trouble or get in the way of your fun. I'm not going to tattle to your daddy or wreck your prom. As soon as I have my diploma in my hand, I'm out of your hair. All this 'we own the school' nonsense is a bit over-the-top. It's a little pathetic, actually. Is it what you do to make yourselves feel good? Because personally, I'd just masturbate more. Especially you." I grinned at Courtney. "A few flicks of the bean would make you so much happier."

It turns out, rich bitches like Courtney didn't find masturbation jokes particularly funny. Courtney made a growling noise in the back of her throat. She lunged at me, but Trey held out a lazy arm and shoved her back. "Leave her," he said. "She's not worth losing points over. We'll get her in our own time."

Their eyes blazed at each other, throwing down a battle of wills. Courtney looked like she was going to argue with him, but she lowered her arm and stepped back. *Probably practicing for when she's a submissive housewife,* I thought, but wisely didn't say. Trey wrung his triumph from her with an easy smile that made my knees wobble. Above our heads, a bell clanged.

"Saved by the bell," Trey mused. "You're lucky, Meat."

The school erupted with the rumble of a stampeding herd. Doors banged, lockers jangled, voices echoed around the vaulted ceilings, and expensive soles scuffed the pristine marble. Students surged into the atrium, shoving and talking and laughing and passing notes. Someone bounced a tennis ball off the wall. It ricocheted off one of the portraits along the staircase and smashed a ceramic vase off a side table. The two women in grey smocks – who I guessed were on the cleaning staff – rushed over to pick up the pieces.

A sea of red and gold and tartan ebbed and flowed down the stairs, along the hallways and landing, surging and undulating as it spread to all corners. Students noticed me standing with Trey and Courtney. No one spoke directly to me or them, but a hundred unblinking eyes watched me. Whispers flew in all directions. I swallowed. I wanted to say something witty, but their attention unnerved me. Why did they care so much that I was here? Couldn't they just ignore me?

Courtney waved her arms above her head. The crowd stopped dead. She waited until she had everyone's attention. "This way, New Meat," she trilled, turning on her heel so that her short skirt flared out, giving those below her on the staircase a look at her lacy black underwear and garters. I didn't want to turn my back on the crowd, but I felt like Courtney and Trey were more dangerous, so I followed them up the staircase, across the landing, and down a wide, vaulted corridor lined with classrooms and lockers. Apparently, because the dorms were on the opposite side of the school to the dormitory wing, all the students had lockers as well. *Lazy asses*.

Something hit my back, and the corridor erupted with laughter, but I ignored it.

As we passed the classrooms, I peered inside, surprised at the timeless quality to the school. Everything was extremely fancy – from the elaborate moldings to the thick drapes on the windows and the ornate wooden desks for the teachers, but so *old*. I didn't see a single laptop on a desk or electronic blackboard on the wall. Weren't fancy schools like this supposed to have all the latest tech?

"Hey Courts, Trey. Is that the new meat?" A guy fell in step beside us. Shoulder-length dirty blond hair hung over amber eyes that sparkled with mischief, and his mouth turned up in the corners into one of those dazzling smiles that probably had girls prostrating themselves at his feet. He wasn't as tall or broad as Trey, but he was definitely fit and knew it. I caught a whiff of a distinctive scent – coconut and sugarcane and something spicy. Playful and flirty, like that smile. *Is everyone at this school a movie star?* The new guy licked his bottom lip as he looked me over. "She's tasty."

Ah, so he may be handsome, but he's also a dick. He's dicksome.

"She's barely a morsel," Trey grinned, but there was no mirth in his smile. "She's all yours if you like your pussy ragged and gaping."

Jesus fucking Christ. I glared at Trey, but he either didn't notice or didn't care.

"Hey, all pussy is good pussy. What's your name, Meat?" The guy draped his arm over my shoulder. I shrugged it off, noticing the edge of a tattoo peeking out from his white cuff. It looked a little like a Nordic rune – I knew all about runes because the skinhead gang at my old school used them. But this guy didn't look like a skinhead. For one thing, he had that luscious hair that just begged for fingers to run through it...

New Guy was looking at me with amusement. I realized I'd trailed off into my thoughts without answering his question. "Hazel Waite," I replied.

"Well, Hazel Waite, I'm Quinn Delacorte, and I'm here to show you a good time. I'm your King and resident manwhore.

Any time you get sick of Trey's shit, you come to me. I'll fuck you until you forget his name. I'm not picky. I'll take any pussy, tight and gaping and everything in between."

Quinn's easy smile suddenly felt malicious, threatening. He tried to touch me again, and I shrunk away. He burst out laughing. Trey and Courtney joined in, their guffaws stabbing at my chest.

"See you later, Meat." The swarm of students swallowed Quinn, leaving me at the mercy of Trey and Courtney. We passed over a covered stone footbridge into another building, through a double set of doors, and turned into a long wing. Instead of marble tiles, my feet sank into a deep pile carpet. There were no lockers here, only rows of doorways with looming gilded portraits and cork notice-boards hanging between them. Each door was numbered with a gold plaque bearing a student's name. Students disappeared into the rooms, swinging their bookbags and calling out to their friends. I peeked inside at sumptuous suites filled with four-poster beds, ornate furniture, and framed artwork on the walls. Was this how rich kids lived? The apartment I'd been renting didn't even have a bedroom – I'd just been sleeping on a couch. When I lived with Mom, my room had been barely larger than a closet, with a cheap bedspread and hip hop posters and Dante's artwork stuck to the walls with old chewing gum. These students dorms were what I'd always imagined a palace to look like. If I have a room like this to escape to, I could deal with people like Trey and Courtney.

Maybe Derleth Academy won't be so bad after all.

At the end of the hall, Trey shoved me toward a narrow staircase – the kind installed in medieval houses for servants to use so they'd be seen and not heard. "You're down here," he said.

Confused, I descended with Trey and Courtney at my heels. Down, down, down I trudged. Three narrow flights of winding metal stairs, lit by a single dim bulb. The echoes of laughing teens faded into a dull roar as I reached the base of the stairs. No lights lit the dark chasm. Panic rose in my chest. *Where am I? Did they take me to some kind of basement so they could torture me in secret?*

Trey flicked a switch behind my head, illuminating a line of dim fluorescent lights running along a narrow corridor. On either side were wooden doors, riveted with large iron bolts. With the old candle sconces still hanging from the bare stone walls, the place really did look like a dungeon.

I ran my hand along the stone. It was damp and cold to the touch. "What is this place?"

"Isn't it obvious?" Trey swung me around, pointing my nose to the center of a door. A small number was scrawled directly on the wood in white chalk.

S02.

But that's... my room number. My Derleth welcome pack had identified my room as S02.

"Welcome home, Meat," Trey rasped in my ear. His tongue flicked out and licked my earlobe.

I should have been disgusted, but my body reacted by flushing with heat. Trey's touch was like throwing gasoline on a raging fire—

At the thought of fire, my body tensed up and my skin crawled. Trey sensed my reaction and laughed cruelly. He must have thought that it was him, but it wasn't.

"Stop that." I spun around, my hand swinging up toward his face. I'd learned a few dirty fighting tricks from Dante. You didn't survive in the Badlands of Philly without knowing how to break a few fingers or a nose. Maybe what Mr. King-Of-The-School needed was for someone to ugly him up a bit.

But it wasn't going to be me. At least, not today. Trey grabbed my wrist, stopping my punch midair.

"Tut tut, Meat. You don't raise your hand to your betters," he sneered.

"Let go of me. If you don't want to get punched, don't fucking *lick* people without permission."

Trey sighed, as though he were thoroughly exasperated with me. "I'm going to go easy on you, because you're new and haven't yet learned that in this school, you're not considered a *person*. You're a bag of bones and meat that takes up precious oxygen I could be using. *Tasty* meat," Trey licked the bottom of his lip, mirroring his friend Quinn, only in a more menacing way, "but meat all the same. Now, open your door like a good girl and we'll all see just what my parents' scholarship money will buy a gutter whore."

Do I have to do this with them watching? This room was supposed to be my private space, my sanctuary. I didn't care how shit it was, because obviously I wasn't getting a suite like the students upstairs. *Fine, whatever. I don't care*. But it was supposed to be *mine*. I didn't want them invading it.

Trey folded his arms. Courtney cocked out her hip. My monarchs had spoken. *Guess I've got no choice*. My hand trembled as I inserted the key into the lock. It took me three tries to get it to turn. Trey's cruel eyes crawled up my back.

The room was dark when I stepped inside. I fumbled along the wall for a light switch and flicked it on.

The room wasn't as bad as I expected. In that, it contained a bed with an actual mattress and not one of nails or a torture rack. Two beds, in fact. I must have a roommate, judging by the clothing hanging in the closet and books already stacked on one end of the desk.

A really boring roommate. Apart from the books and a small pink ribbon tied around the iron bedpost, there was no sign of personality in the room. No pictures on the walls, no books on the nightstand or band stickers on the binders. Nothing to tell me who I'd been stuck with.

"Let me guess," I said dryly. "Scholarship students are on this floor?"

"Suites go to the students who can afford them. My parents already pay enough to charity cases like you – they're not going to deprive my trust fund just so you can enjoy luxuries you didn't earn."

"What do you mean?" I said sarcastically. "This *is* the ultimate luxury. I'm used to living in the gutter, remember. You telling me the dungeon was occupied?" I surveyed the bare walls and the single tiny window. It really did look like a prison cell.

"I wouldn't make suggestions you don't want to come true," Trey growled. Courtney tossed her hair over her shoulder and wrinkled her nose.

"I'm bored, Trey. And the damp down here is flattening my hair. Let's go."

Trey followed Courtney to the door. *What are you, her lap-dog?* I wanted to say, but I bit my tongue.

"Wait, you're supposed to show me where my classes—"

The door slammed shut behind me. *Guess I'll be finding my own way around.* I sat on the edge of my bed, turning my hand over and running my finger over the small raised stain on my skin, the only reminder of the burns on my hands. As I touched it I could almost feel the heat on my skin, the pain of holding fire in my hands paling in comparison to hearing my mother's screams. I dug my nails into the palm of my hand until the pain cut through my nerves and I could breathe normally again.

Don't let them bother you. They're just basic bitch bullies. You've dealt with bullies before, and these ones don't even have knives.

Why did they need knives? Trey Bloomberg had money and power and he had the top position in the class list, the position I needed to get a good scholarship. He didn't need a blade to cut me down.

"Ouch." My voice rang in the empty, cold room. I stared down at my palm. My nail had cut through the skin, and I'd drawn blood. Droplets of red pooled in my palm.

A rush of relief hit me. The pain drew me back to the present, reminding me that I was here, that I'd already survived the worst thing that could possibly happen to me. *Nothing Trey or his minions can do to me will ever hurt me like losing Mom and Dante...*

I turned away, looking for something to distract me. My suitcase lay on my bed, the zippers pulled open.

I flipped open the lid, and my heart thudded in my chest. Someone had riffled through my things, unfolding the clothes, tearing open the side pockets, unscrewing the lid from my dread wax, scrunching up my underwear. *Someone touched my underwear.*

Hang on. I don't see the journal—

Panic rose in my throat. I tore through the case, strewing my clothes around the room. *Please let it be here... please...*

But it wasn't. I tipped the entire case upside down and turned the pockets inside out, but it wasn't there. Someone had taken my journal.

"No." I blinked back tears. That doe-eyed woman must have gone through my case when she dropped it off here. She was probably looking for contraband.

But that journal wasn't contraband. Apart from my phone, it was the most precious thing I owned. I knew the school didn't allow outside stimuli like computers and phones and magazines, but surely, a book of scribbles and drawings wasn't going to harm anyone.

I slumped down on the bed. A single tear spilled over, carving a salty trail down my cheek. I wiped it away angrily. Another tear followed, and another.

I'm supposed to be strong. But I don't know if I'm strong enough for this school.

More tears fell. I didn't wipe them away. I let them drop onto Dante's tank. The tiny dots of liquid would remind me that crying was a sign of weakness, and I couldn't show any weakness here, not in front of Trey or Courtney or Quinn or any of the other monarchs – and certainly not in front of my roommate, whoever they were. This might be the only private moment I had left.

The springs sagged under my weight, poking into my thighs.

Behind my head, a faint scritch-scritch sounded inside the wall. Which was weird, because the walls looked to be solid stone, but I knew that in old places like this there was often a gap between the walls for drainage. *Probably just rats. How lovely.*

Scritch-scritch. Scritch-scritch—

Creak!

The door swung open. My chest tightened as I turned toward it. *What now?*

CHAPTER THREE

I expected to see Trey in the doorway, gloating over the tears streaking down my cheeks. Instead, a short girl stood in the hall with her mouth open in shock. Her dark skin glowed like ebony beneath the fluorescent light, and she wore her frizzy hair in a bob cropped close to her head. The expensive tailored uniform of Derleth clung to her like a sack. Deep brown eyes widened as she took me in. She looked like she was about to keel over with fright.

If this girl had spent the day dealing with Trey and Courtney and their cronies, I couldn't blame her for being afraid. At a guess, I'd say I was looking at my roommate. It was nice to see someone who looked like me – a little slice of home in this terrifying school. I stood up and offered my hand. "Hi, I'm Hazel. We're gonna be sharing a room until one or both of us is eaten by the rats in the walls."

She didn't react to my joke or even take my hand. She remained rooted in place, her right foot shuffling backward as though preparing herself to make a run for it. Her bookbag slid down her shoulder and dropped to the floor. "I... I didn't know I was getting a roommate."

"The second bed didn't give it away?" I grinned to show I was kidding. This girl was gonna have to get used to me mouthing off, because I was like Niagara Falls when I got going. A constant stream of filth you couldn't shut off.

She still didn't move from the door, rocking her weight to her back foot. At any moment I expected her to spring away like a deer. I tried again. "As I said, my name is Hazel. Hazel Waite. I've come up from Philly. I won the Derleth scholarship, although I'm starting to doubt that it was actually a prize worth winning. It took them a while to track me down, which is why I'm late starting."

"I won a Derleth scholarship, too," she blurted out in a thick accent. "My name is Loretta Putnam. I'm from Louisiana."

"Hey, Loretta Putnam from Louisiana. You can come in, you know. I won't bite."

She winced. I wondered if my choice of words was triggering, given all the talk about 'new meat' from Trey. I bet he gave her the same treatment when she arrived at school.

Without turning her back on me, Loretta skated around the edge of the room and perched on the corner of her bed. "You should run away while you have the chance."

"It's tempting, but nah. I got nowhere *to* run."

She nodded. "Yeah, me neither."

"You an orphan too?" My boots clattered against the bare floorboards as I kicked them off and folded my legs underneath me.

She nodded, but didn't volunteer any more information.

"Loretta, I don't know if you're aware, but this is the part of the conversation where we bond over our mutually fucked up pasts. You want to elaborate on your story there?"

She stared at the floor, forcing out every word like it was a battle. "My mom died when I was three. My dad was never in the picture. I've been living with my grandparents, but..." she trailed off, her features going blank as she shut down. Whatever it was that filled in the blank at the end of her sentence, it was clearly so traumatic for her that she couldn't speak it aloud.

"That's cool," I shrugged, giving her the chance to focus on me instead. I wanted to ask her how her mom died, but she clearly wasn't up to talking about it, even though it was so long ago. *Does it really never get better?* "I was raised by a single parent, too. My mom was a dancer, and I guess sometimes she did... other stuff. My dad was one of her clients. He doesn't even know I exist. It was just Mom and me against the world until two months ago, when she was killed in a house fire along with my best friend. I dropped out of school to get a fake ID and work a couple of shit jobs so I wouldn't have to go into foster care, but these bozos found me, so I guess I wasn't very good at hiding."

It seemed impossible, but Loretta's eyes widened even further. "You could go back. Just walk out the gates and go back to your jobs."

"Nah." I shrugged. "I'm just going to tough it out."

Loretta nodded, swallowing hard. "You look tough," she whispered, staring at my scuffed Docs and ghetto outfit. For some reason I couldn't identify, her scrutiny made me feel self-conscious.

An awkward silence settled between us.

Loretta wrung her hands together. I noticed her nails were ragged, bitten down nearly to the quick. I didn't want to upset her further, but I was desperate for more information. "I am tough. I can show you how to be tough, too. How have your first three weeks been? What's the school like?"

She winced. "Bad. Who did you get as your student hosts?"

"Trey Bloomberg and Courtney Haynes."

Loretta winced again. "I'm sorry. They're the worst."

"Really? They seem like such *lovely* people. I think we're gonna be BFFs." I held up the top of my suitcase. "Did you go through this? A woman in a grey smock took it from the car.

Supposedly she also delivered it here, but someone's gone through it and taken something of mine."

She shook her head. "Anyone wearing grey is maintenance staff. They clean the rooms and take care of the grounds. I haven't touched your bag. I haven't returned to the room since breakfast. One of the teachers probably searched it."

"They did more than search it. They stole something. I understand if I packed a bottle of liquor or a t-shirt that said 'Derleth Academy Sucks Balls,' but my friend's journal is missing."

Loretta gave a faint smile at my joke. "A journal? Why did you bring something like that?"

I lifted up one of my boots to show her the gaping hole in the sole. "I couldn't exactly afford to rent a safe deposit box."

Loretta took in my outfit with her wide, terrified eyes, as though she was only seeing my clothes for the first time. *What are the chances it's that I'm just too amazing to take in all at once?* "You have to change. You can't wear that to the dining hall. They'll crucify you."

Ah, so not amazing, then.

"They'll literally hang me on a cross with nails through my hands because I'm wearing these pants?" I lifted an eyebrow as I tugged on the drawstring waist. *I'd like to see them try.*

"You met Courtney Haynes. Her mother is the designer Gloria Haynes. Tillie's dad makes gold watches for the super-rich. Amber's parents are in men's fashion. People at this school *really* care about fashion. Please, wear your uniform," Loretta crossed her arms. "Or I can't sit with you."

"Jesus fucking Christ." I flipped open my suitcase. "It's like I'm living in a bad teen movie. Here, look." I threw off Dante's tank and tugged on the starched white shirt. Loretta ducked as my pants flew at her head. I deliberately misbuttoned my blazer and struck a model's pose. "How do I look? Like the next valedictorian of Derleth Academy?"

That earned a derisive snort from Loretta. "You're never going to catch up."

Her comment confused me, but then I realized she must be talking about the class list. The first quarter started three weeks ago (Derleth used a quarter system instead of two semesters, because they were super rich and fancy and could do whatever the hell they wanted, I guess?). Luckily, I hadn't missed any major tests or assignments, but I'd have to put in some long hours at the library if I wanted to stay on track academically.

"So I have to study a little harder." I shrugged. "I have the time. Based off the warm welcome I've received so far, I'm guessing I'm not going to be inundated with social invitations."

"It doesn't matter how hard you study. I've been pulling all-nighters since I got here." Loretta glanced toward the huge stack of textbooks on the desk. "I've had perfect scores on three pop quizzes, and I'm only up to 58 points."

58? I remembered that Trey Bloomberg already had over eleven-hundred. "Do the points accumulate over years or something? I saw the list in the atrium. Some of the other students have quite a lot more than that."

"They're awarded points based on how much money their parents donate to the school," Loretta whispered. "They call it 'service' to the school, but really they're buying their way to the top."

"That's not fair."

"You have no idea." A loud bell rang. Loretta jumped up. "I've got to go."

"What is it now?" My hand flew to my pocket to check the time on my phone. Pain stabbed at my gut as I came up with thin air.

Loretta grabbed a book from her desk and sprinted for the steps. "It's electives. If you're still wearing your uniform, you can find me in the dining hall tonight."

That's right. I had to eat in the dining hall this evening. That sounded like torture. I guessed I couldn't count on my student guides to show me the cool tables.

Loretta hurried off. Sighing, I smoothed down my tartan skirt, picked up a blank notebook, pen, and my room key. *I guess it's up to me to figure out this school by myself.*

CHAPTER FOUR

Turns out I was right to leave my room. I needed the whole hour to find the dining hall. Derleth Academy was a *labyrinth*. Sometimes it seemed as if hallways changed places, or doors opened into different rooms than before. I walked up and down the dormitory wing, locating a laundromat, a long dark cupboard filled with starched linen, and a common room for seniors with a toaster and microwave ovens, designer sofas, and an ancient-looking vending machine. I started drawing a map in my notebook but I had to make so many crosses and corrections it looked more like a Picasso sketch.

As I stalked the classroom corridors, the bell rang again. I got swept up in a mob of students heading toward the dormitories. Bodies slammed into me, turning me around and crashing me about.

A rough hand grabbed me, pulling me out of the fray. Quinn's emerald eyes met mine as he dragged me into an alcove – a brief respite from the crush of the crowd.

"Hello again, Meat," he grinned, raking a hand through his hair. I wondered how he got away with keeping his hair long like that when I wasn't allowed dreadlocks. "I love your dreadlocks. Totally badass. Can I pull on them?"

I shook off his arm. "Why are you talking to me? Didn't Trey forbid it or something?"

"Trey's only one of the Kings at this school. He's not the boss of me. Where are you going? You looked like you were trying to swim against the tide out there."

Quinn watched me with interest. Unlike his buddy Trey, he didn't seem outwardly hostile. He was clearly one of those guys who was just out for a good time. I'd even consider going there – he looked so delicious, all surfer hair and soft puppy eyes and that heart-melting smile. But there was something in the upward tug of his mouth that told me I'd better watch him, that his indifference could be just as cruel as Trey's malice.

"I was trying to find the dining hall and my classes for tomorrow," I rolled my eyes. "My student guides haven't exactly been forthcoming with information."

"Allow me to escort you." He gave a deep bow and held out his hand, like a prince asking a princess for a dance at the ball. I guess he was a King, so I should be flattered.

"No thanks." I wasn't about to trust a friend of Trey's, even one with surfer hair. For all I knew, Quinn would lock me in a closet somewhere and I'd miss dinner completely. As if anticipating that move, my stomach growled in protest. I hadn't eaten all day. I shoved off the wall and launched myself into the cascade of students.

Quinn yanked me back again, wrenching my arm nearly out of its socket. "You don't want my company?"

"Not really." I rubbed my shoulder. "I would like my arm back."

He dropped my arm. "Too bad. I just saved you from being crushed, and now you owe me a favor. Two favors, actually, since I saved you twice."

I rolled my shoulder in circles, trying to get feeling back in my arm. "You just jerked me around like a dick and probably pulled a muscle. I'd hardly call that worthy of a medal, let alone a *favor*."

"You think your favors are worth shit at this school?" he sneered, and a hint of that cruelty I knew he was hiding flashed in his emerald eyes. Dicksome as he was, he did raise a valid point.

"I'm just trying to get to the dining hall. Thanks for the shoulder injury." I turned back to the hallway. The crowd had thinned a little. A group of girls stopped in front of the lockers opposite us. They kept darting glances at Quinn and me and giggling. *Jesus, no need to act like total sluts. He's not that good looking.*

Okay, he was, but *still*—

"Meat, wait!"

I turned. I never should have turned.

"If I tell you where the dining hall is, what do I get in return?" Quinn waggled his eyebrows.

"I said forget it. I'll find it on my own." I shoved past him. I was able to fight my way down to a narrow corridor that led to a set of steps I hadn't noticed before. There were no lights on in the stairwell, but they weren't blocked off or anything. *Odd. I wonder where these lead.*

As I searched the walls for a sign or map, a familiar *scritch-scritch* noise sounded from behind the wood paneling. At least I knew the rats are everywhere. They weren't something blocked into the basement walls for the sole purpose of terrorizing scholarship students.

It seemed weird, though. I wouldn't have guessed rich bitches like Courtney would put up with rats in the walls.

"I wouldn't go that way if I were you."

I whirled around. Quinn leaned against the wall, watching me with an amused expression. He stepped toward me. The light in the hallway backlit his silhouette, highlighting his muscled shoulders and the curve of his ass. Damn, that boy made dress slacks look fine—

I lifted an eyebrow. "Oh yeah?"

"Yeah. That's the gym. It's off limits because of contamination. Didn't you read your rulebook?"

"That thing's a Tolstoy novel – long and boring and filled with communist plots. How do you mean, contaminated?"

"It started a few years ago – this horrible smell like rotting meat wafting up from under the gymnasium. It seeps out of the vents in that wing. It got so bad that students were fainting. They had experts in to perform tests to try and figure out what was causing it."

"My mom couldn't even get a HVAC repair person to come to our second-floor apartment. You rich bastards managed to get someone to drive up that demented road just because some idiot left his sandwich in a vent?"

"It was a whole team of guys in hazmat suits," Quinn beamed. His smile sent a burst of flame through my chest. "But they couldn't figure out what was making the smell. The best they could come up with was that there's a pocket of gas under there that's been disturbed. Parents were complaining." Quinn put on a faux high voice. "'My little Sissy won't be attending school in a toxic waste dump.' That kind of thing. So the faculty had to close that wing until they could fumigate it. Now we have gym outside in all weather. It's interesting in winter with four inches of snow on the ground."

"Something to look forward to."

"It makes all the girls' nipples hard, so no complaints from me." Quinn's eyes traveled over my body, stopping at my chest. His gaze made me feel naked, like he could somehow see my nipples through my blazer and shirt. I hated that I liked it, but I liked it. "That uniform is working for you."

"My fist will be working for your face if you don't quit eye-fucking me," I growled.

"You have a mouth from the gutter, that's for sure." Quinn held out his arm. "Come on, I'll show you the dining hall. Walk in there on my arm and your social status will be a notch or two above amoeba. It'll be a hoot, and I'll even consider it one of your favors."

I entertained Quinn's offer for a moment. So far, he'd been the friendliest person I'd encountered today, which wasn't saying much. He clearly wasn't lying about his manwhore status, but he was one of the Kings, which meant that he could protect me. If he felt like it.

But that was just the thing. No way did I trust this guy, especially not when he was cut from the same cloth as Trey and Courtney. I didn't want any part of their world, especially not if it meant trying to suck up to dicksome jerks like Trey. *Especially* when I couldn't earn merit points for it. I was here at Derleth for one reason only – to stay out of foster care, to get a scholarship to a good college, and build a new life for myself. Okay, that was three reasons, but none of them included making nice with dicksome surfer boys. I shook my head. "No thanks. I'll find it myself."

I shoved past him. As I rounded the corner of the hallway, I dared a glance back over my shoulder. Quinn stood in at the top of the dark staircase, his elbow still jutting out in offer, a bewildered expression on his face.

I followed a group of junior girls across the quad to the dining hall, which was housed in the East Tower at the rear of the school. As I climbed the steps and entered under the arched wooden doors, my breath caught in my throat. The hall was straight out of a Harry Potter movie – a dark wood gothic ceiling arched high over rows of narrow banquet tables, set with gleaming silverware, crystal glasses, and candles in silver holders. The teachers ate their meals on a raised dais at the far end of the room below three screens that displayed the class lists. Delicious smells wafted from swinging kitchen doors, where a line of wait staff in grey uniforms emerged with large trays.

The only time I'd ever eaten meals served by a waiter was when my mom took me to Denny's every year for my birthday. And Denny's was nothing like this.

I scanned the room and noticed Loretta sitting at a table in the far corner. As I filed up the center of the room toward her, sniggers reached my ears from the tables on either side of me. I caught a few whispers of conversation, "... gutter whore... selling her services... they'll let anyone in these days... bet she fucked the whole scholarship committee..."

Ignore them. Keep walking. They can't do anything to you here where the teachers are watching, or risk losing their precious merit points.

I kept my head high and focused on Loretta. Just three more tables to pass. From the dais at the head of the room, Headmistress West loomed down, her dark eyes following my advance.

Trey and Quinn sat with another boy – another King I guessed, judging by his fierce good looks. Our third monarch had rich brown skin, dark hair cropped short, and a smattering of dark stubble along his strong jaw. His aquiline features and arresting eyes – so dark they appeared almost black, reflecting the flickering candlelight – suggested a non-American origin, but I couldn't place it. His gaze followed me across the room, his face locked in an expression of such fierce hostility a shiver of fear ran down my spine. That guy hadn't even met me and already he seemed to hate me more than Trey. I hoped I'd never run into him, but I knew that was too much to wish for at this school.

The girls in front of me filed past Trey's table. As they did, Trey held up a piece of bread. The self-satisfied smirk never left his face. His friends followed suit, holding up their bread and snickering. Then they'd put their bread down again, reach for the butter and jam, and hold them up for each other. Each time a piece of bread was raised, the guys would crack up laughing.

As I moved behind their table, I could see that Trey was

using the jam to write a number on his toast. As a cute junior girl with blonde braids and a slightly turned-up nose walked past, he held up his toast so his friends could see the number – an eight.

My cheeks burned. I understood immediately what was going on. They were ranking the girls out of ten. Holding up numbers scratched into their toast like we were swimwear models.

My skin itched. Even though I was covered in the expensive Derleth Academy uniform, I felt completely naked, and not in a good way. Trey saw me staring at him, and he flashed me an evil grin before bending over his toast.

I gulped. I had no choice but to keep walking if I wanted to reach Loretta. There was an empty chair on the end of Trey's table, but it was next to Courtney, so that wasn't an option. I just had to go.

I sucked in a breath, held my head high, and walked past their table. Trey's laughter boomed over the hall, echoed by guys throughout the whole room. My cheeks flushed with heat.

I wasn't going to dignify his behavior by trying to see my number, but he'd turned it around and shoved it in front of my face so I couldn't help but see it.

A six.

Part of me was happy they'd given me a six. *Trey Bloomberg thinks I'm a six.*

How messed up is that?

With his other hand, Trey held up a pickle on his fork, placing it in front of the toast. "That's the minus sign," he called to me. "You're a *negative six.* You've got no chance of scoring in this school, gutter whore. You'd have to pay one of us to fuck you, and we know you don't have the cash."

My heart hammered. Laughter rippled around the room. The walls leaned in, moving closer, boxing me in with these horrible people. *Don't cry don't cry don't—*

Thinking fast, I swiped the bread off his fork and bit into it.

"Thanks for the handout," I muttered with my mouth full as I headed toward my place.

Students gasped. Hundreds of eyes followed me as I slumped down in the seat opposite Loretta and took another bite of the bread. Shocked murmurs passed through the students, but none looked more surprised than Trey Bloomberg. He sat down quickly, snapping his fingers to one of the servers, who rushed to fill his plate with more fresh bread. Quinn was laughing, and the third guy... he looked positively *murderous*.

"You shouldn't have done that," Loretta mumbled, not looking up from the bowl of soup in front of her.

"Did you see what they're doing?" I demanded, dunking Trey's bread into my soup and taking another huge bite. The flavors of the sweet and slightly spicy pumpkin burst in my mouth. *Oh wow.* I didn't remember the last time I'd ever eaten something so delicious. At home, we usually had ramen noodles or pasta – cheap and filling, but my stomach would growl half an hour later.

"Of course I saw. Just ignore them," she whispered.

I mopped up more of the soup with the last of Trey's bread. "I can't do that. It's insulting and sexist. We should at least tell a teacher—"

"No!" Loretta's hand flew out, clamping down over my wrist. "You don't want to do that."

"Why not?"

"Those guys' parents give a lot of money to this school. The teachers will bend over backward to give them exactly what they want." She pushed her tray away.

"Sometimes, that means literally," a guy beside us piped up. He leaned over to join the conversation. He had white-blond hair cut into a preppy style, a friendly smile and one of those voices that sounded like he should be in showbiz. I smiled back at him, grateful for the first friendly interaction I'd had since arriving at Derleth Academy. Quinn Delacorte didn't count.

I picked up the new guy's innuendo right away. I was my

mother's daughter, after all. "Are you saying one of them is sleeping with a teacher?"

"Ayaz Demir. At least, that's the rumor. I'm Greg Lambert, by the way." Greg's eyes glittered as he indicated the cruel prince sitting between Trey and Quinn. Loretta busied herself with her soup, deliberately ignoring us both. *Greg sounds as if he's wanted someone to gossip with ever since he arrived at school.* I was happy to oblige. Since the Kings had decided they were out to get me, I wanted all the ammunition on them I could get. "Ayaz might not even be the only one. Courtney Haynes has been trying to get into Coach Carter's gym shorts, but even her considerable charms don't seem to be working. I suspect he might have eyes for his star lacrosse captain." He nodded toward Trey.

Of course Trey's captain of the lacrosse team. According to the brochure, Derleth's lacrosse team were national champions. The dude really did rule the school. "Are Trey and Courtney an item?" I asked.

"Nope. Courtney's had an on-again, off-again thing with Quinn Delacorte. Rumor has it that she wants to be serious, but Quinn doesn't do serious. He's a manwhore of the first order. See the girl with the jet-black hair and flawless ebony skin and pouty lips next to her? That's Tillie Fairchild. She's Trey's girl. Don't let her catch you making eyes for Trey, because their parents have been arranging their wedding since they were in diapers."

"Yeah, that's not going to be a problem." I accepted a plate piled high with roast beef, carrots, mashed potatoes, and a dark, rich gravy from a server with downcast eyes. My mouth watered. I remembered my mom making roast beef when I was a kid. For a time there she had a boyfriend, and it was his favorite. But after he left, we never had it since. I figured it was because we were too poor to afford it, but it could also have been the memory of the food was too painful for her. But that wasn't my pain, and this food was too delicious to turn down. I shoveled mashed potato into my mouth. "Wheeooodetrepparratsberranggggamarr?"

"Manners." Greg smiled, digging into his own food.

I swallowed. "Sorry. Why would Trey's parents be arranging his marriage? Are they crazy religious?"

"I don't think so. Their families are both big deal names in international shipping, and the marriage is the first step in merging their kingdoms. Rich people's lives are very different from ours."

"I'll say. Although, they sure do know how to eat." I took a gulp from the sparkling water in my crystal glass. "I had the pleasure of meeting Trey and Quinn today. Is that other guy any different?"

"Ayaz? He's Turkish and he has a temper. If he tells you to do something, you do it." Greg pointed to Loretta's soup. "Are you going to finish that?"

"Ayaz put Greg's head through a wall in the Senior Common room on the first day of school," Loretta said. She shoved her soup toward Greg, who didn't eat it himself, but passed it down to a hulk of an African American kid with the friendly smile and high cheekbones sitting next to him.

Greg lifted up his floppy blond hair to reveal a long scar. "I've been marked by Ayaz. Doesn't make me special, though. I bet everyone in the school's got a similar scar from that guy."

"Wow." That scar looked nasty. I thought I'd left fights and violence behind in Philly. At my old school in the Badlands, we had to enter through metal detectors to make sure no one was carrying weapons. "Did he have a reason, or was this just a random act of head-smashing?"

"Because Greg's gay," Loretta muttered, poking at her potatoes.

"Because I flirted with him. I was joking around, but apparently, it wasn't funny." Greg gestured around at the table of scholarship students. "They already knew I was gay. The scholarship committee pulled together these extensive files on each of us.

Somehow, the monarchs must've seen them. They know everything about us and our old lives. So that's terrifying."

Anger seethed inside me as I watched the three Kings laughing with their friends. "I know they're Kings of the school and they're richer than Croesus, but that doesn't mean this Ayaz guy can go around being a homophobe."

"I agree, but I'm not going to be the one to do anything about it," Greg shrugged. "I worked my ass off to get here, and I won't let the Kings or Queens jeopardize it."

"How could they jeopardize your place?"

"Andre here—" Greg patted his friend on the shoulder, "is mute. He can't talk because of a head trauma sustained some years ago. Despite this, he reported Quinn Delacorte for making inappropriate comments to Loretta. Instead of investigating it, Headmistress West gave him a lecture about focusing on his own studies instead of concerning himself reporting other students, and docked him 20 merit points. 20 points are nothing to a rich kid like Trey or Ayaz, but it could be a disaster for us. If any of us drop too low, they rescind our scholarship. Any one of us could be kicked out at any moment. And Trey and Courtney and their posse know it."

What the Kings and Queens giveth, they can also taketh away.

I scraped the gravy residue off my plate, wondering if it would be a demeritable offense to lift up the dish in my hands and lick off the last morsels. Loretta leaned forward and shoved her potatoes onto my plate, and I dug in gratefully, Greg's words playing across my mind. For the first time, I understood why Loretta was so frightened. The Kings and Queens on the table opposite really *did* rule the school.

The wait staff moved around the room, topping up bread plates and taking drink orders. While everyone ate, teachers stood up to give announcements about sports teams and extracurriculars. I noticed that all the teachers were doctors or professors, almost as if this was a college instead of a school. A plump woman at the end of the row introduced herself as Dr. Halsey and invited anyone who wanted to try out for the school production to come to auditions in the auditorium on Thursday.

"Are any of you guys going to audition?" I asked.

Around the table, three scholarship students shook their heads. Loretta jerked hers so hard I was afraid it would fall off.

"Well, I'm gonna try out." I chewed a mouthful of potato and gravy. "I used to write plays and perform them with the theatre troupe at my old school. My best friend made these elaborate sets – he was an amazing artist. It was heaps of fun. Even though we had no funding for a proper theatre department, we won a couple of competitions. According to the brochure, I need extracurricular activities if I have any hope of being top of the list, so I figure—"

Loretta was shaking her head.

"What?" I demanded.

"Courtney plays all the lead roles in school productions, unless she's directing," Loretta said sourly. "She's been taking acting lessons from some Hollywood star since she was three. She won't like you there."

"I don't care what Courtney likes." I turned to Greg. "You want to come with me? I'd love to duet?"

"Are you assuming that because I'm gay I sing and love musicals?"

"A little bit, yeah."

"Well, you assume correctly." Greg grinned. "I'm a walking fucking cliché, and I do a mean Ryan from *High School Musical*."

There's a hint of something in his voice when he speaks, a touch of darkness behind his carefree exterior. There was more to Greg than a tired cliché, I was certain. That made me want to be his friend even more.

"Of course you do. I was thinking more *Phantom of the Opera*—"

Or with this school, maybe Sweeney Todd. *We could pretend to slit*

Courtney's throat and bake her into a pie.

Loretta glared at Greg. "Didn't you learn anything from Ayaz? Just keep your head down, stay out of trouble, and hope you don't come dead last."

"Why?" I demanded. "What happens if you come last—"

Something sharp slammed into my forehead, knocking my head back. A paper plane fell into my gravy. It was covered in doodles and handwriting. Familiar handwriting.

No. Oh no.

I picked up the sodden page and unfolded it carefully. It was a pen and ink drawing done in a tattoo style of a woman in a slinky teddy and heels holding a three-headed snake that coiled around her body. The words 'snake charmer' wrapped around the image. A ragged edge along one side cut off the end of the word and one of the snake's heads.

I'd recognize that image anywhere. I'd stared at it so many nights, thinking about whether I should tell Dante how I felt about him, whether I should risk our friendship...

It was a page torn from Dante's journal. The journal that was taken from my room.

Loretta called my name, but it seemed muffled, as though she was speaking to me through water. My eyes clouded over as the paper crumbled in my hands, turning into a pile of wood pulp.

I stood up, heedless to the teachers who ordered me to get back in my seat. My fingers flew to the burn on my wrist. All around me, students laughed. Not the nervous titters of before, but cruel, mocking laughter.

My vision narrowed, focusing on three faces. Trey. Quinn. Ayaz. They stared at me with hands behind their heads and angelic, innocent smiles on their faces, while all around them, their Queens and subjects rolled about with laughter.

I balled my hands into fists. But there was nothing I could do. *Nothing.* It was like standing on the footpath in front of my apartment all over again, watching it burn, hearing my mom screaming inside and not being able to do a thing to save her.

Only this time, it was me who was burning up.

As I shuffled toward the door, Courtney stood. A candy-sweet smile plastered across her face. She came around her table and placed a hand on my shoulder, giving me a gentle shove toward the courtyard. "We're your *friends*, gutter whore. We *care* about raising trash like you out of the ghetto. And that starts by getting rid of your ghetto junk."

My knees locked. My body froze. Inside my mind, flames leaped up from the floor, their heat tearing at my skin.

Courtney gave me another shove. "Go on, Hazel. Go look. Remember to thank us, because we did this for your own good."

I staggered down the stone steps, their laughter following me. At the foot of the steps, French doors opened out onto the quad. Dusk streaked across the open sky – the spires of the Academy's towers piercing a band of burnt orange. *Fire. Fire blazing in the sky*.

Rubbish fluttered across the quad, catching on the columns and tumbling over the steps of the ornate fountain. Mostly rectangular sheets of paper fluttering and skittering between the fallen leaves. *Weird. I wouldn't have thought in a school like this they'd allow all this trash to accumulate.*

I stepped onto the path leading across the lawn, up to the fountain in the center. More papers floated inside, the ink turning the water a muddy brown. A paper fluttered against my knee. I picked it up, and even without looking at it, I *knew* what I'd see. I blinked. Through a haze of unshed tears and imagined flames, the scribbles resolved themselves into familiar shapes. More drawings. Band logos. Tattoo designs. Wild animals leaping off the page.

Dante's journal.

Pages and pages of his drawings, his thoughts and dreams, his doodles and love letters floated in the fountain. Ink and paper dissolving. Ruined.

Laughter rolled over me like a wave, dragging me under so I

drowned in that murky water. I tore my gaze away from the fountain, bent down and grabbed the pages on the ground, chasing them down as they skittered across the cobbles.

Tears burned in the corners of my eyes, desperate to spill over. The name-calling and the insults and the shitty room and the numbers on toast I could handle. But this... they'd destroyed my most cherished possession. And for what? *For nothing.*

I spun around to face them. Trey stood at the bottom of the stairs, a wicked grin on his face. His girlfriend, the beautiful Tillie, glared at me, her arms possessively circling his torso. Trey had his arms around his buddies, Quinn and Ayaz. Quinn looked at me with a hint of pity in his green eyes, but his laugh was loud and boisterous – the loudest of all, rising straight from his belly and echoing off the spires. Under his arm, Courtney chortled, tears streaming down her doll-like face. Only hers were happy tears – happy because she'd taught me this valuable lesson.

Ayaz didn't laugh, but he smiled a cruel smile that froze the blood in my veins. His eyes swept over me with a look that was part hunger, part venom.

The tears spilled over. I rubbed at my cheek, trying to stop them, but I couldn't push them back into my ducts. I opened my mouth to shout some witty retort, some one-liner that would bring them all to their knees. But nothing came except more tears.

That was all I had left of Dante, and you took it from me. White-hot rage burned in my veins. The same fire that had consumed my life now burned inside me, and it was desperate for revenge.

Fucking Derleth Kings, I hope you're ready. Because this is war. And I am going to tear your kingdom down.

CHAPTER FIVE

Even after what the Kings had done, I wasn't allowed to leave the dining hall. A teacher named Dr. Armitage caught me as I fled across the quad and turned me back. When I walked back into the hall, everyone was silent, but I could feel their laughter buzzing in the air, like a swarm of locusts stripping a fertile field. I returned to my seat, stared at my plate of congealed potatoes until Greg whisked it away and handed it to Andre. I left as soon as dessert was served.

Echoes of laughter followed me as I slunk through the halls with the scraps of Dante's drawings clenched in my hand. Courtney passed me in the hallway and hissed in my ear. "I hope you didn't think you would top Art class with those ghetto scribbles, gutter whore."

I wanted to tell her that they weren't mine, that they were done by my best friend, and that he had more talent in his pinkie finger than she had in her entire airhead brain. But a) she wouldn't care and b) I didn't know if that was true. Kids at this school tended to be overachievers, so Courtney was probably being hailed as the next Rembrandt.

I escaped to the peace and quiet of my staircase without

running into any of the Kings. I slammed the door of my room, enjoying the satisfying crack as the wooden frame trembled. I flopped down on my bed, holding up the salvaged pages to the dim light, running my fingers along the jagged edges, wishing like hell things could be different.

Dante slid the journal across the cafeteria table. "History class was boring as fuck today."

"What'd you draw me?" I flipped open the book, thumbing past pages of his distinctive scrawls. I found the new image immediately – a sultry snake charmer holding a three-headed snake that coiled lewdly around her body. "That's so wicked. I'd have that as a tattoo."

"Yeah?" Dante leaned in, his eyes sparkling. "I could do it for you, if you want. Your first and my first."

My heart skipped at his words, but of course, I was thinking of a different kind of first. "I don't know. Drawing sketches on paper is one thing, but I don't trust you with a needle."

"I've been practicing," he protested, his nostrils flaring. Dante dreamed of being a tattoo artist ever since he got his first ink at age eleven. His thick arms were already covered in tats, and he'd recently scored an after-school and weekend job cleaning up at a tattoo parlor. The guy who owned the place said Dante could start a full apprenticeship at the end of the school year, so Dante wasn't even planning to return to school to finish senior year. He was leaving me alone, but it was for a good cause, so I couldn't blame him. But that didn't mean I wanted to be his guinea pig. He'd be dying to get his hands on my virgin, ink-free skin for years.

I wished there was another reason he wanted my virgin body, but every time I thought we might get close, or felt a spark light up between us, he'd pull away or make a joke and the moment would pass. He was giving me serious blue bean syndrome.

"You've been practicing on oranges," I shot back, stabbing at my lumpy macaroni and cheese with more force than I'd intended. "Not the same thing. Sorry man, you know I love you, but I don't want your first wobbly tattoo permanently etched on my skin."

We were sitting on the steps outside the cafeteria. It was bitter cold, and we had to balance our trays on our knees, but it was easier than choosing a table inside. Kids at our school tended to stick to their own kind – Puerto Ricans in one corner, African Americans in another, Dominicans in the middle, skinheads at the back, Irish mob smoking behind the school. But Dante and I didn't fit – no one wanted us in their group. So we were outcasts together.

Two cheerleaders walked past, one sporting a leather jacket covered in gang patches. She hissed an insult at me, something about my mother – empty words that stung my skin. Dante and I pretended we didn't hear—

"At least they didn't hurt you like they hurt Greg."

Loretta's voice snapped me out of my memory. She sat on the corner of her bed, her body rigid, ready to leap away if I made any sudden movement.

"If I'd had the choice, I'd rather have my head shoved through a wall," I said, tracing a line across the page with the tip of my finger.

"They do this to all of us, all the scholarship kids."

"How many of us are there?"

"Only the four of us – you, me, Greg, Andre. They only offer scholarships for the senior year."

Four torture victims.

Or three allies in my plot for revenge.

We lapsed into silence. Above my head, the now-familiar noise scuttled through the walls. *Scritch-scritch. Scritch-scritch.*

"Loretta?"

"Yeah?" She'd sat herself down at the desk, bending over her books. She'd already forgotten about me.

"What's that sound?"

"Oh." She paused, her pen dancing in midair. We both listened to the scritch-scritch-scritch move across the ceiling and down the wall beside her bed. "I don't know. Rats, I guess? Or maybe old ducting? I hear it most nights. I don't really think about it that much."

How can you not think about it? But then I remember Ayaz's cruel smile and Trey's glittering eyes and Quinn's belly laugh. There was so much more at this school that would hurt me than a few rats in the walls. Maybe Loretta had the right idea. Keep her head down, work to keep her grades up, and let the name of Derleth Academy on her transcript open doors for her in the future.

Loretta buried her face in her books. I lay back on my bed and held Dante's drawings to my chest, over my broken heart.

CHAPTER SIX

Buzzzz. Buzzzzzzzzz.

My eyes flew open, my whole body rigid with fright. *What's that?* My mind immediately pictured monstrous flying beetles breaking through the walls and dive-bombing my head. I threw my hands up to protect my face.

Loretta groaned. Her bedsprings creaked as she rolled over, picked up the old-school clock on the nightstand, and turned off the alarm. I lowered my arms, sucking in a few deep breaths to calm myself. *Of course. It's just the alarm. I forgot we had to have that stupid clock because we're not allowed phones at this ridiculous school.*

I rubbed my eyes. The room slowly came into focus. The faint square of grey light from our single high window illuminated a patch on the floor. The basic furniture – the bed, a single night-stand, the desk and hard wooden chairs, the old-fashioned wardrobe with a mirror in the door – stretched in long shadows up the walls.

I'd barely slept. All night, the scratching at the walls grew louder and louder until it pounded against my skull. It moved around the room – starting low down beside the door, scritching along past the desk, across the ceiling, and down beside my bed. My imagination flared, thinking back to all the horror films Dante and I had watched where starving rats chewed through wood in order to consume a human whole.

The last time I'd looked at that ancient alarm clock, it read 3:16AM. The weariness in my body must've overwhelmed my imagination and allowed me a few hours sleep. As I sat up, a pounding headache flared at my temple.

My first official day at Derleth Academy was off to a winning start.

Loretta was already out of bed, throwing on her Derleth Academy uniform – the knee-length red-and-black tartan skirt, a starched white shirt, a black tailored blazer edged with red piping and sporting the school's emblem – the crest containing a crooked five-pointed star and a weird eye thing – and a black-and-red striped tie. "We usually walk to breakfast together," she said, indicating the guys across the hall with a nod of her head. "It's safer that way."

"Noted." I swung myself out of bed and pulled on my own uniform. The itchy wool skirt raised prickles on my skin. As I shoved my foot into the stockings, my toenail tore a hole in the foot. *Hooray*.

I finished changing, wrapped my dreadlocks in a black bandana on Loretta's insistence, and shoved the stack of textbooks off the desk into my bookbag. A couple of stapled pages fluttered to the floor.

Loretta bent down and grabbed the paper. She handed it to me. "Don't lose your schedule."

"Thanks." I folded the paper and shoved it into my blazer pocket. Loretta pushed open the door.

Greg and Andre already waited in the hallway. Greg ran his fingers through his white-blond hair and beamed at me. Andre hung back in the shadows, his jaw set in a firm line. He nodded at me by way of greeting.

"Hey, Loretta, Hazel," Greg greeted us. "Love the headscarf. Very Islam-chic."

"Thanks. That was the look I was aiming for." I touched the fabric. "The headmistress said I couldn't show my hair until I got my locs combed out. I'm not keen on doing it myself, so this is my solution."

Greg opened his arms and wrapped me in a tight hug. The gesture knocked me off-guard. I'd had far too much physical touching since arriving at Derleth, none of it pleasant. Unless I counted Trey's arm brushing mine, his hand on my shoulder, his soft lips just scraping my earlobe while fire raced down my spine...

But I didn't count that, not at all.

It felt good to be hugged, even if it was by a stranger. Greg had one of those smiles that put people instantly at ease. He was flashing it at me now, all white teeth and earnestness. "Today is a new day, and we're gonna get you through it."

Behind him, Andre shrugged, sweeping me with wary eyes. I didn't blame him for being on guard. I guessed all the scholarship students had to be at this school, especially one who couldn't cry for help. Still, with his enormous frame, he didn't look like the kind of guy monarchs would want to mess with.

Greg held out his hand. "Schedule. I want to see if we have any classes together."

I dug out the crumpled paper and handed it to him.

"We've got homeroom together, as well as history, geography, and physics. You've got gym with Andre, which is good because that class is a special kind of torture. Loretta's taking English lit with you, as well as Andre... hmmm, according to this, you haven't chosen your elective yet."

"Elective?" I craned my head to see the blank space on Thursday afternoon.

"Derleth offers all kinds of interesting courses 'designed to foster individual interests and well-rounded scholars,'" Greg used air quotes as he recited from the brochure. "All the teachers have their own academic subjects. There are all sorts of different classes you can take. I'm taking textile arts, aka sewing. It's going to be useful for when I'm a world famous fashion designer. Andre is in anthropology."

"I take feminist studies," Loretta said.

Feminist studies? This school is a whole other world. "What are my other options?" I asked.

Greg flipped to the second page in my schedule where several electives were listed. I scanned the classes. *Ancient Greek, Political Economy, Folklore, Alchemy...*

I snorted. "Some of these are fucking weird. Why do the Sons and Daughters of the American Revolution need to learn *alchemy?*"

Greg shrugged. We filed one after the other up the narrow staircase, emerging into the dormitory corridor, where the other students gave us a wide berth as we all made our way across the quad to the dining hall. "Honey, one thing you're gonna learn is that rich people *are* fucking weird. Wasn't it Courtney's dad who demanded the alchemy class?"

Andre nodded as he grabbed plates from the stack and handed them around to us. We joined the end of the line for the breakfast line. Breakfast was buffet style, with a table of silver chafing dishes holding Spanish omelettes, roasted vegetables, grilled tomatoes, and stacks of bacon. My mouth watered just waiting for it.

"Really?" I glanced across the dining hall, where Courtney held court at her table, surrounded by her friends, including Trey, Ayaz, and Quinn.

"I've heard he's a bonafide flat-earther. He believes the moon landing was faked and the twin towers were a conspiracy – that kind of douche," Greg said in a rush. We moved up a couple of places in the line. "Apparently, he made his fortune with silicon chips before they were cool and now he practically owns the valley. He's new money, but Courtney is desperate to be in the same league as the other monarchs. That's why she puts up with Quinn's manwhoring – she needs him for legitimacy."

"This school is nuts." The line moved up and at last, at last, I was let loose on Mount Bacon.

"Agreed, but at least the food is decent." Greg was making his own dent in the mountain.

"Amen to that." I piled my plate with food, and we made our way over to our table in the corner. Greg and Andre chatted about an upcoming chemistry test (Well, Greg chatted and used the basic sign language Andre had taught him. Andre wrote notes). I listened with half an ear, my mind whirring through potential revenge plots, most of which I pulled directly from teen movies and then promptly dismissed.

"I've been thinking about our audition song for Thursday," Greg said. "What about 'Mungojerrie and Rumpleteazer'?"

"From *Cats?*" I wrinkled my nose. "I'm not sure rolling around on stage in a pair of leg warmers is going to improve either of our social positions. I was thinking about—"

"Morning, Meat," a voice rasped in my ear.

A rich, silky voice caressed my ear, sending a shockwave through my body and an ache pooling between my thighs. I'd never heard a voice that hot before.

As the voice rumbled down my spine, a heady scent wrapped around my body, filling my head with all sorts of images. Sweet honey dripping over skin, blush roses painting the air of a pagan temple, soft lips on mine, fingers like fire curling around my neck...

Ayaz.

My back stiffened. His scent... it was like being kissed by sin itself. I couldn't describe how it blew up my senses, teasing me with temptations I didn't even understand. That scent carried forbidden pleasure, but it also bore an edge – a knife blade that would draw blood as surely as it could draw ecstasy. Ayaz *hated* me. He couldn't be standing behind me, his body pressed up against me, for any good reason.

My fingers curled around the edge of the table. Across from me, Loretta froze, her spoon halfway to her mouth. Greg and Andre looked down at their meals. The entire dining hall lapsed into silence, waiting to see what the King would do next.

"If you can't afford to pay your own school fees, then you shouldn't be eating *our* food. But don't worry, I've got your breakfast right here," Ayaz rasped. Before I could figure out what he was talking about, he dumped something on top of my plate and backed away.

My heart hammered in my chest. I peered down at my plate. A pile of brown sludge now sat on top of my bacon, emitting a fecal smell. Tiny white things crawled from inside it and over my bacon, rolling off the side of my plate and wriggling across the table.

Across the table, Loretta shoved her chair back and stumbled away.

Bile rose in my throat as I stared down at the heaving, wriggling mess. My ears rang. I knew everyone in the dining hall was laughing at me, but I couldn't hear them over the roar of my own heart.

All I could do was watch, frozen and helpless, as a pile of maggots crawled from stinking shit to devour my breakfast.

CHAPTER SEVEN

"Fuck. Fuck!" Greg grabbed my arm and yanked me back from the table. "We're leaving. Now."

I could barely hear him over the ringing in my ears, the pounding of my heart in my chest. I tore my eyes away from the pile on my plate, but the maggots remained etched in my mind. *Wriggling, squirming, twisting...*

I let Greg drag me toward the exit. The ringing dulled, and the laughter rolled over me, shaking me inside and out. Students pounded their spoons against the tables. A chant started up, "You don't belong, gutter whore. You don't belong!"

In the corner, two teachers on duty had their heads bent together. They didn't seem to have noticed the horror. As Greg yanked me out of the dining hall, my eyes fell on Ayaz. He was back sitting with the other monarchs, basking in the aftermath of this latest assault. His mouth was set in a cruel line, but his eyes...

He looked sad. Tragically, impossibly sad.

My whole body stiffened. I couldn't understand it. What would a guy like that have to be *sad* about? And why would he have that look after he pulled off such a successful humiliation?

And worse, why do I care? Why do I want to know about the secrets behind those dark eyes? Why do I want to hear that silky voice tearing through my veins again, or yield to the temptation of that intoxicating scent...

"Fuck." Greg jumped on the cobbles, frantically dusting off his jeans. "Can you see any on me?"

I shook my head, although I didn't really look. Greg wiped down the front of my skirt and blazer, wincing the entire time.

"I think we're both de-maggoted," he said, his shoulders relaxing.

"Did you see him?" I whispered.

"Ayaz? Yes, I saw him dump a whole bowl of shit and maggots over your breakfast—"

"No, I mean, did you see his face? He looked upset."

"He probably got a maggot on his shoe. Bastard!" Greg kicked the edge of the path. "That was *sick*. The monarchs haven't done anything like this to me or Loretta or Andre. You must've really pissed them off. What did you do?"

A laugh escaped my throat. It rumbled in my stomach until it became a wild cackle. I doubled over, aware that I must look nuts, but I couldn't stop. "What did I do? Fuck, I don't know. I exist?"

"Are you... are you okay?" Greg looked at me with concern.

I gripped his shoulder as I finished my laugh with a gasp. I wiped tears from my eyes. "Oh, it's been a while since I laughed like that. You should go into comedy, Greg. To answer you, I'm fine. They can't hurt me with maggots. I live to tackle Mount Bacon another day. And I have no idea what I did. For all I know, Courtney's put them all up to this because I ate Trey's toast and she's on some gluten-free diet and has a hard-on for anyone eating carbs in front of her. People like that don't need a reason to torment people like us."

"Agreed. But you've gotta find a way to get them off your ass," Greg looked pained. "Because I can't stand to see good bacon wasted."

"Me neither." I wrapped my arms around his neck and

returned the hug he'd given me before breakfast. "I promise, the monarchs are going to regret the day they ruined my breakfast."

Greg's smile wobbled a little. "It's when you say things like that, I start to worry."

"Why?"

"Because you look like you could do some serious damage to them. And the monarchs aren't the kind of people to take retaliation lying down."

"Good." I linked arms with his and dragged him away from the dining hall. "Bring it the fuck on."

The rest of the day, I barely heard a word of my classes. My eyes kept flicking to Ayaz, trying to glimpse that penetrating sadness I'd seen at breakfast, trying to understand what was going on in his head. But he gave me no glimpse behind the cruel mask he wore. The memory of his scent itched at the back of my throat, and I had the stupid urge to walk past him and inhale deeply. That was insane, so of course, I didn't. But I wanted to, and I hated that I wanted to.

Tuesday was a non-elective day, which meant that after our final class students were required to spend time on extracurricular activities before dinner. It was when clubs and societies met and sports teams practiced on the fields. Greg and I had booked one of the music suites to practice our song for the audition. As soon as we shut and locked the door, I slumped onto the piano stool, kicked off my shoes and wiggled my toes. The run in my stocking now stretched all the way up to my knee. Super classy, Hazel. Oh yeah, I definitely fit in here.

"What are you doing?" Greg whispered. "Being seen without full uniform is an automatic 10-point demerit."

"Look around. No one's watching. We're safe in here," I

reminded him. "No teachers. No Kings or Queens or court jesters. No maggots."

"Hey, yeah." Greg kicked off his own shoes and sat cross-legged on the floor beside the piano. "So, how are we going to wow them at this audition?"

I tapped on the piano keys. "I was thinking something from *Heathers*. 'Dead Girl Walking' or 'Seventeen,' or maybe a medley?"

"How meta. I love it." Greg gestured to the piano. "Let's hear your chops."

Grinning, I pressed my fingers to the keys and let rip with the melody for 'Dead Girl Walking.' Even though I'd never been able to afford tickets to see a live show, I loved musicals, especially *Heathers*. The songs were punchy, rock-infused, dripping with high school angst and dark humor. I opened my mouth and belted out the words from main character Veronica, as she realizes she's going to be crucified at school the next day, and she goes to bed with the dark, mysterious JD. I close my eyes when I sing, remembering the pages of Dante's journal floating in the fountain and the flames engulfing my home as my mom screamed from inside, until her screams stopped and I became a dead girl walking. I poured all of my pain into the song, loving the way my voice soared in the bright room. When I finished, I opened my eyes. Greg was standing up, clapping like mad.

"That was brilliant. Where did you learn to sing like that?" he asked.

"My mother taught me," I said. "She sang like an angel. She used to perform at a jazz club in Philly on Friday and Saturday nights. I'd hide in the dressing room and listen to her entertain the whole room. Men would send her flowers backstage. But stripping paid more so she had to give up singing."

"And now she's dead, right? And your dad, too?"

What? My hand flew to my wrist, touching the faded scar. "How did you—"

Greg looked horrified. "I didn't mean to sound insensitive. I just meant that the other scholarship students are orphans, so I assumed you are, too."

"All of us?" That could *not* be a coincidence.

"Yeah." He rolled his eyes. "I guess that's one of the criteria for the scholarship. Rich pricks throwing the poor orphans a bone so they can feel good about themselves. Thing is, I never applied for the scholarship, and when I looked it up online I couldn't find anything about it."

"Me too. They said that my school had put me forward for it. I wasn't in a position to go back and ask."

"They told Loretta that, too. But she asked her old principal on her last day and he didn't know anything about it."

"That's weird." Why would the scholarship committee lie about that? It didn't make sense. The scholarship definitely wasn't a scam. We were here at Derleth Academy, our books and board and fees paid. And if Trey's father put up money for it, then it must be a legitimate affair.

"Yep. But what can we do?" Greg shrugged. "This school is a dream come true. Too bad it's also a nightmare."

"You can say that again." I leaned over the piano. "Hey, since you know so much about me, what's your story?"

"Me? Oh, what you see is what you get." Greg spread his arms wide. "I'm a show tune-loving, fashion-obsessed *fabulous* gay teen with dead parents. I'm not going to be able to help you climb the social ladder, but I will paint your nails and gossip when we're both alone on a Saturday night."

"Suits me." I smiled. Greg was the opposite of Dante in so many ways, and yet, he reminded me of my old best friend. Something in the way I felt instantly comfortable around him, like we'd been friends for years instead of less than twenty-four hours. I knew Greg had my back, and I had his – and that started with taking down every miserable rich snob who treated him like shit, starting with Ayaz Demir.

"I've been thinking," I twirled a dreadlock around my fingers.

"I want to get revenge on the Kings for the maggots and the journal. And for putting your head through that wall. And mostly, for taking away your ability to come out in your own time."

"No. No no no." Greg held up his hands. "I'm with Loretta on this one. The Kings are untouchable. The only thing we should do is stay low and hope the monarchs get bored of tormenting you."

Yeah, but what if I'm broken by then?

"Going to this audition isn't lying low," I pointed out.

"Agreed. Taking the leads in the production from Courtney and Trey will be revenge enough. Let's focus on perfecting our song, and we'll wow them with our talent." He smiled at me, but the smile was filled with fear. The monarchs had everyone in this school too terrified to stand against them, but they hadn't counted on Hazel Waite.

"Fine," I agreed, but my mind whirred with plots. *Revenge is a dish best served with a side of maggots.*

CHAPTER EIGHT

Another day, another terrible sleep in the dungeon suite at Derleth Academy. The rats performed their circuit of the room, competing in some kind of rat triathlon between the walls. I imagined little rats with numbered bibs churning their tiny legs while their friends waved flags at the finish line.

"Where are you going?" Loretta asked as I rolled out of bed at 5AM and pulled on my uniform.

"Greg and I booked the practice room before breakfast. We're going to run over our *Heathers* medley until it's perfect."

"It's a bad idea, Hazel. Even if you do win, you're going to incur Courtney's wrath. As horrible as the Kings are, she's a hundred times worse. It's not worth it."

"Why are you so against this?" I demanded. "They're mean to you, too. I thought you'd appreciate watching Courtney squirm."

"I'm against it because you seem determined to bring the wrath of the monarchs down on yourself, and Greg's the one who's going to get hurt," she frowned. "He's been through enough already."

I wondered what she meant by that. Was it about Ayaz putting his head through the wall, or something else? "I know you're scared, Loretta, but nothing is going to change at this school if we don't change it."

Loretta rolled over and shoved her pillow over her head.

Guess the conversation's over, then. I stared at Loretta's sleeping figure, wondering if I should say something, but not sure what it would be. I sighed and went out to meet Greg.

Our practice went great, and apart from some sniggers at breakfast time, the monarchy didn't bother us. Unfortunately, I was too on edge to enjoy the reprieve. Every time I looked down at my breakfast burrito, I saw maggots wriggling and crawling all over it. I passed it to Andre, and he demolished it in three bites.

My first class of the day was physics. Despite being three weeks behind and Quinn interrupting the teacher every few minutes by shouting physics-themed pick-up lines at various girls around the room ("Hey Amber, I'm hung like a Foucault pendulum!"), the class was surprisingly interesting. I'd always been good at math, but what Professor Atwood talked about hardly seemed like math at all. I scribbled a ton of notes and was actually looking forward to researching my assignment on gravity and black holes.

"Hey, Meat," Quinn yelled as I packed up my books. "That skirt would look even better accelerating towards my bedroom floor at 9.8 meters per second."

"No thanks. Physics nerds can't please a woman. Friction alone won't get the job done," I shot back. Quinn burst out laughing. If looks could kill, Courtney would have had me in a body-bag.

After physics was geology. Quinn was also in this class, although Trey and Ayaz weren't. Yesterday he sat in the front with Courtney and Tillie and another monarch girl named Madison. I took a seat in the back row beside Greg. When Quinn entered the classroom, he sauntered straight up to Greg, leaned over his desk, and go right up in his face. "Beat it, faggot. I want to sit here."

Greg's back stiffened. Wordlessly, he collected his bag and went to stand up for Quinn, but I held out an arm to block him.

"There are plenty of chairs at the front of the class," I glared at Quinn. "This one's taken."

"I want to sit next to you," he said.

"Tough. I don't want to sit next to you, especially not when you're rude to my friend."

Quinn shrugged. "Fag boy over here knows the rules. I'm a King. I can have whatever seat I want."

Greg tried to stand up again. "It's fine. I'll move—"

I shoved Greg back into his chair. "Here's the new rule. How about you stop being such a homophobic dick? Or are you so concerned about Greg's sex life because you want in on the action?"

Quinn laughed. "You're the only loser charity case who ever talks back. It's refreshing, and a little hot. Will you come back to my room and suck me off?"

Oh, for fuck's sake. "If you talk that way to me again, I will report you for sexual harassment. Even if I did want to be near your dick, which is a hard no, I'm not sure I'd be able to find it. I didn't get a magnifying glass in my student welcome pack."

Quinn laughed again. He glanced down at Greg and ruffled his hair like he was a puppy. "Keep an eye on her," he grinned. "You've got your work cut out for you with that one."

"Quinn," Courtney waved. "Come sit next to me."

Quinn stuck his lip out in an exaggerated pout and flopped down a row over from me, as far away from Courtney as it was possible to be. He started chatting up a girl named Erika, who Greg had informed me was the daughter of a insurance magnate who Quinn had slept with last year.

Greg looked at me with a mixture of awe and fear. "How'd you do that?" he asked, gripping the edge of his desk as if it was the only thing preventing him from melting into a puddle on the floor.

"At my old school, two kids from rival gangs got into a knife fight in the cafeteria, and one stabbed out the other's *eye*." I hid my trembling hands under my desk so Greg couldn't deduce the lie that was about to escape my lips. "I'm not afraid of Quinn Delacorte."

Thanks to a pop quiz in English Lit – which I aced. English was easy – I was up 15 merit points by the end of the day. I stopped in the atrium on the way to meet Greg for practice and studied the charts. I needed to see who to beat.

Loretta had the highest score of all the scholarship students, but Greg and Andre were only 7 and 11 points behind her. I'd started at -13 because of my hair infraction and talking back to Headmistress West. I was now at 2. Surprisingly, I wasn't at the bottom of the table. Several rich kids were firmly in the minuses, including Quinn Delacorte.

Interesting.

At practice, Greg and I firmed up the musical arrangement of our medley, and he grew confident enough to add a bit of choreography. As we reached the crescendo, I kicked out the piano stool and stood up to belt out the final line.

"Yes!" Greg threw his arms around me when we were done. "That was *brilliant*, and I'm not just saying that. We're going to knock their socks off."

I wanted to knock off more than just socks. I wanted to knock Trey Bloomberg and Courtney Hayes off their pedestals. Winning the audition was only the first step.

The next day, Greg and I rushed to the auditorium as soon as the bell rang, not even stopping to put our books in our lockers.

We were the first to arrive, surprising Dr. Halsey as she set up the room.

"You two certainly are enthusiastic," she smiled as we scribbled our names down on the audition list. "I'm excited to hear you perform. We don't often have scholarship students audition. Many of our students have come from years of training in top-rated music and drama programs, but don't let that intimidate you. Today is all about having fun."

Right. Yes. Not intimidated at all. Thanks for that, lady.

Greg and I took seats in the back of the auditorium and watched the other kids file in. Courtney sprawled out in the front row as though she was Cleopatra reclining on her sofa while her courtiers brought her water and snacks. Trey and Ayaz sauntered in with some of the guys from Trey's lacrosse team and took seats behind Courtney. As soon as Tillie saw Trey, she rushed to his seat and draped herself over him. They started making out, Trey's hands sliding under her blazer, his thumb visibly brushing over her breast. He was stroking her nipple, right here in the auditorium where everyone could see. It was gross, but an ache rose up between my legs, and I pressed my knees together.

I'm not jealous. I'm not going to waste any of my precious pre-show energy wishing it was me Trey Bloomberg was touching.

Tillie stopped devouring Trey's lips only long enough to glare up at me in triumph.

You don't have anything to worry about, I wanted to yell at her. *I have no interest in Trey Bloomberg whatsoever.* And yet, my eyes kept trailing over to where he and Ayaz sat. Tillie straddled Trey's chair, grinding her hips against his.

It's like a sex show.

Greg must have noticed too. He elbowed me in the ribs. "Keep your eyes on the prize. You're trying to dethrone a King, not bed him."

I snapped my head back, heat flaring in my cheeks. "That's not—"

Dr. Halsey clapped her hands. "All right, if I could have your attention. Ms. Fairchild, if you could stop dry-humping Mr. Bloomberg for a moment, we can get these auditions started. Each person will perform one spoken piece and one song. You may perform in pairs or groups, but you'll be judged separately. At the end of the audition, I'll announce the lead roles, with supporting cast and backstage crew to be announced on a sheet outside my office tomorrow."

"I'm first." Courtney leaped to her feet and stalked on stage.

"Of course you are," I muttered. Greg squeezed my hand.

Courtney performed Lady Macbeth's famous speech, dropping dramatically to one knee as she delivered her final line. Her voice was clear, musical, and full of power and emotion. She was good, dammit.

Then she sat down behind the piano and sung. She'd chosen a Taylor Swift song, and she performed beautifully, her angelic voice soaring the full height of the auditorium. The way she batted her eyelashes and lifted her hands as she played made her look like she belonged on stage.

My heart leaped in my chest. "She's good," I whispered to Greg.

"Duh. Of course she is. She's been acting in commercials since she was three. But you're better."

After Courtney took her bow, Trey and Ayaz got up with three other guys and performed a scene from *Bugsy Malone*. They'd even nabbed some bowler hats to use as props. Their accents had everyone in hysterics. Everyone except me.

I don't think I heard a single word of dialogue. If Greg asked me what the scene was about, I wouldn't have been able to tell him. I was transfixed by the two dicksome Kings.

My eyes followed Trey and Ayaz around the stage, mesmerized by their strong, dramatic voices and the transformation in their features. When Trey rested that bowler hat on his face, every muscle in his body transformed. He stood differently, his inflection and accent changed, his face lit up with a passion I had no idea he could possess. He was in his element, but in a different way from Courtney. Where she craved the adoration of the crowd, the chance, Trey's joy came from immersing himself in someone else's story and using his own body to bring that story to life.

While Trey was a fox, Ayaz looked *stunning*. Something about the cut of that suit on his fit body and the way the black brought out his dark eyes made my chest tight. When he performed his lines, his features softened, his face losing its characteristic cruelty. I thought again of that sadness I'd seen in Ayaz's eyes after the maggot incident and wondered what was going on in his life that made him who he was.

After their scene was done, Trey and Ayaz took their turn at a duet. Trey sat behind the piano and pounded out the jaunty tune while the pair of them sang about taking back New York City. They were amazing – their voices deep and resonant and note-perfect. Each note thrummed between my legs like foreplay.

Their polished performance made it clear to me just how much professional training they'd had. When Trey sang the last perfect note, the gathered students erupted into applause. Despite myself, I clapped, too. Greg gave me an odd look, and I lowered my hands.

One by one, the other students performed. It was a real mix of talent levels, with some obvious stars and some even more obvious uses for the vaudeville hook. Tillie's screeching rendition of Lady Gaga's 'Poker Face' was so awful Dr. Halsey stopped her after the second verse.

"Is there anyone else to audition?" Dr. Halsey called out.

"No." Courtney leaped to her feet. "I'm obviously the lead, so I'm happy to start by—"

"We'd like to audition," I called down from the back row.

"Of course. I'd forgotten you two were there." Dr. Halsey smiled. "Please, take your turn now."

As Greg and I descended the steps to the stage, Courtney's girlfriends hissed at us. I heard someone mutter the word 'fag-hag.' Greg blanched and I resisted the urge to start punching monarchs.

Calm down. Beat them on stage instead.

Greg and I opened with a dramatic conversation between the main characters Veronica and JD – we'd drawn from the musical and the 90s film to create a cohesive short scene that showed off both our talents. Then I sat down at the piano, and we launched into our medley.

Greg's voice had never sounded better. He shimmied and shuffled around the stage. Seeing him having so much fun spurred me on, and my notes rang brighter and carried more power. I closed my eyes, picturing my mom sitting at her piano at the jazz bar, playing and singing along with me. The notes flew off my fingers, and I knew I'd played and sang flawlessly.

We finished with our grand flourish. I kicked the stool so hard it toppled off the front of the stage. When we took our bow, only Dr. Halsey clapped. I opened my eyes and the first person I saw was Trey. He leaned against a folded seat, his arms folded, his head tilted to the side as he studied me. He didn't look pissed off, just... curious.

Beside him, both Ayaz and Courtney were competing in the best Kanye West impersonation. They both looked livid, like their heads would explode.

"Congratulations, you two," Dr. Halsey exclaimed. "I've seen enough. You've won the lead parts in our school production."

Wow. I beamed. *We did it! Two poor scholarship kids actually beat the monarchs.* Sweet revenge bubbled in my stomach, and I couldn't keep the smile off my face. It took everything I had not to poke my tongue out at Courtney.

"But they're scholarship students," Courtney screeched. "They can't take our roles—"

"The roles go to the best performers. Hazel and Greg did an

amazing job. Well done." Dr. Halsey looked genuinely pleased, which made a rare bubble of gratitude float through my chest. I wanted to have a teacher that I actually looked up to. "You've each earned 50 merit points, and an additional 10 points for every week you turn up to rehearsals on time and learn your lines."

Wow. 50 points, just like that. Greg wrapped his arms around me in one of his comforting hugs. We did a little gleeful dance. As I stared over my shoulder, Courtney met my eyes. Her cheeks burned with red fire, and a cold smile played across her lips.

I beat her. My triumph turned to dust in my mouth. *She's never been beaten before.*

I'm going to pay for this.

CHAPTER NINE

Word that Greg and I had landed the lead roles spread across school like herpes. As we made our way into the classroom wing the next morning, students tossed wadded-up balls of paper at us, yelling things like 'gutter whore' and 'maggot faggot.'

Can't they think up more imaginative insults?

One spitball hit Greg's temple and stuck there. He raised a hand to brush it off, and the corner of a condom wrapper hit him in the side of the face.

I picked the wrapper off Greg's shoulder and inspected it. Something about it looked strange – the company's logo was more retro than I remembered it. Maybe it was some kind of limited edition condom. It would figure rich people would have something like that.

Courtney's cruel eyes followed me all over the school. My stomach rumbled, but I didn't dare eat anything in the dining hall in case she'd poisoned it. Adrenaline burned through my body as I sprinted between classes. Around every corner, I expected her to be waiting to visit some new torture on me.

The whole school buzzed about the news that two scholarship students would be playing the leads. Apparently, this production was bigger news than I'd thought – it formed part of a week-long arts festival the school put on for parents, alumni, and specially invited guests in the second semester. A few years ago, the president came.

As Greg, Andre, and I walked into physics class, a hand fell around my shoulder. Quinn's dazzling eyes met mine, and his whole face broke into a smile. I pulled away. Quinn's smiles meant trouble.

"Hey, Meat," he cooed, wrapping his arm around my shoulders. The touch sent a shiver of desire through my body. When I overlooked Quinn's crass comments, he was a funny, fun-loving and fucking *gorgeous* guy who was the life of a party. When he smiled, I got lost for a moment. In the real world, a guy like this taking an interest in me would have made me the luckiest girl in the world. But Derleth wasn't the real world – it was a strange and mysterious realm where up was down, down was up, and all the hot guys were completely *dicksome*. "You know what they say about a *prima donna* – the most famous have the voice of an angel, but scream like a devil between the sheets. Want to come up to my room and serenade me?"

"Get off me," I growled, even though that was honestly the last thing I wanted. Quinn's fingers traced a circle on my shoulder, sending a line of fire straight through my body. All three of the Kings seemed to have the ability to set my body alight with heat.

Good thing I knew firsthand just how dangerous fire could be. I shrugged his hand away.

"Quinn, get over here," Courtney said frostily from across the classroom.

"I'm chatting with someone," Quinn called back.

"Silly boy." She flashed him a smile that was laced with venom. "Don't you know it's bad manners to toy with your food?"

"Are you saying you want me to eat Hazel out?" Quinn's lips grazed along my cheek, and my body buzzed with electricity. *Yes, please.* "Because I'm more than happy to oblige. I bet she hits the high notes when she comes—"

"*Quinn!*" Courtney screeched. She turned her desk away from him and whispered furiously to Tillie and Madison.

"Never mind her," Quinn smiled at me. "Sour grapes. So, Hazy, are you ready for me to cash in the first of my favors?"

I stopped in my tracks. "Did you just call me Hazy?"

"I'm testing out nicknames for you."

"Nicknames are generally given to a person by someone they like."

Quinn clutched his heart. "And you don't like me? Why, Hazy, I'm mortally wounded. To make it up to me, you're coming to a party next weekend."

Behind me, Courtney's breath sucked in. I had to admit, I kind of liked that.

"I'll see," I shrugged. My heart thudded against my chest so loud he must've been able to hear it. "I might be busy."

"That would be too bad, Hazy," Quinn's voice lowered, his words soft against my ear, so only I could hear them. "I wouldn't want you to miss out on all the *fun*."

His lips formed the last word against my cheek, the touch lingering for a moment. In that moment was everything – a promise, a temptation, a blazing fire igniting inside me. Heat shot along my veins and pooled into a deep need within my belly.

Instinctively, my fingers reached to press the mark on my wrist. *Why is it the Kings always make me think of fire?*

"I'll see you next Saturday." Quinn's face broke out into a smile as he gave me a wave and slid into a seat.

I took my seat at the back of the class, aware that every eye in the room followed me. Courtney and Tillie stared daggers at me. Greg leaned over and whispered. "You just got asked on a date by Quinn Delacorte."

"No, I didn't," I rubbed the spot on my cheek where Quinn

kissed me. It still burned with that intoxicating fire. "He wants me to go to some stupid party so he can torture me."

"Close, but not true. He wants you to go to some stupid party so he can bed you in a manly fashion." Greg's eyes glittered. "I'm so excited. You have to let me do your hair."

"That's not—" My words died in my throat as Quinn turned around and flashed me another smile. I studied his features but could see no hint of malice in him. He looked excited, like this party was actually something he was looking forward to.

Looking forward to trying to get into my panties, more like.

Maybe Greg's right. I would have to ponder this new development. Kings and peasants weren't supposed to mix. That was probably the appeal I held for Quinn. He'd already had his pick of the Queens and their courtesans, several times over if the rumors about him were even a quarter true. They weren't a challenge anymore, and Quinn was the kind of guy who chased pleasure and sport wherever he could find it.

I was the new girl. I was the one taking on the monarchs. I was forbidden fruit. I just didn't know yet how *I* felt about being Quinn's new sport.

The rest of the day passed in a blur. I felt eyes on me wherever I went, but the whispers of 'gutter whore' had mostly stopped. Instead, everyone seemed to be talking about how Courtney and Quinn were on the rocks. I wouldn't have guessed from watching Quinn, who was even louder and funnier in class than usual. I knew now why he had a negative number of points – he never did any assignments and spent all his time talking back to the teachers.

I glimpsed the Queen herself across the dining hall at lunch, sitting on the end of the monarchs' table. She poked at her salad and whispered to Tillie, the pair of them shooting filthy glances at *me* even though Quinn flung his arm around Amber's neck.

I hated to admit it, but watching Quinn cozy up to Amber after he'd asked me to that party made me feel prickly inside.

My afternoon class was my elective. I chose Ancient History because it sounded interesting and was taught by Dr. Morgan, the general history teacher who I adored with his patched tweed jacket and rambling asides into the darker parts of history. I'd checked the textbook out from the library, but I needed to swing by my locker to pick it up. As I shoved my way through the press of students, Greg came up alongside me.

"Rumor has it that Courtney is out for your blood," he purred.

"Tell me something I don't know," I muttered, hugging my books closer to my chest.

"I want to know all the details about that party. They hold them in a secret location – no outsiders allowed. You've got to report back – who hooks up with who? What did everyone wear? I'll do your makeup, of course, and we'll see what we can do about that hair of yours." He touched a dreadlock that had fallen out the side of my bandana and shuddered.

I tucked the dreadlock back inside my bandana. "We *could* do all that stuff, except that I'm not going."

"You have to go. You owe it to me, your new best friend." Greg leaned against the door beside my locker, holding his hand over his heart. "Can you take a camera? Or maybe just your notebook... make a few quick sketches..."

"Maybe Quinn will take you instead of me. I think you'd make a hot couple." I swung open my locker door.

"What the fuck?"

Something heavy and cold and wet slid from the top shelf and covered the front of my blazer. A foul smell rose up from the lumpy mess, death and blood and fetor.

Meat.

Someone filled my locker with rotting meat.

CHAPTER TEN

Bile rose in my throat. I stepped back. More of the vile meat slid from the shelf and splattered on the floor, splashing up my stockings. I wiped lumps of it from my blazer, fighting back the urge to scream.

Faces turned toward me, leering and jeering, sniffing and shuffling, laughing their hyena laughs as they circled their prey. Tears stung the backs of my eyes, but I wouldn't give them the satisfaction of crying. I wouldn't.

My vision narrowed, the world blurring into a haze of laughing hyenas and sinewy panthers poised for the kill. My blood whooshed in my ears. I felt as though I'd stepped outside my body, as though I was no longer in control. *This isn't me they did this to. It's someone else. I'm watching it happen to someone else.*

Behind me, two voices rose over the rest – dragging me back inside my body, to the reality of my humiliation. *Trey and Courtney*.

Don't turn around. Don't give them the satisfaction.

The rancid smell filled my nostrils, and I coughed and spluttered, backing away from my locker. Blood and juices ran over my books, warping the pages and sticking the covers together.

"Hey, that meat isn't fresh," Trey's voice punctured my heart. Fresh peals of cruel laughter echoed along the hall.

"It's rancid meat," Courtney said. "Better not touch her, guys. She'll rot your dick off."

I stared at the dripping ichor on the walls of my locker, hot rage welling up inside me. My finger touched the burn on my wrist.

If they think I'm going to sit back and take this shit, then they're dead wrong.

I picked up a handful of raw meat. The slimy ichor dripped between my fingers as I drew my arm back and spun on my heel, letting the handful fly at Courtney's face. She wasn't expecting it, because the wad hit her square in the jaw. Her mouth was wide open with laughter, which cut off mid-chortle to become a loud, piercing shriek.

"That went in my mouth, you bitch!" she screamed.

"Maybe you should have thought of that before you filled my locker with it," I shot back, winding up for another toss. Blood boiled in my veins. I was so *angry*, I didn't care about anything except getting her back, watching her suffer. Maybe I'd stuff some in her mouth, force her to eat it while everyone watched.

Courtney shrieked and jerked away, slapping her hands on her book bag, flapping the fabric satchel. "My books...they're so hot, like they're on fire. How did—"

Another handful left my hand. Courtney twisted to the right, and the meat sailed past her and hit the person standing directly behind her.

Headmistress West.

Oh, shit.

The headmistress had crept up so silently, I hadn't even known she was there. Now, bloody meat dripped down her face, staining her velvet gown. The entire hallway fell silent. My locker door creaked on its hinges.

I'm dead. I'm fucking dead—

"Ms. Waite," she spoke in a pleasant voice that turned my heart to ice. "If you would follow me."

"But Courtney—"

Headmistress West curled one taloned finger over, beckoning me. The tears spilled over as I slammed my foot into my locker door, kicking it shut with a loud *BANG*. Several hyenas jumped. I glared at them through tear-soaked eyes as I followed the headmistress down the hall to my doom.

As I trudged past him, Trey leaned over, his eyes dancing with glee as he whispered in my ear. "You're not new meat any longer. You're dead meat."

CHAPTER ELEVEN

After the locker incident, I was left mostly alone. Apart from snickers and insults that followed me everywhere, no one did anything massively cruel. I wanted to enjoy this lull in the bullying while it lasted, but instead, I walked everywhere with a knot in my stomach, wondering what they'd throw at me next.

It didn't help that I still wasn't sleeping. The *scritch-scritch-scritch* on our walls wouldn't stop. I went to one of the women in the grey smocks to see if they could lay some traps for the rats, but she merely shook her head and scurried off.

She was right to dismiss me. She was ordered around all day by snobby rich kids who thought they were better than her even though they'd never done an honest day's work in their lives. I hated myself for bothering her. Of course I could deal with the rats in the walls. I'd dealt with far worse in my life.

The only bright spots in my day were rehearsals for the school production with Greg, and watching my name jump up several places on the points board. Despite the headmistress docking me 20 points for the mess in my locker, which she made me clean up myself, two more perfect test scores and the school production had put me over 150 points. It wasn't anywhere near Trey's 1305, but I was gaining.

I spent most of Friday dreading the weekend and the new tortures the royal court dreamed up, but actually, it was two of the most pleasant days at Derleth. Trey and Courtney and their friends were off doing their own thing, so they weren't around to torment us. Loretta and I spent most of Saturday in the library, trying to catch up on assignments. Greg and Andre joined us for some of it, but Greg kept shifting in his seat and fidgeting. The dude could not sit still. After two hours he let out a huge sigh and said, "Let's go do some archery."

I'd never even seen an archery set up close before. My school back in Philly didn't even have a field. We had to use a nearby park for outdoor sports – and you always had to watch out in case you stood on a used needle. Derleth not only had two perfectly manicured lawns to play on, but an entire room filled with expensive sports equipment students were free to use. Greg dragged out two targets and four bows and showed us how to set them up along the west field.

Greg started us all on the thirty-foot line. He showed us how to attach the arm guards, notch the bow and stand with our feet lined up with the target and our bodies rigid. I let loose my first arrow, enjoying the satisfying *THWACK* as it slammed into the target. A cool breeze rustled my dreadlocks, and I felt badass, like Katniss in the Hunger Games. It was Dante's favorite film, so I'd seen it a hundred times.

"Where did you learn how to do this?" I asked Greg as I notched another arrow.

"My father taught me. He loved to hunt. I shot my first deer with a bow when I was six years old." A dark cloud shifted over Greg's eyes for a moment.

I found it so hard to picture gentle, caring Greg who loved show tunes and wanted to be a fashion designer going hunting with his dad. Not for the first time, I wondered how he lost his parents, but I didn't want to ask. This school already knew too many of his secrets. He needed to keep his pain for himself, as I did.

We shot all our arrows and went to collect them. Loretta's arrows had all overshot the target and stuck out of the earth like porcupine quills. We found all but one of them. "It must have gone into the bushes," Loretta said, reaching toward the row of small shrubs bordering the field. As I looked closer I realized they were rose bushes, with thorns on the branches and a few drooping blood-red flowers remaining on the plants, between large red fruits. The ground around them was littered with red petals and dropped fruits.

Greg grabbed my arm. "Don't go in there!"

"Why?"

Greg pointed at the fruits on the ground. "You mean aside from the fact that you're walking into thorn rose bushes? These are rose hips. They contain prickly hairs that are the main ingredient in itching powder. If you got those on your skin, you'll be in agony. Just leave the arrow, no one will notice."

As we went back to the line and I lifted the bow, I noticed movement on the field beside us. A lacrosse game was getting underway. Guys ran up and down the field, swinging their silly stick things. Trey, of course, took up position in the mid-field, calling instructions to the other guys. Courtney and her friends stood on the sidelines, jumping up and down in tiny skirts.

"Courtney's legs must be freezing," Greg said, pulling the collar of his jacket up against the icy wind. "They're turning blue."

"Maybe that's why she's doing all that jumping," I said. "Trying to stay warm."

"Nah, she's just imagining herself jiggling up and down on Trey's cock," Greg piped up. Andre and I cracked up.

I grinned. "Shall we cause some trouble?"

Loretta stared at me in concern. "What are you going to do?"

"I'm just going to cheer on my fellow students, in the spirit of school camaraderie." I set down the bow. "You guys coming?"

Loretta shook her head. "I'm going back to the library," she muttered, sprinting across the lawn before I had a chance to reply.

"Ignore her," Greg said. "She's afraid. People are being worse to her because she's your roommate."

I didn't know that. I only had one class with Loretta, and she never sat with me. I wondered if that was the reason. "That makes me so angry. Why would they pick on someone who can't defend herself? What are they doing to her?"

"Just the usual, saying lewd things, calling her your lesbian lover. Trey printed out pornographic images and glued her class photograph on them. Loretta's mom killed herself when Loretta was really young because she was raised in one of those Southern Baptist families and she couldn't live with the shame of being gay. So Loretta takes it kind of personal."

"Wow," I breathed. Loretta's mom *killed herself?* That was some dark, dark shit. No wonder Loretta had closed off when I'd asked about it. "I'm guessing the monarchs know about this?"

"It was in her file," Greg's features darkened.

It wasn't really Greg's place to tell me Loretta's story, but he couldn't help being who he was – a hopeless gossip. As I watched her tiny figure running in the direction of the school buildings, I felt as though I understood her a little better. The way she would stiffen any time someone said something dirty, her fervent wish to stay under the radar, the way she kept worrying about Greg. My chest tightened. *What a shit thing to happen, and then to have your tormentors throw it back in your face.*

My blood boiled. Loretta had already been through the worst thing to ever happen to a person, and then to have to relive it over and over every time she walked down the halls or went to class. *Fuck the monarchs. They deserve to learn that they can't do this to people and get away with it.*

I just wished I had some power to make it all go away for Loretta, and Greg, and all of us, to make Trey and all the other monarchs understand what it was like to walk in our shoes. Sure, Greg and I had taken the leads in the production, but it didn't feel like enough. It pissed them off, but it hadn't made them understand that what they were doing was *wrong*.

Revenge plans circled in my head as we wandered over to the edge of the field, twenty feet from where Courtney and her friends huddled. Quinn, on the opposite team, intercepted Trey's pass and tried for a goal, but Ayaz – who was the goalie for Trey's team – stopped him. The boys yelled insults at each other in a friendly way as they returned to their starting positions.

Quinn had his hair pulled back into a messy bun. Tendrils pulled free and whipped around his face. His muscles rippled under his shirt. I thought about his invitation to the party next weekend and found myself wishing it was real, that he actually wanted to spend time with me as a person.

Why am I such a sucker for guys like that?

As I watched him, it occurred to me that Quinn was the key to any revenge plot – to any hope of stopping the bullying. He wasn't like Trey and Courtney and the others. He was a bully, but he wasn't doing it because he felt threatened. He did it because he craved stimulation. I could probably use that.

Plus, when he wasn't being gross or horrible, his smile made butterflies dance in my chest. And I hadn't felt that in a long, long time.

"Hey Delacorte," I yelled as he jogged back to his place. "Looking good!"

Quinn flashed me a dazzling smile. Courtney's head whipped around so fast she broke the sound barrier. She stalked toward us, claws sharpened, feline body coiled, ready to pounce. Beside me, Greg stiffened.

"Are you sure you know what you're doing?" he muttered.

Courtney stopped a few feet from me, her hands on her hips.

Two of her fellow Queens, Amber and Tillie, stood on either side of her. Courtney's voice dripped with false sweetness. "Poor little gutter whore, thinking Quinn's interested in you. He's *my* boyfriend, and he only asked you to the party as a joke. You're so pathetic, of course you'd think it was real."

"He told me you're not even dating," I said. "I'm not the one who's acting pathetic, hanging on to a guy who obviously doesn't want me."

Courtney's eyes flashed. "And you think Quinn wants you? Oh, gutter whore, you are so deluded. Quinn doesn't give a fuck. He's a poor little rich boy trying to stick it to his parents by slumming it with you."

"Is that what he's been doing with you, slumming it with the new money?" I yawned as if the whole thing was totally boring. Which it kind of was. "I don't really care what you and your not-boyfriend get up to, Courtney."

"Why. Too busy being a fag-hag?" Courtney glared at Greg, who shrunk from her gaze. Behind us, Andre remained bone-still, not saying anything but not giving her any ground, either. *That guy is a total rock.*

"Is that really all you got?" I growled, sensing the anger flaring inside me, tearing through my veins like a flame, consuming everything in its path. "You're going to stand there giving basic bitch homophobia and you think that intimidates us?"

"Of course it does." She smiled, and her smile was so certain and so satisfied that my fingers itched to punch it off her face. "Gutter trash like you and your friends."

"Hey, Courts," Trey called from the field. Courtney's head whipped around. To my surprise, the guys had stopped play, and were standing in their positions, watching our stand-off with interest. "Back off. They're just watching the game."

What? I searched Trey's face for some trick, some sign that he was building me up for an epic fall. He frowned at Courtney, his body angled toward her in a power stance, staring her down. King versus Queen. Some understanding flickered between them – a silent battle for power that had nothing to do with me or the other scholarship students.

Tension crackled in the air as Courtney directed her glare at Trey. "You're not the boss of me," she hissed like a cat, her shoulders squaring off and her chest thrust out. There was a threat in her voice that sent a chill down my spine.

Trey shrugged, his eyes never leaving Courtney's face. "Suit yourself. Personally, if Hazel and her friends want to watch me, I'm not gonna complain."

Damn you, Trey Bloomberg.

His teammates laughed, some of them cruelly. Quinn's infectious laugh rose over them all. At the sound of it, Courtney bristled. I tried to imagine the two of them together, lips locked, skin on skin, Quinn's hands sweeping her sharp angles and touching her feline face. But it just... didn't work. Did Courtney even *like* Quinn? In class, she always sighed when he made jokes, and she never joked back. Did she see him, or did she just see a fast-track to legitimizing her family in the eyes of the elite?

As if answering my question, Quinn's eyes fell on me. I winked at him and he laughed even harder. He wasn't the only one watching me. In the goal, Ayaz had removed his helmet, running his hand through his hair while two dark pools swept over my body, burning into my soul. When Ayaz looked at you, he peeled away layers; he saw more than just the mask I wore for Courtney. If his eyes had been kind, I might have thrown myself at him, laid my deepest fears and my darkest secrets bare. But since he was a vicious, maggot-wielding bastard, he could go to hell.

In the center of it all, Trey's gaze narrowed on me. But before I could get a read on him, he'd turned back to the game, running off down the field with the ball, his muscled legs pumping as he slammed through the distracted midfield defense. My chest fluttered as he ducked under Quinn's stick, his broad shoulders stretching and straining to make the pass to his teammate. As he lifted his arm, I caught a glimpse of something on his wrist. It was fast, but I thought it was a twin to the rune tattoo I'd seen on Quinn earlier. Did the two of them get friendship tattoos? That was kind of... cute. Adorably cute, actually.

My gaze flicked back to Trey's face, and I forgot all about the tattoo. The curl of his lip, the sparkle in his eyes as he jogged after his teammates, reminded me of the way he looked on stage – transformed to another place, another body. His features softened, his icicle eyes focused on the ball and nothing else.

Trey Bloomberg was only happy when he stepped outside of himself, when he could pretend for a minute or an hour that he was someone else. But why? What was so awful in his life that the perfect rich boy was desperate to escape?

"See? I told you she's been making eyes at Trey, too," Tillie hissed to Courtney.

Shit. Too late, I snapped my attention back to the girls. They'd seen me looking at Trey. They could read my guilt all over my face.

"You have no shame," Tillie snarled. "You're looking at my boyfriend. You're practically drooling. It's *disgusting*. Even if he was single, he'd never be into a pig like you."

"We've been *nice* to you, gutter whore." Courtney's voice dripped with saccharine sweetness. "We've tried to welcome you to this school and make sure you know what to do if you want to survive. But you haven't learned your place, so I see we're going to have to take drastic measures."

"Oooh, I'm so scared," I held myself and pretended to shudder.

"You won't be laughing soon," Courtney's eyes flashed. "We're going to make you wish you'd never been born."

CHAPTER TWELVE

I figured Courtney would focus her energy on humiliating me at the party, which despite what I'd implied at the lacrosse game I had no intention of attending. She'd be at the venue with a bucket of pig's blood just waiting for Quinn to lead me to a certain spot. I figured if I stayed in my room and taught Loretta how to play blackjack then I'd avoid the whole thing.

I figured wrong.

On Monday morning, Ayaz shoved his way past me as I walked into homeroom, a cloud of honey and roses and fury. He whipped the black bandana off my head. My locs tumbled free, flopping down over my eyes.

"Give that back." I grabbed for the bandana. Ayaz smirked and tossed it to Quinn, who flung it at Courtney, who balled it up and shoved it into her purse.

Snickers erupted from the royal court. Mr. Dexter looked up from his papers and surveyed the class. He zeroed in on me in the doorway, trying to hold my dreadlocks back from my face. "Ms. Waite, that's not a regulation haircut."

Twenty pairs of eyes swiveled toward me. My cheeks burned

as a dreadlock fell over my eye. Courtney sniggered behind her hand.

"I know, Mr. Dexter. I've already discussed it with Ms. West. I'll be fixing it as soon as I've earned a pass-out to go into Arkham for a haircut. Headmistress West said I could wear a bandana until then."

"If this is true, where is your bandana?" he demanded.

"It's... " I glanced over at Courtney, who had her head buried in her notebook. I knew better than to demand she return the bandana. "I must have left it in my locker."

"Very well. Make sure you pick it up before your first class, or you'll be facing the loss of your merit points." He nodded and returned to his papers.

I slumped down beside Greg. "Do you have a bandana or scarf or oversized novelty handkerchief I could borrow? I doubt every teacher is going to be as understanding as Dexter."

I'd finally crossed 200 merit points and I didn't want a single one taken away. I reached up and touched my hair, longing for the comfort the weight of my hand usually brought. But there was no comfort to be had – not with judgmental eyes burning into my skin and Mom and Dante dead and buried forever.

I loved my locs. They reminded me of where I came from, of who I'd been and who I'd loved before the fire that had taken my life away. But looking around the room at the preppy haircuts and perfectly-styled bangs, the blow-waves and the highlights that cost more than a month's rent, a ball of shame lodged in my throat. I saw what they saw when they looked at me – dirty hair, cheap nail polish... a gutter whore pretending to be royalty.

I don't belong here.

Never had it been more obvious than with my hair on display. My dreadlocks hadn't been touched up in months – stuck in the same state they'd been in before the fire. Even though time stopped for me, my hair kept growing, and now they were ratty and unkempt. I'd waxed them yesterday, rolling them as tight as I could, but the ends were unraveling and the regrowth made the tips lumpy. Scorn rolled over me as I realized I looked like shit, and I cared, I fucking *cared*, and I hated it.

This school... it would make me into something I wasn't. It would crush the gutter whore out of me.

"I'm sorry." Greg glanced across at the monarchs, who watched me with hungry expressions. "Even if I did have something, I don't think it would do much good. They'd only steal it, too."

Across the room, Courtney smirked at me. With a sinking feeling, I realized this was only phase one of their attack. The warning shots. They were gearing up for the big push.

After homeroom, I dug through my whole locker, but I couldn't find anything to cover my hair that wouldn't get me in more trouble. My first class was history. I raced in early and sat right at the back. Dr. Morgan didn't seem to notice. But the physics teacher, Professor Atwood, frowned at me as soon as I entered the classroom.

"Ms. Waite, that hairstyle is against school rules."

"Please, Mr. Atwood, I have dispensation from Headmistress West until I can get it cut—"

"Rules are rules." He cut me off, as he clicked away on his ancient-looking laptop. I squeezed my eyes shut so I wouldn't have to watch my points total drop on the screen behind his desk.

I worked so fucking hard to crawl my way up the rankings, and the monarchs were determined to ruin what little progress I'd made. Even though they started life with every advantage, they weren't going to let me have an inch. Not even 200 measly fucking points. Everything felt like too much today – I longed to throw my bookbag at Professor Atwood, storm out of Derleth Academy, and never come back. At least working in the diner was honest. At least I knew where I stood. At least I earned every fucking cent I made.

"By the end of the day, I'm going to lose all my points." I

slumped down next to Greg, balling my hands into fists and resting them against my eye sockets, trying to stop the tears itching behind my eyes from flowing down my cheeks and ruining my tough girl reputation. "I don't even get what the big deal is with my hair. Why do they care what my hair looks like? It doesn't affect my grades in any way."

"Here they want everyone to look like perfect little minions," Greg said. "I'm not allowed to wear makeup. Haven't you noticed how the students wander around looking dead to the world in their perfect identical hairstyles? They want to make sure people like us are stomped back down where we belong."

I flashed back to the scholarship advisor, looking over my shabby clothes and poor neighborhood with barely-concealed glee. "You'll find the school forward-looking and diverse," she'd said. "We believe in lifting up those who haven't had a privileged start in life."

Sure you do. As long as we remember our place.

At lunchtime, I went back to my room to hunt out something else to cover my head. At the bottom of my suitcase I found another bandana – a blue one this time, an old one of Dante's that he must've left at my place one day. It was so threadbare it was practically see-through, but it was better than nothing. I tied it on and rushed to the dining hall in time to hit the tail end of the buffet line.

"I can't believe they let her in the dining hall like that. It can't be hygienic." Courtney strode past me in the buffet line and pretended to peer into my hair. "Yuck. I can see nits! Nits and beetles!"

"Nits and beetles!" Other students took up the chant. I focused on shoveling piles of quiche and salad onto my plate, not acknowledging her.

If you ignore her, she'll just go away.

But that wasn't Courtney. Ignoring her made her angrier. She grabbed a handful of my hair, wrenching my head backward. I dropped the plate in my hands as I lost my balance and listed over. Ceramic shards flew everywhere and bits of egg and bacon stuck to my stockings.

"Nits and beetles! Nits and beetles!" The chant rang in my ears. My scalp burned as I clawed at Courtney's hands, trying to free myself. Instead, she twisted her grip, tearing at my hair, and I howled with agony.

Hot, white pain arced through my scalp as Courtney dragged me backward. Ceiling beams swung above me as my whole world flipped upside down. She flung me around and slammed me hard against the end of the monarch's table. My head cracked against the wood, and white dots flared across my vision.

"Don't come near any of us ever again," she hissed. "You're *diseased*."

More gobs of wet quiche slapped against my body as I dragged myself up. Students hurled food and abuse at me until I managed to stagger down the steps of the great hall. Their taunts followed me into the bathroom, where I scrubbed the food off my uniform as best I could. My temples throbbed from cracking my head on the table, and my whole head flared with fire. Clumps of torn hair came away in my hands.

A lump rose in my throat as I fought the urge to cry. I gulped several times, forcing down the bile that rose in my throat.

I'm not strong enough for this.

I leaned against the wall and stared at my reflection in the mirror. Dreadlocks fell over my face, the ends unraveling now that I hadn't had them redone. Gobs of quiche clung to the thick locks.

I'd survived seventeen years living in the Philly Badlands – attending school with gang members, hiding alone in our apartment while I waited for my mom to get home from the club, being best friends with a guy who seemed to incite death threats on a daily basis just because he liked art more than knives. I watched the two people I loved most in the world burn in a fire. I'd seen more in my life than Courtney Haynes could ever know.

Now I had the opportunity other kids in my neighborhood could never have dreamed of – a free ride at a prestigious school, a basically guaranteed spot at the college of my choice. Never in a million years did I ever expect to see my reflection staring back at me wearing an expensive private school uniform.

But the girl inside that uniform was still the same.

I didn't fit here. I didn't belong. Dressing me up in an ugly tartan skirt didn't change the girl inside.

No matter how much I fought Courtney and Trey and all the other monarchs, it would never change the fact that they were *born* for this life and I'd landed here by luck. Outside of these walls, I didn't have a name that inspired awe or a mansion in the right part of town or a close personal friendship with the president. These kids were going to grow up to run the country, the *world*, and even if they had to stare at my face on the other end of a boardroom, I would still be the gutter whore who served their fries.

They were never, ever going to stop until I was back where I belonged.

I was my mother's daughter. I hoped and I hoped and I put on a brave face and I pretended that things were better than they were. And I almost believed my own bullshit, until something like this happened and the cracks showed. Tears welled in my eyes.

"I miss you, Mama," I whispered to my reflection, to the hazel eyes I inherited from her, the eyes she'd used to tempt a thousand men out of their one-dollar bills, the eyes that had inspired my name. I wished I could see her staring back at me, her lips curled into one of her secret smiles, her eyes crinkling at the edges, her arms wide open, ready to wrap me in a hug that could crush my ribs.

But all that looked out of that mirror was a sad, broken girl with no one and nothing left in the world.

Grief roared up inside me, hot like the fire that took her. It wasn't fair. It wasn't fair that they had everything and I had nothing. That they had the whole world and I was completely alone.

I pulled my arm back, and I slammed my fist into the mirror. Pain flared across my knuckles. The sound shattered the grief from my bones, the pain carving out the horror like a knife. The girl in the mirror disintegrated into a thousand tiny pieces.

Shards of glass littered the floor at my feet. I picked my way around them, heading for the door. Blood dripped down my knuckles as I bent down to examine a perfect triangle of glass, a single hazel eye staring back at me – not kind like my mother's, but hard as flint.

Carefully, I picked up the piece of glass, folded it in one of the fluffy paper towels, and slid it into my skirt pocket.

Bring it on, Courtney. If you want to break me, then you'd better be prepared for a fight. And us gutter whores fight dirty.

The bell rang. Wiping my face and patting the glass shard in my pocket, I ducked into the hall and made my way to English literature. When I took my seat in the back corner, Courtney and her friends moved their desks away, creating a plague circle around my desk. The teacher didn't say anything, because this was Derleth Academy and Courtney Haynes was Queen.

"Got the bubonic plague?" Trey smirked at me, drumming his fingers on my desk as he strode past on the way to the back row. I stared at my hands. I didn't have an answer. The shard weighed heavy in my pocket.

The shunning continued through the rest of the day. As I wrote a quote on the board in class, Amber muttered the ring-around-the-rosie nursery rhyme under her breath. Students crossed themselves in the hallway as I went past, as though I was a vampire. When I arrived at my locker, a symbol had been drawn on it in red paint.

What was weird was that the symbol looked almost *exactly* like the rune I'd seen tattooed on Quinn and Trey's wrists.

"It's to ward off evil," Courtney hissed as she sauntered past, her arm looped in Quinn's. She dragged him away before he could say anything, but his eyes met mine over his shoulder. He looked almost... sheepish. But I was probably imagining that.

Why is Quinn's tattoo on my locker door?

When my last class was finished I went straight to my room, slipping a note in Greg's locker asking him to cover for me at rehearsal. I collapsed on my bed, staring at the ceiling and listening to the rats scrabbling through the walls. For once, I found them a comfort. The rats had infiltrated this school and were devouring it from the inside out – they didn't ask for permission.

I must have drifted off to sleep. I didn't even hear Loretta come in. The next thing I knew, I found myself standing somewhere cold and damp, a slippery darkness wrapping around me. A rancid smell that was too much like the rotting meat in my locker invaded my nostrils until I choked for air.

I thrust my hands out in front of me, stumbling forward until I touched a wall. My fingers scraped cold stone. *Where am I? Am I in the corridor? Where's the door to our room?* My eyes strained to see the gloom. Something flickered in the distance. A flame? Was something on fire?

My chest tightened. The hairs on my arms stood on end. *If there's a fire, then why am I so cold?*

And where am I that the very air seems drenched with death?

A sound penetrated the gloom. Scritching, like the sound that came from the walls in my bedroom, only louder and brighter and more terrifying as it echoed through vast chambers and deep crevices, through all the dark places where nightmares dwelled.

Scritch-scritch-scritch-scritch.

Hundreds of tiny feet descended upon me. The incessant scratch and scrape of claws on stone crawled on my consciousness. My head swam with dizzying fear, a fear all the greater because I could not confirm it. I could not see what descended upon me.

Was it death, visiting me at last to take me to my mother, to place me into Dante's arms? Then why, instead of opening myself up to it, did my mind rebel from it? Why did my skin itch and my throat close as if it wasn't death that came scritching for me along the walls, but some nameless, unheard-of thing even more abhorrent?

They're coming for me... The rats in the walls...

I woke with a start, my heart pounding in my chest. A thin shaft of golden light had started its journey across our bedroom wall, indicating the path of the rising sun. The ancient alarm clock read 4:45. Rats *scritch-scritched* across the ceiling. Everything perfectly normal, perfectly as it should be.

It was just a nightmare. It wasn't real...

The cold, clamminess of my dream still clung to my skin. I struggled to suck in a breath, my throat still closed from the foul smell my imagination had conjured up. I tried to sit up. Something like a rubber band grabbed the back of my head and snapped it back against the pillow. There was a *squelching* sound and a warm wetness around my ears, like my head was resting on Jell-O.

I raised a hand to my face, swiping it through something wet and sticky under my head, and sniffed. My head swam from the fumes. It smelled like a road.

Tar. It's tar.

But why is there tar on my pillow...

I swung myself out of bed and grabbed the door handle. Locked tight. But I knew that didn't mean anything. Courtney and Trey had someone sneak in here and take my journal. I thought they had bribed the woman who took my suitcase, but I realized that they could easily have made a copy of my key.

They broke in here in the night and put tar on my pillow. But why—

My eyes struggled to make out the shapes of furniture. The fumes closed my nose, choking me. White lights danced in front of my eyes. My steps felt slow, sluggish, as though I was moving through molasses.

I staggered into the corner of Loretta's bed. She sat up, her arm *slooooowly* reaching out, grabbing my wrist. The movement nearly sent me sprawling.

"What's going on? Who's in here? Oh, Hazel, it's just you—" Loretta's words died. She choked. "Hazel, the fumes... your hair—"

My hair?

My hand flew to my head, for the first time taking stock of what they'd done. When I felt my dreadlocks, I screamed and screamed and screamed.

CHAPTER THIRTEEN

"Lookin' good, dyke." Trey smirked as I entered homeroom.

I stared at my shoes, my hand touching the bare base of my neck and wishing I could just sink into the floor.

Did they have to take everything?

I'd spent two hours in the bathroom, trying to rinse the sticky tar from my hair. It was like someone had dipped my head in a pot of honey. The tar clung to every dreadlock and I tore large clumps of hair out before I realized what I had to do.

My stomach churned from the fumes and my hands trembled as I took Loretta's scissors and chopped off my hair. Dreadlocks fell to the floor like limp, dead worms. My beautiful hair – a gift from Dante's sister before she got shuffled to another home – gone, just like every other thing in my life.

I didn't cry. I had no tears left.

After I was done, I was left with a thin, matted mess. Combing the tar out of the roots had torn out half my hair, and what was left was thin and fine – longer on top where the roots had grown out. But at least I still had some hair. Luckily, I'd been cutting my own hair since I was eight, and Dante's sister had taught me a trick or two. I evened it out as best I could, keeping it longer on top in a kind of punk-rock mini-hawk, and used some styling product I borrowed from Greg to make it sit on top of my head in spikes. If Dante were here, he'd have said it looked fierce.

But Dante wasn't here, and fierce was the last thing I felt right now.

Trey's knowing look punched me in the chest. I wanted to shout something, but I was too raw, too broken. Courtney was right – she was going to win this. I took my seat without answering Trey, staring down at my book and listening to the whispers swirl around me.

"Today, you'll be starting your main assignment for the year. I'll assign you to work in pairs. You'll each research a historical event that caused a paradigm shift in society. Please avoid the world wars, as we'll be dealing with them in the third quarter." Dr. Morgan came through the class and paired everyone up. I shuffled my seat closer to Greg, hoping we'd be paired together. But she paired Greg with Amber, and I got... Ayaz Demir.

No, no.

I couldn't face talking to one of the Kings today, let alone working with one on an important assignment.

But the assignment was twenty percent of our final grade. Dr. Morgan explained that each pair would create a display about their event that would focus on the impact it had on future generations and its impact on the world today. The top displays would be showcased at the end-of-year graduation event for parents and alumni, and the students who submitted that project would each be awarded 200 points.

200 points. My heart hammered. That would jump me ahead. That kind of gain could help me close the gap between the high-achieving students. If I did everything right, it could shoot me past Trey Bloomberg when the time came.

"Join up with your partners and start brainstorming ideas," Dr. Morgan said. "You have the rest of the hour to decide on a topic and create a plan. Most of the work will need to be done outside class time, so you'll need to set a schedule and divide tasks evenly—"

I didn't look up from my desk as Ayaz pulled his desk opposite mine, but I could *feel* the ambivalence rolling off him. "Trust Morgan to stick me with the circus freak dyke plague victim," he muttered. His book hit the desk with a metallic *clang* that rang through my chest.

"Let's just focus on this assignment," I said, pulling out my books.

"If you wish," he said. His words sounded curiously old-fashioned. I wondered about Ayaz. He was a King of the school, and yet his foreign-ness, the odd way he spoke sometimes… everything about him should have made him someone who was ridiculed, like me. And yet here he was, a monarch. Even though he sat only a foot away from me, he was on another planet.

I touched my hair, expecting to feel the weight of my fingers in my dreadlocks, but instead, I touched the bare skin on the base of my neck. A few thin strands of hair came away in my fingers, and I shuddered at the violation that'd been done to me. *Did you do it? Did you sneak into my room and paint tar all over my hair? Did you take the last piece of my old life away from me?*

"I think we should do the Salem witch trials," I said, surprised by the venom in my voice.

"Feeling a little persecuted, are we?" Ayaz sneered.

"Let's say I have an affinity for those who are tortured for being different." My fingers reached up to touch my hair again.

"And how did the deaths of some witches change anything?" Ayaz said. "It's not exactly relevant."

"You mean how the Salem trials have been used ever since as political rhetoric and in popular culture to warn against the danger of mass hysteria and false accusations? What about the transition from medieval to post-medieval culture? What about identity and religion in our colonial past? What about the witch as a symbol both of patriarchal oppression and of early feminist thought—"

Ayaz's eyes burned into mine. "You really give a shit about this stuff."

"I give a shit about those 200 points," I said.

Ayaz's mouth twisted. "So do I," he said. He seemed like he wanted to say more, so I waited, but he didn't.

"Good." I nodded. "I know you hate me or whatever, but can we just agree that we want to win, so we'll both do the work and neither of us will sabotage this assignment?"

Ayaz stared at me for a long moment, and I could feel myself shrinking in my chair. His honey and roses scent wafted around me, sending a flame down my spine. After what seemed like a century, he nodded. "You might be right about this witch trial thing. You know there's a connection to the school?"

I raised an eyebrow. "I did not know that. The website wasn't exactly forthcoming about that particular part of the school's history."

A muscle tugged at the corner of Ayaz's mouth. Was that the beginning of a smile? My heart thudded, but I couldn't dear hope. "The school was founded by Thomas Parris, the son of the Reverend Samuel Parris who was responsible for a lot of finger-pointing during the trials. Rumor has it that following the trials, the good Reverend was haunted for the rest of his days by the innocent souls he condemned. They invaded his body and mind, made him hurt himself, and made him frightful to others. Thomas Parris did everything he could to free his father of these malevolent spirits. When he exhausted the resources of the church, he turned to Jewish mysticism and then to the very dark magic against which his father had fought."

I leaned forward, enraptured by Ayaz's voice and this insane story. "Parris' occult studies and the strange people he attracted started to gain attention in Salem. There were stirrings that he had been corrupted by the lure of witchcraft. All his studies were in vain, for Samuel Parris died that winter in agony, passing a small sugar plantation in Barbados to his son. Thomas Parris fled Salem, sold the plantation, and came here. In his diaries, he said that this site called to him. He spoke of a sign from the spirits that he should have this land and that he should build a great house that honored his pagan gods.

"Parris built this house based on the principles of sacred geometry, designing it to align with heavenly bodies and for certain rooms to draw energy from the earth in order to channel spirits and other things. He dug underground caverns and tunnels into the bedrock, and worked sigils into the architecture – sigils are symbols that represent certain demons or gods, and it's believed that by drawing them the magician has a degree of control over the being."

"You mean this whole building was like a demonic house of worship?" I asked. "What's the sacred geometry about?"

"It's like this." Ayaz tore off a sheet of paper. His hand flew across the page as he drew a quick outline of the school – the wings and the central buildings surrounding the courtyard, the fields and the long, winding drive. He added a U-shape to indicate the peninsula. Over this, he added a series of swooping lines and symbols. He finished it by linking the corners of the buildings into a crooked five-point star.

"Some of this I've seen in Parris' diaries, some I figured out from stuff I learned in alchemy class. But basically, Parris thought of his home as this conduit of energy. He wanted to communicate with beings from other dimensions or whatever. But the building also had to be able to contain these demonic energies. He couldn't very well call up all these dark things and just let them loose upon the world, so his home also had to serve as a prison. Hence why your room only has that one, tiny window covered with bars."

"You're telling me that my dorm room used to be a prison cell for demons?" I scoffed. "If you're trying to scare me, this is not the way to do it."

"Demons, and other things." The gravitas in Ayaz's voice drew me in. He seriously believed this stuff. "In Parris' diaries, he speaks about communing with the 'other' gods – Ancient Gods of gods who have fallen into a deathlike sleep but whom he hoped to awaken. He invited magicians and occultists from all over the world to his home to attempt to summon these Great Old Gods. Like all good occultists, they threw violent parties and held orgies under the stars. The newspapers reported strange happenings in Arkham village – herds of cattle mysteriously dying, earthquakes that seemed to originate from the house on the hill, reports of participants in Parris' rituals carried away to asylums, turned insane by what they had seen.

"Eventually, the locals in Arkham got sick of all the strange happenings and of the influx of weirdos heading up the hill to dance naked in the moonlight. They stormed the house one night, set fire to it, threw Parris off the cliff, and ran his coven out of town. The place lay abandoned for a hundred years or so, until some ancestor of Trey's bought it and turned it into this school."

I spun the page around to face me, picking out details of the drawing. Ayaz had rendered the school beautifully, even adding architectural details like the carved gothic arches and gnarled trees along the edge of the cliffs. "You're quite a good artist."

"How would you know?" he snapped. "You've probably never even been to an art gallery."

"My best friend is a tattoo artist. Instead of shutting away his art in elitist buildings, he drew it on people's skin." I shrugged as if it was no big deal. "Actually, I should say that he *was* a tattoo artist. He's dead now. He died trying to hide from bullies like you. The only thing I had of his was his journal – you know, that notebook you destroyed in the fountain for the amusement of your loyal subjects."

"I didn't ask for your life story," Ayaz snarled. I nodded mutely. *I guess that conversation is over.* We got to work building out a plan of our project based on the knowledge we already had about the trials and what we needed to research. Ayaz jotted notes, his hand moving across the page in swift circles as he doodled a plan for our presentation. Then we each opened our books and worked in silence.

A few moments later, a pen tapped against the page under my nose. I looked up, startled.

"That wasn't me," Ayaz said, his expression unreadable. "I didn't destroy your friend's book."

I searched his face for any sign that he was messing with me, but he was, as usual, impossible to read. All I saw in his eyes was barely subdued rage. Was that anger for me, or was it about something else entirely?

I shrugged, because what was I supposed to say?

"I don't go in for property damage," Ayaz added. "That's more Trey and Courtney's style."

"You're more of a maggots-in-my-breakfast and tar-my-hair guy," I shot back, my hand flying to my head again. "Sorry, if you're looking for some kind of moral high-ground, you're not getting it from me."

"I didn't touch your hair. That was all Courtney." Ayaz looked away. It was odd, almost as if he didn't want to think about the maggots. Well, tough. I didn't want to think about them either, but the vision of their wriggling bodies entered my mind every morning as I took my seat in the dining hall.

"Even if you weren't the one who tarred my hair or destroyed the journal, you stood there while they did it. You didn't stop them. Seems like I'm the only one around here standing up to the bullies at this school, and look what I have to show for it?" I pointed at my head.

"Trey's not a bad guy," Ayaz said.

I snorted. "You've met him, right?"

"There are things you don't know."

"Fine, whatever. What I do know doesn't exactly fill me with warm fuzzies."

"Courts is a piece of work. Tillie and Amber will follow her lead. But Trey... he and his family kind of adopted me when I came to this country, when I was alone. He's like a brother to me. He has his own issues. There's more to him than what you see."

I snorted. "Oh yes. I'd love to have a heart-to-heart with Trey Bloomberg, find out what deep secrets in his heart make him want to torment me. Are you going to be an artist?"

Ayaz bristled. "That's a swift change of subject."

"Yeah, well, maybe I don't want to waste the one mildly pleasant conversation we'd had talking about Trey fucking Bloomberg. I'm dying to know what people are going to do when they're done with this stupid school. Are you all going to be fucking monarchs in the real world, too? Answer the question. Artist, or maybe architect?" I pointed to the perfect floorplan in front of me.

"No." Something flashed in Ayaz's eyes that I couldn't place. Something like a real human emotion. "I'll be a doctor."

I tilted my head to the side. "I can't imagine you as a doctor. You're going to have to work on your bedside manner."

"Yeah, well." Ayaz's body locked down, whatever emotion I'd seen locked tightly away again, replaced by the simmering resentment that I was beginning to suspect was a cover for something much deeper and darker. "You don't know everything."

"Not much time to draw pictures as a doctor."

"Correct." Ayaz's tone said that he wasn't up for discussing it further.

"I'm going to business school. One day I'm going to look at all the monarchs from across a boardroom table, and I'll be able to buy and sell the lot of you, and maybe then you'll know what it means to be treated like shit just because of what you look like or where you came from."

Ayaz's eyes burned into mine. "There's a lot you don't know about this school."

"What's there to know? It's a bunch of snobby kids who are

going to be snobby adults in unhappy marriages, breeding the next generation of snobby, unhappy kids."

"You think you know what's going on," Ayaz hissed. "But you can't even begin to imagine. The future of the modern world is decided in this school. There are kids here with the power to topple nations, to bankrupt the world's financial institutions, to commit unspeakable acts of evil. If you knew the truth of who you'd face across the boardroom, or the source of their power, you wouldn't want to be any part of it. You'd either go mad from the revelation or flee into the peace and safety of the ghetto from where you came."

I snorted. "You sound like Thomas Parris, talking about his Great Old Gods. You don't know me. You don't know what I can handle. I'm not afraid of you or Trey or anyone else at this school."

Ayaz's face darkened. When he spoke, his voice had this dead, resigned tone that sent a chill through my body. "You should be."

CHAPTER FOURTEEN

Ayaz's warning echoed in my head for the rest of the week. Every time I thought of it, and the way he'd said it in that dead, hopeless voice with his eyes flashing, a chill ran over the back of my neck.

Or maybe that was just me getting used to my new haircut. Greg hadn't stopped praising it ever since I unveiled it at rehearsal. I hadn't told him about the tar. The look of abject pity on Loretta's face as she watched me cutting my hair off had been burned into my brain. I couldn't bear it if Greg looked at me in the same way. I told him that Headmistress West forced me to cut off my locs, and left it at that.

As the weekend drew close, people lost interest in me in lieu of gossip about Saturday's party – who was going, what were they wearing, what alcohol and drugs had been smuggled in courtesy of staff members amenable to bribery. Quinn hadn't spoken to me since the previous week, so I assumed Courtney had made her point and he was back licking her boots.

After Saturday dinner, I went to the library with Greg and Andre to study for a couple of hours. We got next to nothing done because all he wanted to do was berate me for not going to the party. I was starting to appreciate Andre's company more – he would wiggle his eyebrows at me and make funny faces while Greg yammered on. His stone-faced demeanor was a mask, just like the masks we all wore. Underneath, Andre had a wicked sense of humor, and I almost forgot that he was mute. It was nice to hang around someone who didn't expect you to fill in the silences or bombard you with a hundred questions.

Finally, I gave up and suggested we turn in for the night. We walked back through the dorms toward our staircase. I couldn't help but notice how empty it was, all the doors shut, no music thumping or voices laughing. We stopped outside Quinn's door – it was locked when I tried the handle, and there was no loud music or fucking sounds coming from within. "See?" I beamed at Greg. "He's already left for the party. I'm off the hook."

Greg looked gutted. "Damn, I was rooting for you."

"Yeah, well..." We descended our staircase into the gloom. "At least this way I don't have to wear some uncomfortable, ill-fitting party dress. I can just chill out with a book and—holy shit!"

I swore as a shadowed figure moved in the darkness, reaching for me. Quinn's laugh rolled from the gloom, deep and throaty and intoxicating.

"Fuck!" I flicked on the hallway light. Quinn leaned against the bare stone wall, rolling a joint between his fingers. With his emerald dress shirt untucked at the waist, matching his dancing eyes, and a leather jacket slung casually over his shoulder, he looked every bit the bad boy cliche.

He also made my chest tighten and a warm fire flicker to life in my core. Quinn's coconut and sugar scent combined with the sweetness of the weed and swirled inside my head, turning me about, making me dizzy and disoriented. Smoke tendrils curled around his face, giving him a sinister quality that was utterly irresistible.

"I've been waiting for you," he said.

"I couldn't think why." I pulled my key from my pocket, then stopped, waving it in his face. "Wait, I don't need this. You've got a key to my room. Why didn't you just go in, make yourself at home, destroy a few more of my possessions."

Quinn shrugged. "Not me." He grinned. "None of that shit was me."

"I don't believe you. Go away, Quinn."

"No can do. You said you'd be my date."

"That was before you put tar in my hair." Behind me, Greg gasped. Andre made a choking sound. Shit, I hadn't meant for them to find out.

"Like I said, wasn't me. You owe me a favor, Hazy, and I'm cashing in. Put something sexy on, you're coming to a party."

"No, I'm not."

"Yes," Greg shoved me toward the door. "She's going. Put on that black dress I saw hanging in your closet. It's gorgeous." Andre was nodding vigorously.

"Listen to bum boy and the mime here," Quinn jerked his thumb at Greg and Andre.

I unlocked my door and slid into the room, peering out at Quinn through the gap. "Fine. I'm only going if Greg, Loretta, and Andre can come too."

"Sorry, Hazy, that's not a good idea."

"Bye, then." I tried to shut the door in his face. But Quinn shoved an expensive boot into the door, jamming it open.

"If it were up to me, we'd bring along your merry crew. I literally do not give a shit. I'm sick of partying with the same old boring people, anyway. But Courts has got a price on your head, and she's going to bring them all down with you. At least while you're there, you're under my protection. If your friends come, they're sticking their own heads above the parapets, because I can't protect everyone. You got me?"

Greg held his hands up. "My head looks much better on my shoulders. I'll stay behind."

Andre hesitated for a moment, then stepped closer to Greg. I glared at them both. *Fucking traitors.*

Quinn lifted an eyebrow. "C'mon, Hazy. What if I promise nothing bad will happen to you?"

"A promise from Quinn Delacorte doesn't mean anything to me."

"Fine, then can I appeal to your curiosity? Just for one night, wouldn't you like to know how the other half live?"

He got me. I didn't care about their expensive clothes or fancy alcohol or illegal party drugs, but I was desperate to understand what made Courtney and Trey and Ayaz and even Quinn tick. What had Ayaz been talking about in the library, about the real secrets of this school? What made all these people so much better than me and my friends?

I sighed. "Fine. I have to change. Wait out here." I kicked the door against his foot.

Quinn didn't move his boot, although he winced as the door slammed against it. He stuck out his lower lip. "Let me in, Hazy. I'll help you change."

"No."

Please?" Quinn blew out smoke. "It's cold, and I can hear rats crawling through the walls. I'm too pretty to be mauled to death by rats."

"I beg to differ." I yanked the door back and slammed it hard against his boot, which for all its expensive leather tooling didn't look as though it was very tough. I guessed right. Quinn yelped and jerked away, and I managed to shut and lock the door.

"What's going on?" Loretta glanced up from the desk, her eyes wide. "Was that Quinn Delacorte?"

"The one and only. He's invited us to a party tonight." I riffled through the clothes in my closet. What did I own that I could wear to a Derleth party? I held up the black jersey knit bodycon dress that I'd found in a thrift store back in Philly, the dress I knew perfectly set off my dark skin an hazel eyes. For a second, I imagined Quinn's face when I walked out in this, his lips curling back into that infectious smile as his eyes lingered on my body, devouring me. My skin tingled with the anticipation of it.

Hang on... what am I doing? I don't want Quinn to look at me like that. I might be his date, but I wasn't trying to snare him, especially not when Courtney had her claws in him.

Then why are you going to this party? I admonished myself. *Why is your heart racing at the thought of him perving at you in a dress?*

"Us?" Loretta's voice held a note of suspicion. "And you're going? Come on, Hazel, it's another trick. They're trying to lure you out so they can do something terrible."

Probably. Her words stabbed at my chest, like a knife twisting in my heart. The fire Quinn had stoked within me fizzed out.

"Why would you trust Quinn after what they did to your hair?" Loretta added, twisting that knife deeper.

But Loretta was also asking a very good question, one I should have already answered for myself. My fingers folded over the hanger. Why *did* I trust Quinn? Why was I going? Just because Quinn said I owed him a favor? What was he going to do to me if I refused? It couldn't be any worse than the things they'd already done.

I *wanted* to go to the party, and I wanted to go *with Quinn*. I wanted his eyes on me and his hands on my body and I wanted to see his face light up with that beguiling smile because of something I said. That was fucking ridiculous and impossible because Quinn was a King and I was the nobody, the gutter whore, but there it was.

Well, fuck Quinn and his smile. I might be going to his party but that didn't mean I'd play by his rules. I shoved the dress back in the closet and settled on a pair of skinny jeans, a white tank, and my leather jacket. I secured the chain holding my room and locker keys around my neck and lifted up the corner of the mattress, where I kept the mirror shard. I shoved it into my pocket. With my new short haircut, I looked more like a Badlands street fighter than a prep school girl.

At least I'm me.

When I opened the door again, Quinn's eyes bugged out of his head. "Yeah, you looking damn fine, Hazy, but that's not going to cut it as an outfit."

"Oh, I'm sorry. I left all my cocktail dresses and Louboutin heels at my summer house in the Hamptons." I pulled up the collar of my leather jacket. "This is what you get. So either deal, or go to the party by yourself. Personally, I couldn't care less."

"You're always a surprise, Hazy." Quinn cocked an eyebrow at me. He stuck out his hand and pulled me through the door, crushing my body against his. My breath caught in my throat as he pressed his chest against mine, as his scent invaded my nostrils and his lips danced tantalizingly close to mine. The air between us crackled with fire.

"Mmmmm." Quinn's voice rumbled in my chest as he ran a finger over my lips. "You know, we could just skip the party altogether, go up to my room."

It took all my self-control to tear my body from Quinn's and dart away. With my face hidden from Quinn by the gloom of the corridor, I sucked in a deep breath, trying to get my pattering heart and flame-kissed skin under control. "Let's hit the party. I'm dying to see the rich kids of Derleth trying to tap a keg without ruining their manicures."

"Ladies choice. We're going this way." Quinn grabbed my hand and led me in the opposite direction, away from the stairs. At the end of the hall, he jiggled the handle on the last door until it opened. This room didn't have a number scrawled on the door. Quinn picked something metal off the floor, and after a few flicks, a small flame inside an old-fashioned lantern leaped to life.

I gasped and staggered back, shocked by the fire, but after a moment I realized it was under control, of course it was, and my breathing calmed.

In the flickering light, I recognized the space as a mirror image of the room Loretta and I shared, except instead of beds and a desk and closet, there were old desks and boxes stacked around the walls. There was no window on the other end, only a tall mirror coated in dust.

Quinn went straight up to the mirror and slid his fingers under the frame. After a moment, the glass swung out into the room, revealing a set of dark stone steps twisting upward.

"Ladies first," Quinn gestured with a bow.

A shiver ran down my spine. "Fuck no. Your favor was for a party, not stepping into Narnia."

Quinn sighed. "It's a secret passage. Old rich eccentric people like the family that built this house had them installed so they could escape if the Japanese invaded or some shit. It'll drop us out near the party and I won't have to sneak you through the halls with teachers on duty."

Scritch-scritch-scritch, went the rats in the walls as they scurried along the roof and circled the walls of the tunnel.

I didn't move. My mind raced with all the things that could go wrong if I stepped into that dark passage with Quinn.

"Come on, Hazy. We're missing the party."

"I'm not going first so that you can slam the door on me and leave me trapped in a hole in the wall." *Especially not with those rats scritch-scritch-scritching inside.*

"You're so paranoid." Quinn stepped inside with the lantern, folding his bulk into the narrow space. He moved up two steps and then held his hand out for me.

"Gee, what reason would I have for being paranoid, I couldn't even think." Thinking about the shard in my pocket, I accepted his hand, climbing into the mirror. His fingers were hot against mine, sending a line of fire straight into my core.

Inside the cramped space, Quinn's coconut-and-sugarcane scent rushed over me, tropical and tantalizing. The lantern light flickered in front of us, illuminating just enough so that I could see the curve of his ass in his designer jeans.

After twenty steps, we entered a narrow tunnel. The rough stone floor sloped downward. Somewhere in the distance, water dripped, and the air had a damp quality that made my sinuses itch. "This runs under the fields," Quinn explained, holding the lantern high so that I could see as well.

I remembered what Ayaz had said about Thomas Parris building secret caverns and tunnels into the bedrock beneath the house, so that his coven could meet in secret to perform their rituals. Was this one of them? A faint chill wafted over my bare neck, but it did nothing to quell the fire inside me ignited by Quinn's touch.

We walked for what seemed like ages before I could see a faint dot of light. Quinn pulled me forward, and we exited the mouth of the cave. A freezing wind whipped up from below us, and I pressed my back against a rock face.

"Here's the rule, if you use this tunnel, you've got to cover up the entrance," Quinn swung a mess of vines and branches over the cave. "We don't want anyone else finding it."

"Who's we?"

"Trey, Ayaz, and me. There are three secret tunnels that lead out of school. We're the only ones who know about this one. And now you."

Why was he sharing this with me? What made him think that he could trust me when his friends so obviously hated me? "Quinn, what is—"

He held a finger to his lips. "I know what you're going to ask, Hazy. I'll tell you one day, but it's a long story. Tonight, we party."

Confused, I let Quinn grip my hand and led me away from the cave entrance. "Where are we?" I asked, suddenly afraid. In front of me, there was only a narrow ledge. Below my feet, waves crashed against the cliffs below, the ocean rumbling through my bones, deep and resonant, like Ayaz's voice.

"We're on the eastern tip of the peninsula," he said. "The eminent Thomas Parris created a pleasure garden here for his Bacchanalian orgies. You know about the history of the school?"

I nodded, then realized he wouldn't be able to see me. "Yes. Ayaz told me, in a rare moment when he wasn't scowling."

"I wouldn't take it personally. Ayaz scowls at everyone. Even Trey, and they're practically brothers. So yeah, apparently, this Parris guy loved to party. The shindigs here used to be out of this world. It's said that they summoned all kinds of demons and dark things that terrorized the whole area. The school owns it now, of course, and we're not supposed to go down here. It's too dangerous, which of course is part of the appeal. Hold on. I've got you." His hand tight around mine, Quinn made his way down the narrow path. I kept my eyes on my feet. One wrong move and I'd slide over the edge and dash myself across the rocks below.

Is that such a bad thing?

I pushed the dark thought aside. I hadn't thought something like that in a couple of months, not since I watched the flames tear through the apartment and wondered if I should throw myself upon them. *I'm a survivor. I don't give up.*

But was I? Being at Derleth made me doubt everything I thought I knew, even about myself.

Our path joined others snaking around the cliffs. The paths joined and widened, and I started to notice details of the garden. Deliberate beds and niches were set into the rocks, housing weird statues and wilting plants. Nature had re-asserted herself after the garden had fallen into ruin – weeds twisted through the rocks, overtaking the beds and choking the statues.

The cold stole my breath. Bitter wind rushed up from the ocean below. Salt water misted my legs as I picked my way down the path after Quinn. Despite the cold, girls sauntered past in sleeveless dresses and towering heels. *How are they not human Popsicles?* I rubbed my arms through my leather jacket as I surveyed the party.

We stood on a wide, oddly-shaped terrace carved from the cliff. Students spread out along the craggy rocks, laughing and drinking from red plastic cups or passing around pipes filled with God knows what. The terrace had been set up with a dance floor along one end. No shitty playlist from someone's phone at this elite party, but an actual live band made up of juniors I recognized from the drama department played weirdly out-of-date 90s emo music while girls swayed and ground against each other. Behind the band was an elaborate grotto carved into the rocks, inlaid with a frieze depicting satyrs and maenads in all kinds of lewd poses. A waterfall cascaded off the rock-face and trickled through a series of pools, where students bathed surrounded by hundreds of twinkling candles.

At the other end of the terrace, a stone gazebo stood on top of a rock ledge, appearing to float above the ocean. The roof had caved in, leaving the structure open to the sky. A brazier in the center held a blazing fire, and I could see students huddled around, covered with blankets and talking in low voices. In the darkness, I couldn't make out any faces. I didn't like not knowing where Courtney was, not when I stood this close to the edge of a precarious cliff.

I followed Quinn through a crowd, glancing back over my shoulder every few steps in case she snuck up behind me. Quinn led me straight to a folding table heaped with alcohol. He grabbed us both cups and set about mixing a couple of drinks. I watched his movements like a hawk. If he put something in my drink, I didn't see it. But I swapped our cups around and waited until he took a sip first before I did the same.

"You're paranoid," he grinned, clinking his plastic cup against mine.

"I've seen *Carrie*. You and your girlfriend could have planned some humiliating stunt."

Quinn rolled his eyes in an adorable way, and despite myself, a laugh rumbled up through my belly. "If you're talking about Courtney, she's not my girlfriend."

"She believes she is. And I'm probably going over a cliff or drinking rat poison tonight because of it."

Quinn threw his arm around me and thumped his chest. "She'll have to get through me first."

My heart soared, and I hated myself for being sucked in by Quinn's charm. I wanted so badly to believe that this guy actually genuinely wanted to hang out with me. I was even starting to like the silly nickname he'd given me. But the wind bit against my bare neck and I stiffened, sliding out from under his arm. "Is there any food?"

Quinn pointed to another table, where someone had laid out platters of food. Lots of weird-looking fishy stuff on crackers, no thank you. *Ooh, cocktail sausages.* I popped two in my mouth. *Wheeee, they're quite spicy.*

I grabbed a handful of chips and munched on them while Quinn watched, mouth agape.

I stared at him, mouth still filled with sausage and chips. "What? You never seen a girl eat before?"

Quinn whistled. "No, not really. Most of the girls here are on some annoying diet. No starch! Only two hundred calories! No sugar! Boring, boring, boring. I've never seen a chick plow through a bowl of chips like that."

"Yeah, well, where I come from, you never say no to food, because you don't know how long it will be until your next meal." I licked salt off my fingers and reached for another cocktail sausage.

"I can't even imagine," he said. The way he said it, it wasn't mean. It was just a statement of fact. He literally *couldn't imagine*, because being hungry was so far out of his realm of experience.

"I can't imagine living the way you do, where you could have anything you possibly wanted and every opportunity at your fingertips. I can't imagine snapping my fingers and having people jump to do my housework or make my food or get me off."

"When you put it like that, it does sound pretty amazing," Quinn agreed. He flashed me a smile, but it didn't reach his eyes.

Ah, now there's something real behind the trickster King's mask. "Isn't it?"

"You want to swim?" Quinn asked, changing the subject with a swiftness I couldn't help but notice. "The pool is fed from a natural spring. It's actually quite toasty once you get your clothes off."

"I'd love to swim." The words came out too fast. It was reckless to risk taking my clothes off here, but the thought of seeing Quinn with his shirt off, in the water, all those muscles and tattoos on display... I glanced around again. Courtney was nowhere in sight. In fact, no one seemed to have noticed Quinn here with me. I dared to believe it might be okay.

Quinn grinned and grabbed my hand, dragging me to the edge of the rocks. Clothes and shoes were strewn everywhere. I peered into the water, noting the number of couples pressed together in the dark corners. In the middle of the pool, where the water was so deep the bottom was only a black abyss, Amber and Madison splashed around with a couple of guys. My chest tightened. If they were around, then Courtney and Tillie couldn't be far away—

Quinn tugged off his jacket and laid it down on the rocks, stepping out of his jeans to reveal those lean, muscular legs. My mouth dried as he shrugged off his shirt, revealing broad shoulders and a tight, toned chest crisscrossed with tattoos. My finger flew to the burn on my wrist as he looped a finger into his boxers and tossed them aside, too.

"You coming, Hazy?" He grinned at me, enjoying himself.

I tried to stop looking, but I couldn't. I'd never seen a guy completely naked before. And here was Quinn, standing around all tight muscle and bad-boy swagger like it was the most natural thing in the world. His cock bounced as he clambered up the rocks. *How can he be that big? How can something that big fit inside a girl?*

I pressed my finger into the scar as my body flushed with heat, jamming my thighs together in a vain attempt to quash the violent urge that flared inside me. *I do not want to find out. That's not why I'm here. I do not want to find out...* "Quinn, wait—"

He sat on the edge of the rocks, swinging his legs, giving me ample view of that glorious cock. "Yes, Hazy?"

"I didn't bring my bathing suit."

"Too bad." Quinn couldn't have sounded less upset if he tried. He swung his legs over the side and lowered himself into the water. My mouth dried as his taut buttocks disappeared beneath the surface.

Oh, fuck it.

Before I could change my mind, I slipped out of my jeans, tank top and jacket and balled them up inside Quinn's clothes. I left my room key and locker key on the chain around my neck. Luckily, I'd chosen a black bra and underwear that, while not exactly Victoria's Secret, at least wasn't sagging or riddled with holes. I was more covered up than most of the other girls in string bikinis.

Cold ocean air caressed my arms, raising rows of goose pimples across my skin. I scrambled up the edge of the rocks and sank into the hot water beside Quinn. I gasped as heat pooled in my body, partly from the hot water and steam, partly from Quinn's fingers trailing along my arm.

Only water separated us – a few flimsy molecules between his completely naked body and my nearly naked one. I was grateful for the cloak of darkness that hid the heat flooding my cheeks. I crossed my arms over my chest, anxious to pretend everything was cool, that I wasn't falling apart because I was sitting in a hot spring with Quinn Delacorte.

I settled onto a shelf of rock that acted as a seat and looked around, trying to recognize the other faces in the candlelight.

Ayaz sat opposite us across the pool, with a girl under each of his arms. He talked to them in his low, sexy voice, and even across the water, the sound of it vibrated through my body. Something about the Kings of Derleth was impossible to resist.

Quinn's arm went around my shoulders. A thread of panic rose up inside me, and I pushed myself off from the edge to give myself space. I needed to breathe. I needed to figure out what I was doing here, how I'd let myself be tempted into this grotto, in my *underwear*.

I blamed Quinn Delacorte's fucking *smile*.

The rocks were slippery, and the middle of the pool was deeper and hotter than I'd expected. I couldn't see or feel the bottom, just a black hole of water stretching down into infinity. I tried not to think about eels and other things that might lurk down there.

Quinn swam up beside me. "I'll beat you to the other side," he said, dog-paddling toward a crag of rocks near Ayaz.

I followed him, hauling myself on the rocks. Here, I could see over the edge of the pool. Surprisingly, the garden carried on beyond, the terraces stepping down through an avenue of trees to a heavily wooded area at the bottom enclosed in a high metal fence.

"What's that?" I asked, pointing at the metal gate.

"Oh, that's the cemetery."

"What?" *Why would a school need a cemetery?*

"It started off as the Parris family plot. Once the school took over the land, some of the early alumni wanted to be buried there, and the school allowed it provided they were sufficient benefactors. Mine and Trey's grandfathers are both buried there. There was an accident here a few years back, and some kids died. They're buried there, too."

"What kind of accident?" In all the internet searches I'd done about the school, I never saw anything about a fatal accident.

Quinn avoided my eyes. "I don't really know. It was ages ago."

I shuddered. "I can't imagine being buried at a *school*. That seems really sick to me. Will you be buried there?"

"Nope. I intend to go out in a blaze of glory crashing my father's plane into a mountain," Quinn grinned. "There won't be anything left to bury."

"That's gross. Can we go down and look?" Something about those metal gates tugged me forward. I don't know why. It wasn't as if I hadn't already seen too much of cemeteries. My mom and Dante had been cremated, both their bodies and their spirits consumed by flames. They each had a tiny plot in an inner-city cemetery – it was all I could afford. But being buried on the edge of a cliff facing the rolling surf, it seemed different somehow. I wanted to see, to understand.

"What are you, morbid or something? We're not going down there." Quinn wrapped his arm around my shoulders again, his fingers hanging dangerously close to my breast. My body gave in to the heat of his touch, sinking back into the water, forgetting all about the cemetery in the haze of his emerald eyes.

"Why not?" The words came out in a whisper.

"Because I had something different in mind." Quinn trailed a finger along my cheek, stopping for just a moment over my lips. His touch left a trail of fire against my skin.

I gulped. "Quinn, maybe we should—"

Quinn's lips were on mine, hot and needy, tearing my next words and tossing them to the breeze. His heat melted something in me, something that had been cold and frozen for too long. I melted against him, skin on skin. My hands gripped his shoulders, relying on his taut muscles to hold me upright because my whole body had turned to jelly. Quinn parted my lips, and his tongue glanced over mine, and the fire within me ate away at my insides until I was nothing but warm lips and tongue and electric pulses and singed flesh.

Is this really happening? I pressed my hand to Quinn's chest and there was his heart, beating a steady, languid rhythm.

My first kiss.

Was this what kissing felt like? Like jumping off a cliff without a parachute, like falling and never reaching the ground, like standing up really fast and feeling all the blood rush from my head? Or was that just Quinn, the King of the school who took the outcast to a party because he could, who kissed her under the stars because he felt like it?

Hot skin pressed against skin. Steam from the pools twirled around us, like fingers drawing me deeper. My whole body roared with fire. *Why is it always fire?*

A terrible sadness gripped me, because this kiss was the greatest thing that had ever happened to me. It was amazing. It was breathtaking, and it should have been with someone else. But he was dead, consumed by fire. And now here I was, igniting a flame inside myself with another guy before Dante's had been properly put out.

The sadness only made me press harder, my body arching into Quinn's, seeking the solace of his touch. He didn't grope at my breasts, instead trailing his fingers down my spine, over my hips, brushing the edges of my bra. Quinn pressed his thigh against my leg and I could feel his hardness and my throat closed up but my body begged for more, more, *more...*

Through the mists, I saw Ayaz on the other side of the pool. One of his girls was nibbling on his ear, while the other had her hand under the water, pumping up and down and... I could guess what she was doing. He should have been paying attention to them, but his eyes locked on me, those dark irises burning with hate.

A shudder ran through my body that had nothing to do with desire. Quinn sensed it. He pulled back. "What's wrong?"

"I'm sorry," I whispered. "Ayaz."

Quinn glanced over his shoulder and flashed Ayaz the finger. "Hey, bro, stop making eyes at my date. You're putting her off."

"Don't bring plague victims into the grotto," Ayaz shot back, rolling his head back so he stared at the stars. The girl in front of him was really going for it. I slunk away from Quinn, not wanting to see Ayaz get jerked off. Quinn took my hand and pulled me back against him, pressing my back against his chest so that his arms wrapped around my front and my ass pressed up against his... against *him*.

"Don't let Ayaz get to you," Quinn murmured against my ear. My body shuddered in response – the good kind of shudder this time. "It's nothing personal. He hates all scholarship kids."

"Why?" I was finding it hard to speak with Quinn pressed up against me.

"Because he used to be one."

Quinn let that piece of information hang in the air. I opened my mouth to ask more. It didn't make sense ... Ayaz was a King... he had all those merit points... the only scholarship plan was for seniors... so how could he have been like me?

But Quinn was clearly done with talking. He nibbled my earlobe until I gasped, then tilted my head back and pressed his lips to mine, and I forgot all about Ayaz. Quinn's hand pressed against the back of my neck, angling me just so. His mouth devoured mine and I trailed my tongue along his lips. He tasted the way he smelled – like coconut and sugarcane, like the sweetest dessert mingled with a slight tang from the weed. I forgot about Ayaz, forgot about Dante, and lost myself in Quinn's expert arms.

"Quinn! I need to talk to you!"

Courtney's shrill voice pierced my ears, jolting me back to reality. Quinn's whole body tightened. He drew away from me, his eyes drifting to the heavens.

"She hasn't seen you yet. I need to deal with this." He slid out of the water, trailing his fingers along the top of my head in a possessive way I kind of liked. "Wait here for me."

Before I had a chance to reply, Quinn clambered over the wet rocks to where Courtney and her friends were lounging, wearing expensive designer dresses and kicking off their expensive shoes like it didn't matter if they rolled off the cliff. He bent down and planted a kiss on Courtney's ruby red lips. A dark thread of jealousy curled up my spine. I pressed my finger into the burn on my wrist as Courtney sank back against the rocks, giggling as she pulled Quinn on top of her.

I'm so stupid. I thought when Quinn said he was sorting it that he meant he was breaking up with Courtney. *For me.* Fire burned in my cheeks – the fire of humiliation. Of course, Quinn wouldn't be dropping Courtney for me. He'd brought me here specifically because he wanted me to see this. It was all part of a monarch game.

I have to get out of here.

I turned back to the water. The group with Madison and Amber had moved into the center, so I'd have to go around them. I pushed up from the side and dog-paddled my way to where I'd got in. As I neared the edge, Ayaz reached out and wrapped his wrist around my hand. I yelped. He yanked me so hard toward him I nearly kicked the girl between his legs.

"What are you doing here?" he growled, his face inches from mine. Despite myself, his voice still sent flames of desire through me. Behind him, I could see the girl staring at us in confusion. I didn't blame her. I'd be confused too if I was jerking a guy off and he suddenly dragged over the most shunned student in school. Ayaz's second girl was nowhere to be seen.

"Quinn invited me," I said. The words came out more like a question. I berated myself. *You have to be strong around him or he'll eat you alive. Get it together.*

"You don't belong here. You should leave."

"Forget about her, Ayaz," the girl simpered in his ear, running her manicured nails down his naked chest. "I've got something right here you want…"

Ayaz shoved her off him. He leaned right in close, his breath hot against my face, caressing the same places Quinn had just been kissing. My whole body tingled with an electric charge that pulsed between us. If I moved even an inch, we'd be pressed together, skin on skin.

Ayaz tilted his head to the side. "Watch out for Trey tonight," he whispered, his lips grazing my ear.

"Why?" I said, but Ayaz was already floating away, his dark eyes boring down on me, begging me for something I didn't understand.

Why did he tell me that? It sounded like a warning. But if Trey was planning something for me, why would Ayaz bother to warn me?

I flicked my gaze over to him, but he leaned back against the rocks, his blonde friend straddling him and... yeah, my cheeks flushed. It was definitely time to get out of the grotto.

I pressed my hands against the rocks and shoved myself up. Instantly, goosebumps rose on my skin. God, it was cold out here. I scrambled down the rocks, picking through the expensive shoes and discarded designer dresses, searching for where I'd left my clothes balled up inside Quinn's jacket.

Ah. There's Quinn's jacket, and underneath... my hands grasped thin air.

Huh?

Quinn's boxers, jeans, and shirt were there, but my clothes weren't. I tugged everything inside out, then searched the nearby rocks, thinking they might have been kicked aside accidentally. *We definitely left our clothes here, and...*

Cold panic settled on my shoulders. This wasn't an accident. Quinn had talked me into going into the grotto, and now my clothes were missing. And my mirror shard. I was shivering, practically naked, in the middle of this party filled with people who wanted to do me harm.

Shit. Hazel, you're an idiot. You brought along a weapon to defend yourself, and then you let them get their hands on it.

A few feet away, Someone giggled. "Looking for something, gutter whore?"

I looked up to see Trey's girlfriend Tillie, wearing a red bikini that left nothing to the imagination and a matching red silk kimono and Louboutin heels. She stuck her hand on her hip and curled back her lip in amusement.

Terror rose in my throat. It didn't take a genius to figure out that someone had stolen my clothes. A couple of guys wandered over from the band area. I scanned the area for Quinn, panic swirling inside me, growing bigger and more monstrous as I realized just how perilous this situation had become.

No way was I going to stand around in my dripping-wet underwear and wait for whatever attack was coming. I grabbed a black dress at random from the pile and tugged it over my head. It barely covered my ass, but barely was better than nothing.

"Hey, that's mine!" A hand grabbed my shoulder. "Give that back, you bitch! You'll ruin it!"

"Then give me back my clothes," I yelled, my voice too ragged and panicked to carry any authority. I swung Quinn's jacket over my head and shoved my feet into his boots. More bodies moved down the rocks toward me. I heard guys snickering, girls chuckling like hyenas.

I shoved past Tillie and headed toward the dance floor. *Got to find Quinn. Got to get out of here.*

I couldn't see him anywhere. I raced toward the food and drinks area, scanning the crowd. A couple of guys from the lacrosse game were shaking cocktails for a small crowd. No Quinn. Two bodies tangled together in front of the food table. I squinted. Yes, that was them.

Courtney and Quinn. He was still buck-naked. She had her hands all over him, one graceful leg lifted up and curled around his back, staking her claim. My lips burned as I stood frozen, unable to tear myself away.

She's not my girlfriend, Quinn had said. Well, he could have fooled me. Of course I fell for his shit like an idiot, because I wanted to believe a guy like Quinn could choose me. But nothing had changed – he was still King, she was Queen, and I was *nothing*.

Courtney must've noticed me, because she pulled back and licked her lips. "See something you like, gutter whore?"

I like your boyfriend. Too bad he's a big fucking dicksome idiot. "Nope. I was feeling peckish, but you're just having your 'my heart will go on' moment right in front of the food. Are you sure that's not a health code violation?"

Quinn laughed. He ran a hand through his hair and turned to face me. His smile wobbled. He wasn't as sure of himself as he made out. "Hazy, I—"

Courtney gripped his shoulder, digging her nails into his flesh. Quinn snapped his mouth shut. "Back off, dyke," Courtney hissed. My cheeks burned. I spun on my heel and strode away.

I did a circuit of the party area, walking with purpose and barreling through groups like I was desperate to get to someone even though I was completely alone. I needed to get back to that cave, but I couldn't remember the way. The only other people who knew were Quinn, Ayaz, and Trey. Quinn was clearly out-of-bounds, I wasn't exactly going to go near the grotto again, which meant that I had to find Trey. *Great.*

I found myself back near the drinks table. Thankfully, Courtney and Quinn had moved on. I bypassed the glass bottles and pitchers of red-stained punch and loaded myself up a plate of snacks – satay chicken, sushi, chocolate truffles, little crab cakes with cream cheese. Even if everything else at Derleth Academy sucked, the food was top notch, absolutely amazing. I had no idea how the students got their hands on these expensive ingredients, but I wasn't going to let them go to waste.

I took my plate and wandered over to the moon temple, hoping that the food would calm my churning stomach and give me something to do with my hands so they'd stop shaking. I stood as close to the fire as I dared, enough to catch a scrap of its warmth, but far enough away from the huddled couples that no one would notice me. Far enough that I could pretend the sight of flames curling up toward the sky didn't give me horrible flashbacks.

I finished my food and found the corner of a rock by the edge of the terrace. I swung my legs around, dangling them over the edge and studying the Milky Way splashed across the sky. I imagined Thomas Parris and his friends gathered around a similar fire, wearing robes and chanting in Latin to raise spirits and demons. I felt like the students of Derleth Academy were doing him proud.

A rough hand clamped down on my shoulder, dragging me back against the sharp rocks.

"Quinn—" I gasped.

But it wasn't Quinn. It was Trey. His teeth scraped along my collarbone, biting down against my ear.

"Why can't you listen?" he demanded. "Why can't you stay away from my friends?"

I tried to tear myself from his grasp, but he held me tight against him. I kicked out with my feet, trying to find purchase on the rocks. But all I kicked was thin air as Trey lifted me up, dangling me over the rocks. My wet body welcomed the fire of his skin, even though my heart pattered with fear.

Of course, I never did very well with fear. It tended to make me mouthy.

"You've been coming into my room," I managed to hiss at Trey. He made a growling sound low in his throat, the kind of sound an animal would make if it was being provoked. I knew I should stop talking, but I needed to hear it from him. I needed to know the truth. "You took my journal. You tarred my hair. How did you do it?"

"It doesn't matter *how*," he growled. "It matters why. You had to get the message."

"What message?" My fingers dug into his arm, the only thing stopping me from toppling over the edge.

"That you should give up now. That you should leave this

academy. Just run away, back to your old life, gutter whore. I've tried to make it obvious. I don't know what else to do to make you see…" A wave crashed against the cliffs, spraying us both with dark, cold water. Trey's arm slipped. My feet clipped the edge of a rock. I screamed, but the wind and the sea swallowed my cry.

Trey's arm tightened around my throat. He leaned forward, my whole body tipping, the ocean rushing up to meet me.

My arms swung wild, grasping at air. My feet slipped and skidded against the sharp rocks. The wind whipped up, spraying my naked legs with salt tears.

I'm going to die I'm going to die I'm going to—

Stars spun above my head, the band of the Milky Way swirling with the curl of white froth capping the dark waves. The specks of light becoming the flames of dying stars, the faces of my mother, of Dante. Panic collided with my grief, and the grief and guilt swallowed me up into the cold night. My arms went slack. I stopped fighting. *Fine. Let me die.*

Let me find the only people who will ever love me again, after what I've done.

"The fuck?" Trey growled, adjusting his grip as my whole body slackened. "Hazel?"

"Do it," I choked out. "Go on. Give me what I want."

Trey made a noise in the back of his throat that sounded like an animal in pain. He tossed me to the ground. My body slammed into the hard rocks. Pain arced up my side. My head swam and I gripped the earth as it spun around me.

"Fuck. *Fuck.*" I could hear Trey swearing. Other people were talking in quick, hushed voices. They sounded muffled, as though they were shouting underwater. I lifted my head and tried to see what was happening, but white stars burned and exploded and died in front of my eyes. I placed a hand under my shoulder, trying to shove myself upright, but my body refused to obey. My cheek hit the rock, sending a fresh jolt of pain through me.

Hands wrapped around me, hefting me to my feet. "Hazy. Shit. Can you walk? Lean on me."

Quinn. His touch was a shooting star, jetting fire through my body as he dragged me off the ground. He wrapped his flame-skin around me, steadying me as my legs collapsed beneath me. He pulled me up again, his body acting as both crutch and shield.

"That was *sick*," Quinn spat out, his arms squeezing me so hard I gasped for air. Needles stabbed in my chest as I swallowed the cold. I could only make out faint, spidery shadows through the dancing lights in my eyes, but I figured Quinn was talking to Trey. "All these years you've pulled some fucking sadistic shit, but you crossed a line. You said you were going to steal her clothes and scare her a bit, not drop her over a fucking *cliff*."

"We've never had one like her before." Trey's voice pierced my skull, sending new lights dancing in front of my eyes. "None of that small stuff is going to work. She has to *believe*—"

"You've never acted like this before, either," Quinn shot back. "What's wrong, Trey? Why couldn't you finish the deed, then? What's your father going to say when he finds out?"

I didn't have time to contemplate Trey's words, because Quinn scooped me into his arms and stomped away. I could feel my limbs being poked and jostled as he shoved his way through the crowd.

"Fuck, I'm so sorry, Hazel," he murmured. "I'm going to get you out of here."

"Let me down," I begged. His touch burned. The full fury of what happened rolled over me. *I nearly died. I* wanted *to die.*

I'm messed up. This school is breaking me.

Quinn kept walking, wobbling down one of the narrow paths. I kicked my legs, raking my nails at his face. "Let me down!" I yelled.

"All right. Here, let me help you." He tried to hold me up, but I scrambled away. My legs still wouldn't support my weight, so I crawled on my hands and knees down the narrow path.

"Hazy, wait!" Quinn's voice bounced off the cliffs, but I kicked out at his shins and kept crawling. I leaned against the cliff and managed to haul myself to my feet. With every step, fresh agony splintered my body. *Keep going. Find the cave.*

Horrible, disjointed thoughts pounded against my skill.

This isn't a game anymore.

Trey could have killed me.

He wanted *to kill me.*

And I was going to let him.

The cold crept into my bones as I pulled back the vines to expose the cave entrance. I hugged my arms over my body, but I couldn't keep out the cold. The flame inside me had died.

I felt like a ghost – invisible, cursed, shunned.

This is the last time I fall for the Kings of Derleth and their crap.

I will have my revenge.

CHAPTER FIFTEEN

As I crawled back through the mirror in the pitch black, the hardness of my resolve settled over my heart.

Trey's words echoed over in my head. *We've never had one like her before.* He meant scholarship student. He was saying that what they were doing to me – all the shunning and taunting and bullying – they had done to others. How many others suffered because Trey and Courtney and the other monarchs wanted to maintain their positions at the top?

They were all in on it. Trey, Quinn, Courtney, Tillie, Ayaz. I balled my hands into fists as I thought of the kiss in the grotto, the kiss that left me breathless, my body on fire. Of *course* Quinn had done that as part of the plan. Of course. *How could I be so stupid as to think it meant something to him?*

And Ayaz? He warned me about Trey. *Why? Was that part of the plan, too? So I could feel stupid for ignoring him?* Well, it succeeded. I swallowed hard, my throat aching where Trey's arm had pressed.

I paused outside our bedroom door, listening to the rats circling over my head. Adrenaline still surged in my veins, and my whole body ached from being thrown around the rocks. I pulled my key from around my neck, turning it over in my fingers. I knew if I went inside, Loretta would be in bed. If I knocked on Greg's door, he'd want to talk about the party. I didn't want to talk about it. I didn't want to go to sleep. But I had nowhere else to go—

A light moved past on the landing upstairs, casting brief striped shadows across the corridor. *Odd*. Everyone was at that party, so who was upstairs walking around with a light? Did someone come back early?

Did someone come back to try and catch me?

Curious, I crept up the staircase, listening hard. I could hear quiet voices, footsteps moving through the dorm. It was more than one person, and they were moving quickly in the direction of the main academic wing.

I poked my head up and peered between the railings. My heart leaped into my throat as I saw Dr. Morgan striding down the hall, a black robe fluttering around her legs.

"We've checked all the rooms," she told Headmistress West. The headmistress appeared even more formidable than ever in a high-necked black velvet dress beneath a set of elaborate robes edged with gold trim. She clutched a tall silver candelabra – the flickering candlelight highlighting her sharp cheekbones and pale, porcelain skin. "They're all either at that party, or sound asleep."

"And the scholarship students?" she snapped, a note of distaste in her voice.

"No one stirs," Dr. Morgan said.

"Very well." The headmistress spun on her heel and swept down the hall.

Interesting. I had no idea they conducted this nightly inspection. Greg hadn't mentioned it, either. And what was with the robes? Was it some kind of official academic dress? Were they off to a staff meeting?

In the middle of the night? On a *weekend?*

Curious now, I waited until all the teachers filed out of the dorms then crept down the hallway after them. I hid behind one of the stone columns flanking the entry, peering along the corridor as they walked past the empty classrooms. I expected them to head across the atrium to the faculty wing, but instead, they turned off into a small stairwell. Boots clanged on metal stairs. Candlelight flickered along the rows of lockers.

They were heading down to the gymnasium.

My curiosity piqued further, I crouched low and skirted along the wall, pausing at the top of the staircase. *I'm not supposed to go down there, but I have to know what they're doing.*

I dropped down low and peered around the corner, just able to see their flickering light from the top of the stairs. What were they doing down there? I slunk down the first step. *I have to find out—*

A hand clamped over my shoulder.

I jumped. My mouth flew open, but a hand over my face muffled my scream. On the wrist, I could just make out a small runic tattoo.

"Don't cry out," a familiar voice rasped in my ear. "If they hear you, you're dead meat. And I'm not talking metaphorically this time."

"Quinn?" His name came out as a muffled squeak against his hand.

"The one and only." His grin was just visible in the dim light. "I'm going to take my hand away, but you can't scream, okay?"

He sounded so frightened that I nodded. He dropped his hand and started tugging me back into the hall, back in the direction of the dorm.

"You're hurting me," I hissed. "What are you doing here?"

"I came to give these back to you." Quinn dropped my arm and held out my clothes, rolled into a ball. I took the stack and felt for the shard in my jacket pocket. It was still there. "You can't follow them down there. It's not allowed."

"Since when did you get such a hard-on for the rules?" I

demanded. My finger flew to my wrist, pressing at the dark smudge to remind myself not to think about the kiss, not to fall for this guy's bullshit.

He ran a hand through his hair. It stuck out on one side of his head in this disheveled, totally gorgeous way. He looked like he was having some kind of argument with himself. "I don't. I just don't want you to get in trouble."

"Why would I get in trouble? What are they doing, anyway?"

Quinn focused his eyes at a spot over my shoulder. "They have to go down and run air tests in the gymnasium, to see if the toxicity has gone down enough that they can open the wing again. That's why they check we're all sleeping like good little students first. If any of us are caught down there, they'll be sued."

"Uh-huh." Dr. Morgan said all the students were at the party. They knew we were all breaking school rules, and they didn't care. But did Quinn know that? I thought so, but I wasn't sure.

"I'm begging you, Hazy." We crossed over the covered bridge and Quinn held open the dormitory door for me. "Go to bed. The others are starting to head back from the party. If they see you walking around in their dorm..."

"They'll what?" My hand rested on my throat. "They'll try to kill me again?"

Quinn winced. "That was never supposed to happen. Trey got carried away. There's so much you don't know—"

"Yeah, whatever. What I *do* know is that I should be filing assault charges against your friend. Against all of you." Tears pricked at my eyes, but I was too angry to cry. "Don't pretend you weren't under orders to get me to that party, or to kiss me like that so I'd let my guard down. You *let* them steal my clothes."

Quinn's face told me everything I needed to know. "I didn't know he'd do *that*," he said.

I shrugged. "Yeah. Sure. If Trey tells you to throw me off a cliff, you'd do it. You're just his little errand boy."

Quinn's lip curled up. "You don't know, Hazy."

I snorted. "Yup. That's the truth. And I don't want to, either. I just want to get my diploma and get out of this fucking place."

"That's what we all want." Quinn squeezed his eyes shut, and such an expression of pain wrote itself across his face that even though I fucking hated him, my arms itched to slide around his neck and pull him close.

Footsteps echoed in the corridor behind us. Drunken laughter bounced off the walls. Quinn glanced over his shoulder. "Go," he hissed, shoving me down the stairs toward my dorm. "Sweet dreams, Hazy."

"Rot in hell, Quinn."

I crept back down the stairs just as Courtney's trilling laugh blasted overhead. I shoved my key into my room and slipped inside, my heart pounding.

I felt certain that Quinn was lying about the gymnasium. The way he wouldn't look at me, the fact that the teachers were all wearing those black robes and carrying candles, and that flash of pain in Quinn's face when he spoke about graduating, told me that something was off. Something was going on at this school, and it had nothing to do with bullying.

What were the teachers really doing down there?

CHAPTER SIXTEEN

I had to bide my time for revenge on the Kings. The first step was to enlist Greg's help. That was easy – I told him what Trey had done at the party, how Quinn had got me there, and how Ayaz had known about it but chose to give me a feeble warning rather than stop his friend. Greg agreed that the Kings had to pay.

I didn't tell him about the teachers' late night foray to the gymnasium. Something about Headmistress West's face, about the fear in Quinn's eyes as he dragged me back from the staircase, told me this was something that could put my friend the hopeless gossip in danger.

"So we're doing this," Greg whispered from across our library table. He whipped his head around to make sure no one was in earshot before adding, "*How* are we doing this?"

"Can you get access to the chemistry lab for unsupervised experiments?" I asked. I wasn't taking chemistry, but it was Greg's top subject. He said that he might want his own makeup line one day.

Greg screwed up his face. "Not normally, but Dr. Ellery has a fondness for me. I can probably swing something. What do you have in mind?"

I leaned forward. For the first time since we nailed our audition, I was excited about something at this school. I'd thought long and hard about how to make the Kings and Queens pay without getting in trouble ourselves. I didn't want either of us to lose points over this. "Do you remember what you told us about the rose hips being the active ingredient in itching powder?"

A slow smile crept across Greg's face as I outlined my idea. With our plan set, all we had to do was set it up and wait for the perfect time to use it. When we weren't studying or rehearsing, Greg and I were walking around the gardens, picking the last of the fruits before winter hit in earnest.

It was weird, but ever since the party, the monarchs had been... *nicer* isn't the right word. Courtney and her friends still hissed at me in the halls. I still caught Trey and Ayaz looking at me with contempt. But they seemed to have pulled back on the bullying. Quinn still openly flirted with me, even though he seemed to be back with Courtney. Ayaz and I even had a couple of semi-pleasant conversations while working on our history project.

I thought about calling off the revenge plan. This new peace was nice. I wasn't constantly looking over my shoulder. My stomach unknotted itself. I could concentrate more on my schoolwork and the production. I'd even managed to bring my total up to 450 points. I didn't want to go back to having to constantly worry about when they'd strike back.

But Trey had nearly *killed* me. I couldn't let him keep believing he could treat another human like that. All the monarchs thought they could get away with anything because they were rich and powerful, and they needed to know that wasn't true. *I* needed to believe that wasn't true.

I wasn't just doing this for me, I was doing it for Loretta and Greg and Andre and all the other scholarship students they'd tortured.

My opportunity for revenge came three weeks after the party. In homeroom, Mr. Dexter announced that Saturday was our first parents day for the year. Parents were allowed to visit the academy at any time of the year, but I'd noticed very few of them did. I guessed they were all too busy with their perfect rich-people lives.

Twice a year, Derleth held a parents day, where the school would put on special activities. All the parents came, and then went to a big catered alumni party in the evening, with an open bar, so they could all relive their school days.

It seemed to be a day especially concocted to torture poor orphaned scholarship kids, but it would also give us the perfect stage for revenge. In order to hit the Kings where it would hurt most, we couldn't destroy their property – we had to make them feel small. And in front of their powerful parents was just the place to do that.

Both of us had full jars of rose hips hidden under our beds. Greg secured his lab time to process the hairs inside the fruit into a powder. As he passed my locker to collect me for rehearsal, he lifted the flap of his bookbag to show me two jars of dark powder nestled between his textbooks.

"I hope this works," he said. "I'm ready to see Trey Bloomberg squirm."

Members of the silent maintenance staff drove the official school vehicles down to the bottom of the peninsula to pick up the parents from the fancy hotel in Arkham where many of them were staying. Some parents decided to brave the journey in their own vehicles, and a steady stream of Maseratis, Porches, and Lamborghinis rolled into the visitor parking lot.

Derleth Academy pulled out all the stops with a busy schedule of activities throughout the entire day, starting with a Champagne breakfast, then a tour of the school – including demonstrations and presentations of recent student projects – followed by a catered lunch in a tent on the grounds, where many of the music and drama students would provide entertainment. The day would finish with a centuries-old tradition where the lacrosse team would play a team made up of past alumni. All men, of course, because feminism clearly hadn't yet visited the hallowed halls of Derleth.

At breakfast, the scholarship students took our usual table. I tried not to give the monarchs the satisfaction of staring at their rich, perfect families, but curiosity got the better of me. I watched over the top of my orange juice glass as Trey's parents shoved their way to the head of the monarch's table.

"My other son, Wilhem, is interning at my company," the man who I guessed was Trey's dad – Vincent Francis Bloomberg the Second – told Courtney's mother, his voice booming across the room. He looked like an older version of Trey – the same brown hair that changed color under the light, the same ice eyes flecked with gold, the same self-satisfied smirk. "He'll be taking an executive position within the next six months, that's for certain. But then, I'm not surprised. He inherited the brilliant Bloomberg mind. Trey here takes more after his mother."

I understood that comment was a veiled insult by the way Trey's whole body stiffened. It was weird, because Trey was many things – a bully, an asshole, a manwhore with an incredibly hot body – but he was not stupid. I'd seen him answer enough questions and present enough assignments to know he was top of our class for a reason. His father continued talking as if Trey wasn't there, while his mother was deep in conversation with several other women wearing identical beige pantsuits.

Meanwhile, Quinn was cracking jokes like they were going out of style. He had a slim, beautiful woman on his arm with identical emerald eyes, and he looked at her with a serious reverence I'd never seen in him before. He clearly loved his mother a lot. It was kind of nice to see, given how he treated all other women like they were disposable.

A few people down the table, the man I'd identified as Quinn's father leaned over Tillie's mother, his hand practically brushing her cheek as he tucked a strand of her hair behind her ear, lingering for longer than necessary. He had Quinn's dirty blond hair and handsome face, but there was a cruelness in the tug of his mouth that was chilling.

Interesting.

Between his two friends and their families, Ayaz sat with a stiff back and blazing eyes. He didn't have anyone with him, although Trey's father kept leaning over and nudging him into the conversation. Ayaz would always smile for a moment, then return to his stony brooding face.

I remembered that Trey's parents put up most of the money for the scholarship program, and that Quinn had said Ayaz was a scholarship student, and that the two of them were like brothers. Maybe Ayaz had some private arrangement with Trey's family. Vincent Bloomberg II certainly seemed to have some hold over him.

A hand waved in front of my face. "Earth to Hazel," Greg called out. "What's going on in that head of yours? You've been drinking from an empty glass for the last five minutes."

"Nothing." I slammed my glass on the table and focused on my rapidly cooling breakfast. A few moments later, my gaze slid back to their table, drawn by Trey's dad loudly discussing his eldest son's achievements at college. *It's weird the oldest son wasn't called Vincent, too. Why was Trey given that honour instead of his brother if his dad didn't care about him?* Vincent Bloomberg II kept leaning over to Ayaz and talking about which medical schools he should apply for, but he never said anything to Trey.

"Stop staring at them," Loretta hissed. "You'll draw attention to us."

"You mean more than this stupid parents' event already does?" I growled, because surely the school knew how insensitive this could be for people like us, who'd lost our parents. Of course they knew, they just didn't care. We were there to make them look good, end of.

"Personally, I'm enjoying myself," Greg said. "It's fascinating to listen on these conversations. Some of the most powerful people in the world are standing in this room. The deals made over hand-shakes at these events could change our future."

Beside him, Andre nodded. Because of his disability, Andre was always listening. Last week in the library I asked him if he ever got sick of just listening all the time. He wrote me back a note that said, "Sometimes. But then I think about all the things I've learned because I'm not wasting my energy trying to think up a reply." Andre was wiser than all of us.

"They're also dicks," I said, watching Quinn's dad hold a glass of Champagne for the other woman to drink from his hand. He spilled a little into her cleavage, licked his fingers, and *ran it over her breast*, right in front of his wife. Quinn's mouth set in a firm line, but he kept on making his mother laugh.

"No argument," Greg said, flashing me a knowing look. Loretta glanced between the two of us, suspicion in her eyes.

As we left the hall, Greg winked at me and patted his bag. While the rest of the students and parents headed toward the main academic wing for the morning activities, Greg ducked away to the locker room, where the lacrosse team had already stashed their clothing prior to the game.

I didn't see Greg again until our performance. He waved at me from across the wings, and my chest burst with pride. Despite being the leads in the production, Greg and I were placed in the chorus for today because we didn't have any family attending. We danced and sang our hearts out in the back row, and pulled faces at each other from the wings.

At the end of our performance, all the parents clapped. Except for Trey's dad. When Trey and Ayaz walked off the stage, I overheard Vincent Bloomberg II say, "You were excellent, Ayaz. Trey, I can see all that money I spent on voice tutors was wasted. No wonder you didn't win the lead."

Trey had been note-perfect, sweat trailing down his gorgeous face as he performed a complex dance routine. His dad was even more dicksome than his son.

I had to leave to race to the next classroom, where Ayaz and I were giving a short report about the Salem witch trials. Greg shot me a thumbs up and darted off to his next activity.

We're on.

Ayaz was already in the classroom, setting up our display. While I'd spent the week writing up our report, he'd completed five beautiful pen and ink drawings of the trials and of some of our observations about their importance across history. My mouth dropped when he showed me the final products. They were amazing. They looked like they should be in an art gallery, not part of a history assignment where they'd barely get a second glance.

"These are incredible," I breathed, holding one up to the light. "You've got to mention that you drew these. We'll probably get extra points. I'll do it if you feel weird about it—"

"I'll do the talking," Ayaz snapped, snatching the drawing from my hand. "It's me they're here to see. You just stand aside like a charity case so they can feel as though their money is going to a worthy cause."

Not even Ayaz's comments could get me down today, and since we'd already been given 5 merit points each for agreeing to give the presentation, I let him talk the parents through it. In the front row, Trey's parents stood side by side, both beaming at Ayaz. Was that weird? When it came time for questions, a hand shot up at the back of the room. Trey. He looked his dad straight in the eye and asked, "Don't you think that by focusing on the female victims and using the medieval witch archetypes you're playing into a feminist agenda? Four of the victims of the trials were men, and let's not forget Reverend Parris, turned mad with guilt for acting out the will of his parish and the laws of his church."

At the mention of Parris' name, I noticed several parents in the room stiffened. They must hate being reminded of the school's sordid past. I was glad we hadn't focused on the connection in our presentation today.

Ayaz's face flushed with anger at Trey's comment, but he smoothed it over, rattling off an answer that was more profound than anything I could have come up with. Trey's father beamed at Ayaz, and Trey slunk away before our presentation was finished.

I couldn't believe my luck – for whatever reason, the two Kings of the school were competing for the attention of Trey's father. *This is too perfect.*

I could barely contain my excitement as the game drew close and we were directed onto the field. I had to fake an air of nonchalance. The success of our plan relied on no one figuring out we were behind it.

At the side of the field, the fathers pulled on special polo shirts with DERLETH ACADEMY ALUMNI embroidered on them. Both Vincent Bloomberg II and Damon Delacorte were playing. They laughed and slapped each other's shoulders and called out friendly insults to their sons across the field.

On the other side of the field, Trey gathered the team together in a huddle. From his gestures, I gathered he was discussing tactics, but he had to stop every few moments to adjust his shorts. I couldn't see Ayaz from this angle but I hoped he was doing the same.

Greg slumped down beside me, a wide smile on his face. "What are you so happy about?" I asked, elbowing him in the arm.

"Don't be silly, Hazel. I'm always happy to cheer on our school. Go team!" Greg yelled as Trey and his teammates jogged past. I leaned into Greg's shoulder to hide my giggle. Trey's hand flew to his crotch, and his head whipped over his shoulder at us. I gave him my best wide-eyed innocent look, and as soon as he turned back to the field, I stifled my laugh into Greg's shoulder.

Vincent Bloomberg II was elected as his team captain, so he faced off against Trey in the center of the field. Coach Carter placed the ball on the ground between them, stepped back, and blew the whistle.

Sticks whirled through the air. Trey reached the ball first, and he swung to pick it up with his net. His body listed to the side as his other hand flew to his crotch, and he ended up whacking the ball across the ground. His dad scooped it up and ran toward his goal. The midfielders raced after him. Vincent passed the ball to Quinn's dad, who sidestepped another student and hurled the ball at the goal.

Ayaz was in the goal. He reached up to block the ball, but as he did, his face contorted with agony, and his shoulder dropped. The ball glanced off the edge of his stick before bouncing inside the goal.

Dads 1, Students 0.

Trey trudged back to the center of the field. His teammates called encouragement. His dad sneered. "Clearly, this school's team isn't what it used to be if you're the best they've got."

The whistle blew. Vincent got the ball again. Trey's face reddened. He flung his stick up, swinging it like a baseball bat at his dad. Only he'd miscalculated and instead of hitting his Dad's stick, he brought the swing down on his helmet.

"Slash!" called Coach Carter. "Bloomberg, you're off for five."

"Don't you know the rules?" his father's taunts followed him. "You're a disgrace, Trey. Don't even bother getting back on the field. Your team won't miss you."

Trey slumped off the field. On the bench, he ripped off his

helmet, threw it on the ground, and sat down and shoved his hands in his shorts. His face scrunched up in pain as he scratched and scratched.

Greg and I struggled to hold in our laughter. Loretta glanced over at us with a frown. "Did you guys have something to do with this?"

"Who us?" I said angelically. "We wouldn't dare. Why risk the wrath of the Kings? Trey's probably got an STI."

Greg spluttered with laughter. Loretta shot us both a filthy look. "They'll figure out it's you. They'll kill you for this."

They've already tried.

I focused my attention on the field, not wanting to miss a single moment of sweet revenge. Ayaz was having his own problems. He was so busy itching that he missed two easy goals. By the time the first quarter was over, the Dads were winning 4 to 0.

Trey was allowed back on in the second half, but they'd switched him out from the prime position to left midfield. He stood only ten feet or so from where we were sitting. Every few seconds, his hand drifted to his crotch. He slapped it away, his face twisting with agony.

"Trey, stop scratching your balls and play!" his father yelled.

Trey's cheeks reddened. He jogged back on the field, but a few minutes later, he was scratching himself again. The rest of the game was a massacre. After a while, even the Queens stopped jumping around like fools, bearing their team's defeat in stunned silence.

The fathers won, eighteen points to two. I didn't have to understand lacrosse to know that Trey's team had taken a thrashing. The other dads patted Vincent Bloomberg II on the back. He accepted their praise with a greedy smile.

Damon Delacorte placed his arm around Quinn's shoulder and led him off the field. He flashed a playful smile at his son, which I expected Quinn to return. Instead, he stiffened up and stared at his shoes.

As soon as the players started heading for the lockers, Vincent stalked over to face his son. "You're a disgrace to this family," he snarled, grabbing Trey by the collar. Trey's expression never faltered – he still wore the same stone-faced look he wore. But his eyes flashed with hate.

"I don't think this was his fault," Ayaz said from behind Trey. "It might be a practical joke—"

"Of course it's his fault." Vincent glared at his son. "I'm just sorry you were dragged into this, Ayaz. Clearly, Trey isn't in control of this school. This never would have happened if his brother was here."

"Well, he's not here," Trey snarled, his voice dripping with hate. He slammed his arm into his father's hand, breaking his grip. He staggered back, his shoulders tensed, his hands balled into fists. "You decided I was the one who would stay behind while Wilhem went on to glory."

"Don't you *dare* speak of those things here," Vincent's eyes flashed back, the ice in them even. "You know what's at stake. Do your duty to your family, and you will be rewarded. Embarrass me again, and you'll wish you'd never been born."

He turned on his heel and stalked off toward the lockers. Trey watched him leave, his shoulders sagging. Ayaz placed a hand on his arm, but Trey shrugged it away.

Quinn came running over, his head bent low and a hoodie pulled tight around his face. In what had to be the most perfectly serendipitous moment ever, he had his sports bag slung over his shoulder. I leaned forward, my hand finding Greg's and squeezing it.

"What happened, man?" Quinn dumped down his bag in front of Trey. "You were itching like crazy out there. It was hilarious. People are saying you have an STI."

"I don't want to fucking talk about it," Trey growled, his hands still balled into fists.

Quinn shrugged. His hand tugged on his hood, pulling it even lower over his face. "It was just a game. It doesn't matter."

"That so?" Trey leaned forward and shoved the hood off Quinn's head. I gasped as I saw the swelling around Quinn's eye. In a few hours that would turn seriously black.

Who had hit him, and why?

Quinn dipped his head low. He grabbed the edge of the hoodie from Trey and yanked it over his head. "Fuck you," he whispered.

Trey looked like he was going to say something else, but Ayaz stepped forward and nudged Quinn's bag with his toe. Beer cans and snack bars tumbled out onto the grass, along with a familiar-looking jar.

"Quinn, what are those in your bag?" Ayaz frowned.

"Huh?"

Ayaz kicked the bag, and a second jar rolled out onto the grass. "Those. What are they?"

Quinn stared down at his open bag in confusion.

"Just snacks and refreshments from my personal stash. Here, I brought you one, too. It was meant to be a celebratory drink, but you can use it to drown your sorrows. Hey..." he picked up one of the jars of powder. "What the fuck is this?"

Trey grabbed it from his hands, uncorked the cap, and sniffed the dark powder. He instantly broke into a sneezing fit. "Quinn..." he choked. "You bastard."

"What?"

"You put fucking *itching powder* in our fucking shorts!" Trey yelled. "How old are you, five?"

"I didn't—"

"Of course you did. Who else in this school would do something so juvenile, knowing that all our parents were watching? You didn't just embarrass Ayaz and me in front of Dad, but you embarrassed the whole school. If you don't think there's going to be consequences, then you're even stupider than I thought."

Trey upturned the entire container of powder over Quinn's head.

Shit.

Quinn's face registered surprise. The powder streaked his cheeks and stuck to his lips and eyebrows. He reached up to swipe at his eyes, and then he started to scream.

CHAPTER SEVENTEEN

Quinn's scream tore across the field. Parents and students raced over. The coach blew his whistle.

"It burns," Quinn yelled, clutching his face and tearing at his skin. Dark powder clung to his hair and smeared across his cheeks. *And his eyes... oh god, his eyes...*

Trey's face turned white. "Shit, Quinn." He reached out to grab his friend's shoulder, but Quinn flailed wildly, shoving him in the stomach. Trey staggered away, his eyes wide in horror.

"I can't see. I can't—"

Quinn fell to his knees, scraping at his face, his body trembling. His mother rushed over and wrapped her arms around his shoulders, screaming at someone to help him. Headmistress West sprinted across the field, her Morticia Addams gown streaming out behind her.

"Call an ambulance!" Quinn's mother screamed.

"Do stop sniveling, woman," Damon Delacorte drawled. He stood on the edge of the field, his arms swinging at his sides like he didn't have a care in the world. "He's just being dramatic, the way he always is."

The last time I'd seen Quinn, he'd been heading off the field with his dad, and then he came back with that shiner...

Headmistress West picked up the jar and sniffed the contents. Her nose wrinkled and she gave a loud, unladylike sneeze. "Ah, I think some students have been playing a prank. The nurse should be able to handle this."

"I'm blind!" Quinn wailed.

Trey's shoulders sagged as he watched them drag Quinn away. Ayaz moved beside him, but Trey shrugged him off and stormed away toward the lockers.

My stomach twisted up in knots. I remembered what Greg had said about how he had to wear a face mask and goggles while he ground the itching powder. If too much got in his eyes or nose it could cause permanent damage.

Permanent damage.

I wanted the Kings to suffer the way they'd made me and the other scholarship students suffer, but I didn't want Quinn to go blind.

I stood up, dusting grass clippings from my skirt. "I'm going inside."

Greg lifted an eyebrow. "Want to gloat up-close?"

"Something like that." I circled around the groups of gathered parents, dodging wait staff offering canapés and more glasses of Champagne. I noticed Quinn's dad grabbing two glasses. One couldn't have been for his wife, because she'd hurried off to the nurse's station. Which was exactly where I was going.

From the atrium, I headed into the administrative wing, following Mrs. Delacorte's wails to the nurse's station at the end of a long corridor. I peered around the door, not wanting to barge in if the nurse needed space.

Quinn lay on a hospital bed, clutching his face and howling. The nurse – a portly woman with a kind face who the students called Old Waldron – was making up an eye bath, while Quinn's mother wiped at the powder on his face and hair with a damp cloth, her face screwing up as she got it all over her own skin.

Trey's parents stood beside the bed, watching Quinn with worried expressions. Courtney and her parents were there as well, and her dad was speaking in a loud voice about how they shouldn't give Quinn any medicine, because the FDA deliberately suppressed actual cures in order to line the pockets of the pharmaceutical industry, and would in fact make Quinn worse.

"Dad, just shut up!" Courtney yelled. "My boyfriend could be blinded, so no one cares about your crackpot theories!"

At the word 'boyfriend,' Quinn's mother flinched, but she kept on wiping Quinn's face without saying a word.

"Open your eyes and hold this over them," Old Waldron instructed, trying to pry Quinn's hand away.

"Don't hurt him!" Courtney flew at the bed. As she did, she happened to glance up and see me in the doorway. "What are you doing here?" Courtney sneered.

"Nothing. I—"

Quinn's broken voice punctured the tension in the room. "Hazy? Is that you?"

Courtney rocketed across the room and shoved me. "Get out. He's *my* boyfriend. He doesn't want you here."

"If he doesn't want me, then why was he making out with me at the party?" I sneered back at her.

Wrong thing to say. Courtney shrieked and lunged at me, claws raised. Thinking fast, I stepped back into the hallway and slammed the door in her face. She slammed her fist into the glass. "Next time, that's your face, bitch."

I backed away, my stomach all knotted up. *Quinn, I know you can't hear me, but I really hope you're okay. I didn't mean for this to happen.*

There was no way I was getting back into that room. But there was one more stop I had to make.

Trey. I needed to see him. I couldn't explain why, but when I thought of his white face as his father yelled at him, I knew that I'd unwittingly itched my way into the middle of something dark between them.

Where would Trey go?

I knew better than to look for him with his family or back at his room, where anyone might be able to find him. Instead, I asked where I would go if I was King of the school and I wanted to be alone. There were locker rooms on either wing of the school – one to serve the east fields, one for the west. They were using the east field for the match today, so I headed along the west corridor, past the rows of lockers and empty classrooms. I stood outside the locker door and listened.

For a couple of minutes, I heard nothing. Then an odd sound, like a wail. Like a person in pain.

Summoning the courage, I peered around the door, expecting to see one of the showers leaking or something. What I didn't expect was to see Trey Bloomberg slumped on a bench with his head in his hands and tears streaming down his cheeks.

CHAPTER EIGHTEEN

Okay, what do I do? I'm staring at the guy who's made my life hell. I should be dancing around him in triumph. So why do I feel like crawling into the floor?

I could just say nothing and walk away. But that wasn't my style.

"Hey," I said.

Trey jumped, turning his body away from the door in an attempt to hide his face. "Fuck off," he muttered. There was no fight in his voice.

"Is that any way to talk to the only person who's come to see if you're okay?" I took a step toward him. "Something happened on the field today."

"Yeah. Fucking Quinn." Trey laughed, the sound broken, erratic. He wrung his head in his hands. "I bet you feel fantastic, seeing me like this."

"Did you feel good when you destroyed my friend's journal, or when you stuffed my locker full of meat or threw maggots in my food or tarred my hair, or called me and my friends awful names? Did you feel fantastic when you held me over the edge of a cliff? Did that make you feel like a big, awesome person?"

Trey didn't say anything.

"Quinn didn't put that powder in your shorts. I did," I said. *Fuck, where did that come from?* I hadn't intended to tell him the truth. Trey's eyes widened. The corner of his mouth tugged up, and it almost looked like he smiled.

"Damn, Hazy. I underestimated you."

Hearing Quinn's nickname for me on Trey's lips made it seem different somehow, affectionate. I sucked in a deep breath. *Am I really doing this?*

Guess so. I crossed the room and sat on the edge of the bench. "I thought it would feel good to see you suffer. And it did, for a bit. But your dad is an even bigger bully than you are, and I can't stand watching anyone be bullied."

Trey snorted. "I thought maybe this time it would be different, you know? He'd see that I was top of the school, captain of the team. I did everything he asked for, and it wasn't enough. It will never be enough."

"You don't have to measure yourself by his standards."

"What do you know?" Trey snapped.

"Hey, don't snap at me, or next time it'll be you in Old Waldron's bed with your eyes full of itching powder."

As soon as I said it I wished I could take it back. Anger flashed in Trey's eyes and I shrunk away, afraid he'd hit me. But he didn't. He placed his head in his hands and let out a deep, racking sigh.

"I peeked in on him on my way here," I said. "Courtney was there and she wouldn't let me in. They're washing his eyes out and he'll probably be fine, but he's in agony. You should go. Convince them to call an ambulance."

"They won't. Besides, he won't want to see me."

"I bet you're wrong about that. Assholes like you and Quinn tend to stick together. I noticed you didn't ask me why I did this. It was because you nearly killed me, in case you were wondering."

"You said you wanted to die. You're..." Trey didn't finish his sentence. His eyes locked on mine, deep pools of cool blue – no ice this time, only glittering gold crystals and deep water.

A tap dripped.

Trey's lips met mine, hot and hungry. My whole body responded like I'd been plugged into a light socket. My body trembled as fire danced through my veins. His lips were warm and soft, but the kiss itself was frantic, a mash of teeth and tongues. We bled our pain into each other, relishing what we took because it made the other human, vulnerable. Trey's vulnerability was wild, reckless, desperate for affection, for acceptance. And I gave it to him in this moment, so he would return the favor.

Trey's hands reached up, digging into my hair. "I feel like I'm kissing a boy with this haircut," he murmured.

"Are you gay for me, Bloomberg?" I teased him. He responded by kissing me harder, his teeth grazing my lip, arms wrapping around me and drawing me deeper under his spell. I reached up to touch his cheeks, feeling the wetness of his tears as his mouth drew out a roaring fire from inside me.

What am I doing?

This is Trey Bloomberg. We're not supposed to be kissing. I shouldn't be consoling him because his dad's a bastard. I should be gloating over my revenge.

But instead, my body melted into Trey, flame on flame, heart on heart. The more we kissed, the higher the fire raged inside me, the more of Trey I understood, the more I knew exactly why he had hated me – because when he looked at me, he saw a wildness that he longed to embrace. Trey Bloomberg was just as trapped, just as caged, as I was. The only difference was that his cage was made of gold.

Trey's hands skimmed my body, dragging me closer, tugging me so that I straddled him awkwardly on the bench. His finger snaked beneath the hem of my shirt, untucking it from my skirt so his thumbs grazed my skin. Just that touch made my body flare like a star gone supernova, and I moaned against his lips. Trey's fingers trailed higher, pushing up my shirt, grazing the underside of my bra—

"Trey? You back here?"

Trey jerked away from me, his eyes wide, just as Ayaz came around the corner. I yanked my shirt down, my face hot.

If Ayaz saw what we were doing, he had the fortitude not to mention it, or even to acknowledge my presence with more than a flicker of his dark eyes. "I've been looking for you everywhere. Come on, man. Quinn's asking for us."

"Yeah?" Trey stood up and followed Ayaz. The door swung shut behind them, leaving me sitting in an empty boys' locker room with the taste of Trey Bloomberg on my lips, wondering what the hell just happened.

CHAPTER NINETEEN

"What's wrong?" Greg said as I slumped down at the breakfast table. "We should be celebrating, but you've got your sourpuss face on."

He was right. Our plan had gone off without a hitch. Quinn was recovering in the infirmary (his blindness was only temporary, but his eyes were scratched and swollen from irritants in the powder, not to mention his mysterious black eye), and Trey and Ayaz were laughingstocks. One of the yearbook photographers had snapped some pictures of them scratching themselves on the field, and someone copied the photos and plastered them on all the notice-boards in the dormitory. All the parents saw them as they left the school after their all-night alumni party. When I'd glanced at Andre across the table, he'd flashed me a silent, knowing smile.

I shoved my bacon around my plate, checking around and underneath it for any maggots. My lips still tingled from Trey's kiss. The whole thing was insane. *Why did he kiss me? Why did I kiss him back? Why can't I stop thinking about it, and about what might have happened if Ayaz hadn't come in?*

I pushed my food under Andre's nose and shoved my chair

out. "I've got to meet Ayaz in the library. We're working on our project."

Greg's eyes widened. "Wait, Hazel—"

But I was already halfway to the exit. As I walked past the monarch's table, Trey's eyes followed me, burning into my flesh. My lips ached with the shadow of his kiss. The trails his fingers laid over my skin sizzled with fresh desire.

Beside him, Tillie Fairchild glared at me. If her eyes were daggers, I'd be skewered on the wall. *Does she know? Fuck, I hope not.*

She can't know. If she knew, I'd be lying dead in a pile of my own eviscerated organs.

Who am I? Who is this girl who wastes her time lusting after someone else's boyfriend, after the guy who tried to kill her? I'm sick. I need help.

It can't ever happen again. If Trey Bloomberg thought he was going to slum it with me while dating Tillie, he had another thing coming. I wasn't some guy's pity fuck or mistress. *If he wanted me the way he'd made me believe he wanted me during that kiss, then he can break up with her. He won't, so it's over.*

If only... My whole body shuddered with heat at the memory of his fingers trailing the edge of my bra. I rubbed my lips as I jogged across the quad toward the library. There was no use hoping or wishing. I must've imagined the connection between us. What happened in the locker room was an accident, a strange side-effect of Trey's vulnerability over the prank I'd pulled. We weren't attracted to each other. We didn't even *like* each other.

Right?

Right?

I tapped my pen against my paper and checked the clock on the library wall. Ayaz was supposed to meet me twenty minutes ago. He'd never been late before.

He's probably got his tongue down some girl's throat, I thought to myself, remembering Ayaz sitting in the grotto with the two girls. I'd found out from Greg that they were juniors, and that apparently they'd both been in Ayaz's bed that night.

"Hey, Meat." A muscled frame dropped into the seat across from me. But it wasn't Ayaz. It was Quinn.

"Shouldn't you be in the infirmary?"

Quinn looked awful. Both his eyes were swollen and puffy, the skin on his face red with irritation. The bruising around his black eye had darkened into splotches of color, and it looked even worse when combined with his other injuries. I was surprised he could even see enough to find his way here.

"Yes. I should." Quinn placed his chin in his hands and stared at me across the table, like he was trying to unpick my mind. "What are you doing in the library on a Sunday? This is the day of rest."

"Yes, and you should be resting. I'm studying so that I can get into a good college. Unlike some people, I'm not relying on my daddy's purse-strings to open doors for me."

"Touché." Quinn reached across the table and rubbed his finger across my knuckles. The touch sent a river of fire through my arm. "Trey tells me you're to blame for my current condition."

Guilt tightened my chest. If Quinn went blind, I'd never forgive myself. I didn't want anyone to get *hurt*, not like that. "I'm not. Trey was the one who dumped that powder on your head."

"Yeah, total dick move on his part." Quinn kept stroking my knuckles. My hand froze, pen poised mid-stroke. I hated how much I didn't want him to stop.

"Are you going to be okay?"

"They think so. Trey kept insisting they take me to a hospital, but Dad wasn't going to have it. Finally, they agreed to bring a specialist just to shut him up. They flushed out my eyes with saline and dropped in this orange dye so they could see any particles that were left." Quinn rubbed his eye socket and winced.

"Everything's still pretty blurry, and I may have a bit of scarring on my cornea from the fibers, but apparently, I'm going to be fine in a couple of weeks."

Now it was my turn to wince. "I'm so sorry, Quinn. I never meant for this to happen to you."

He shrugged. "Yeah well, you don't know everything that's going on. If you did, you still probably would have done it – under the circumstances, I'd say your actions were justified."

I nodded, but the guilt still twisted in my gut.

"It's not all bad," Quinn added. "I get out of class for a few days and they've got me on these trippy painkillers. Right now I can see three of you. You are literally *Hazy* now." He gave a loud laugh that sounded a bit maniacal.

"Have you seen Ayaz?" I asked, for something else to say.

Quinn tapped his chin. "Maybe. What's it worth to you?"

"Huh?"

"I'll tell you where he is, for a price. I don't want much. Just a little kiss."

"Jesus. Forget it."

"No, seriously." Quinn leaned across the table, his eyes lighting up. "I'm injured, and I think your kiss might be just what I need to cure me. Trey told me what happened in the locker room."

I gulped. "What did he say happened?"

"That you two locked lips, and that it was, to quote his exact words, 'not unpleasant'." Quinn's lopsided grin only made him more adorable. "One kiss from you and Trey's forgotten all about his shitty dad, so you must be working some kind of ghetto magic on him. I could use a little bit of that. So go on, Hazy, pucker up and I'll tell you where Ayaz has got to."

"Why are you bothering me? Don't you already have a girl-friend?" I jerk my thumb toward the library door, where Courtney had just walked in. She stopped in her tracks when she saw the two of us leaning close. Her face turned stormy, and she whirled on her heel and stormed back out.

Quinn grinned. "Just because Courtney believes she's my girl-friend doesn't make it so. I don't do commitment, Hazy. But I do other things remarkably well."

With that, Quinn Delacorte grabbed the collar of my shirt, yanked me across the table, and pressed his lips to mine.

My stomach leaped into my chest and fire danced through my veins. This was as hot and sensuous as our kiss in the grotto, only a hundred times more exciting because we could get caught at any moment. Quinn's tongue slid between my teeth, expertly teasing my mouth open, demanding and inviting at the same time. Against my will, my body folded against his, pulling him closer, ready to taste more, more...

"That's it," Quinn murmured. His thumb brushed my blazer, darting over my nipple. A sliver of fire drove straight through my body.

This is crazy. I tore my lips from Quinn's, gasping for breath. "Why did you do that?"

Quinn tried to raise his eyebrow, but his eye was too swollen, so all he managed was a weird kind of squint. "Blame the drugs?"

"What's this about, Quinn? You already kissed me at the party. You fulfilled your part of the plan by humiliating me. Why would you kiss me again?"

He shrugged. "I wanted to. And see, now I owe you one. Ayaz is in classroom 2F, doing a little extracurricular work for the head-mistress. He must've forgotten to tell you."

I leaped to my feet and rushed to the door, desperate to get away from Quinn and all the confusing emotions swirling around my head. At least Ayaz wasn't confusing like the other two – he made no secret of the fact he despised me. There was something to be said for consistency.

2F? Where is 2F? I think that's in the same wing as history class—

I rounded the corner of the corridor and stopped dead.

Tillie Fairchild had Loretta pinned up against a locker, her arm against Loretta's throat. Behind her stood Courtney, her head

held high, her blonde hair glinting with dappled light as she imagined herself in front of a Hollywood camera. She read dramatically from a small notebook while Loretta stared at a spot on the
ceiling. Her eyes were completely blank, as if she weren't really
there.

"... all ah want is for them to leave me alone," Courtney cooed
in a sing-song voice, affecting Loretta's accent. "Ah don't even
want to be at this school. Ah only came because Grandma made
me, because being invited to a fancy school would help her to
regain face after what Mama did. But they're never going to stop
tormenting me. There's only one escape ah can see, and it looks
brighter and brighter every day."

My heart leaped into my throat. Somehow – probably with the
aid of the copy of the room key – Courtney and Tillie had got
their hands on something private Loretta had written. Now they
were reading it out for the whole school.

My eyes met Loretta's, and what I saw there sickened me even
more than what the monarchs had done. Loretta looked serene,
completely at peace, as if what was happening to her right now
was destined to be. I saw what happened to a person after the
bullying and belittling become too much – Loretta believed the
lies they were telling about her. She accepted that she was
nothing.

It made me sick. It made me see red.

It made fire burn on the tips of my fingers.

"Oh, Mama!" Courtney wailed, reaching a crescendo as the
students around her rolled about with laughter. "Ah wish you
would talk to me. Ah wish ah could be with you right now. Why
did you have to leave? There's no point to any of this without
you—"

Courtney spun around as she read. Her eyes met mine,
glinting with triumph.

No.

I'm not letting this go on.

Courtney was only doing this because of me, because she was still pissed about the party, because she realized she couldn't hurt me the way she wanted to, so she was going after someone who she could crush completely.

"Oh Mama, ah just want to be with you again—"

I marched up to Courtney and snatched the book from her hands. "That doesn't belong to you."

"Silly gutter whore," she smiled. "Everything in this school belongs to me. Everything in this *world* belongs to me. Face it, I'm just better than you in every way. The sooner you and your pathetic little friends understand that, the better off you'll be."

"Hazel," Loretta said, her voice flat. "It's okay. I don't care."

You should care. I wanted to scream at her. *You can't just crawl into a ball and give up because of what they say.*

"We've all learned some very important things about our classmate, Loretta," Courtney said sweetly, addressing the gathered students. "I know we all wish her the best for her latest endeavor. Loretta has failed at everything else in her life. Let us hope that she will find the strength to succeed at this."

"Kill yourself, kill yourself!" Students chanted. I grabbed Loretta under her armpits and dragged her away. Courtney's hyena laugh echoed off the corridor.

"That's it," I growled, pulling Loretta toward the faculty wing. "We're reporting them."

Loretta wrenched her arm away. "No."

"Loretta, they are literally telling you to kill yourself. That's beyond just normal bullying. That's fucking *abuse*. The teachers have to do something about this. They have to—"

"Just leave it alone," Loretta grabbed the journal from my hands, her face flaring to life. "Leave *me* alone. I wish you'd never come to Derleth! Everything was fine before you came."

Clearly it wasn't, if that was the kind of stuff Loretta was writing. I watched her shuffle away, her head hanging low. *Shit, she's in a bad place.*

The sliver of guilt that had been with me since I saw Quinn ripped at my chest. I shared a room with Loretta. I should have seen that she was depressed, but I'd been so busy with my own revenge plans and daydreaming about Trey and Quinn and Ayaz—

Ayaz. Where was he?

He hadn't been in the crowd tormenting Loretta, which was interesting. He loved a good torment as much as the next monarch. He must still be with the headmistress.

I jogged down the hall, searching for the classroom Quinn mentioned. I paused at the door, but the lights were out inside so I couldn't see a thing through the small glass panel. I pushed opened the door. "Ayaz, are you in here? We were supposed—"

The words died in my throat.

Ayaz had Ms. West bent over the desk, her black gown rolled up over white hips. Her graceful neck arched back in ecstasy as he plunged his cock into her.

CHAPTER TWENTY

Shut the door.

I commanded my body to move, but it refused to obey. I was frozen in place, forced to watch Ayaz's cock slide in and pull out, long and sleek and dark and glorious. His hands gripped the headmistress' hips and my body tightened, flushing at the thought of his fingers tangled in my own hair, that long cock sliding between my legs—

Ayaz looked up. His eyes meet mine. He flashed me a smile that had no mirth in it whatsoever, raised a hand, and flipped me off.

"Shit." I slammed the door. My feet pounded on the marble as I ran, gasping, down the hall.

What did I just see?

By dinner, it was all over the school. No one seemed fazed by the fact Ayaz was screwing the headmistress. That was old gossip, and having it confirmed only made him into even more of a god. But the fact that I'd hung off the door, watching like a total perverted dickhead, made me the laughingstock once again.

Ayaz must have spread the rumor himself. It was either that or Headmistress West, and she hadn't even noticed me standing there, watching her get fucked.

The headmistress is sleeping with a student. As experienced as Ayaz was – I gulped and pressed my legs together at the memory of him sliding into her – he was still underage. It was illegal. If their affair was an open secret, how come no one reported it?

The one good thing about my latest disaster was that it diverted everyone's attention from what Courtney had done to Loretta in the corridor. If it helped Loretta, I was happy to be their punching bag.

At dinner time, Ayaz caught my eye across the dining hall, his cruel gaze following me as I shuffled to my seat. I glared back, hating him for torturing me and hating myself for finding him attractive. I seemed determined to sabotage what progress I'd made at this school, all because of three Kings who seemed to have moved on from good old fashioned bullying into this weird mindfuck seduction game.

The one bright spot in my week was physics class. I'd handed in my black hole assignment on Friday, confident that all the research I'd done and equations I'd outlined would earn me a top mark. Professor Atwood had promised to have the marking done by today, and we'd have time in class to discuss the assignments.

I fiddled with my pen as Atwood moved down the aisles, handing back the papers. Courtney frowned at her copy, and as she turned it over I noticed several red marks and comments scrawled over the sheet. Atwood tapped her desk. "You need to focus on your studies," he said. "This isn't like you."

I couldn't help but feel a little surge of triumph at that. It looked like Courtney was letting her bullying plots affect her studies. I couldn't say the same for myself – I knew my assignment was A+ material.

Greg held his up and grinned at me. "B+. Respectable. That's two extra merit points for me."

"Yeah. That's awesome." My heart skipped as the professor skipped past my desk, moving down the next row. *Where's my assignment?*

Professor Atwood handed a paper to every student in the class and sat back at his desk. "If anyone wants to discuss their results, I'm happy to—"

My hand shot in the air. "Um, Professor... you didn't hand me back my paper."

He frowned at me over his glasses. "That's correct. I've only handed back the papers of the students who completed the assignment."

What?

"There's been some mistake. I finished my essay and handed it in. Greg was with me when I did it, weren't you?"

Greg nodded.

"I don't consider the testimony of classmates as irrefutable proof, Miss Waite," Atwood said. "The submission system is impossible to tamper with. The assignments are slid through the letter slot into a locked document box. I am the only one who has a key, so your paper could not have been removed before marking. Your assignment was not in that box, therefore, it has not been marked."

"But I handed it in!" My hands balled into fists. I was dangerously close to crying. "I spent hours on that paper. I asked you all those questions about dark matter, remember? I *swear*, I handed it in."

Titters from the other students reached my ears. Courtney's hyena laugh was unmistakable. Oh right, of course this was her. I squeezed my eyes shut. Top marks on that assignment were worth 30 merit points. I was counting on those points to pull up my total. With it, I would have passed Loretta for top place amongst the scholarship students in one swoop. As I watched in dismay,

Professor Atwood tapped on the keyboard of an old-fashioned brick of a laptop, and my total *decreased* by 30 points, putting me behind all the other scholarship students.

The unfairness of it grated against my skin. I *finished* that assignment. More than that, I knew I *aced* it. I deserved credit for it.

I skipped last period. It was my ancient history elective, which I normally enjoyed, but I couldn't face Dr. Morgan today. So I'd lose three points for ditching; what did it matter now, anyway? I slunk back to our room and flopped down on the bed, too despondent to crack open a textbook or even to look through the few drawings from Dante I'd managed to save. I felt under the edge of the mattress for my mirror shard, but decided not to pull it out, just in case my thoughts spiraled out of control.

Scritch-scritch-scritch. The rats scrambled around me. I wondered if they ever had to deal with bullies.

Evening crept in. Every creak and groan of the building I expected to be Loretta, coming back to our room to tell me that of course this would happen, that I was an idiot for thinking I could take on the Derleth royalty and win. My stomach grumbled and I knew I was missing dinner, but I couldn't bring myself to move from the bed.

The hours ticked by and still Loretta didn't show. *That's weird.* Usually, she came back to the room straight after dinner. She didn't like being in the library late at night because she hated walking back to our room in the dark.

Scritch-scritch. Scritchascritchascritchascritch. The rats were extremely active tonight, running in circles across the ceiling, their movements as agitated as my mind.

Where's Loretta?

CHAPTER TWENTY-ONE

Loretta wasn't in her bed when I woke up in the morning. My stomach churned. I'd slept so fitfully, waking up every hour to hear the rats scratching and scrabbling, I definitely would have heard if she came in. I thumbed through the books on the desk and her neatly folded clothes. Nothing was missing. She hadn't been back to our room all night.

What if the monarchs did something to her? They were so horrible to her, and—

I remembered the expression on Loretta's face as they taunted her. She didn't cry. She wasn't angry or upset. She was beyond that. She accepted what they said, what they taught her. That she was nothing. That she didn't deserve to live.

What if Loretta hurt herself because of what the monarchs did, and it's all my fault?

I tugged on my uniform, stopping only long enough to tie my shoes and tuck in my shirt as I flew out the door and up the stairs.

I knew what I was supposed to be doing – laying low and keeping out of the way. Because even the teachers were in the monarchs' pocket, or the other way around. But that look on

Loretta's face terrified me, and if she hadn't come back to her bed last night, where else could she be?

Students laughed and joked in the halls as they made their way to early morning extracurriculars. Luckily, I didn't cross any monarchs, because I don't know what I would have done if I had. I peered in all the cubbies and corners of the library, checked the music rooms in case Loretta was on some kind of all-night clarinet binge, even poked my head into the common room to see if she'd suddenly decided to bond with Courtney over binge-watching old DVDs of *America's Next Top Model*. But she was nowhere to be found.

That meant I had to do the thing I really didn't want to do.

In the faculty wing, I made an appointment with the secretary to see the headmistress. She phoned through to Headmistress West's office while I swung my legs and coiled and uncoiled my fists.

"Headmistress West will see you now."

My whole body trembled as I stood, partly from rage, partly from fear of the woman I was about to confront. But Loretta could be in trouble, and I had to help her if I could.

"Ms. Waite, it's interesting to see you in this office of your own volition."

After seeing the headmistress bent over that classroom desk with Ayaz's cock buried deep inside it, I found it hard to take her severe act so seriously. "I'm worried about Loretta."

"Your roommate? Can you explain the nature of your concern? Has she been found with contraband?"

"No!" I didn't want anyone to accuse me of reporting other students. "I can't find her. She didn't come back to bed last night. She's not in any of her usual places around the school."

"Is that all?"

"Um... yes. Sorry, I would have thought the disappearance of a student might rate a modicum of concern." I waved a hand. "My mistake."

"Your concern is exemplary, although in this case misguided," the headmistress said in a clipped tone. 'Loretta's grandparents have taken her home."

"Home?" I didn't understand. "But there's still a week of class before the end of the quarter. She wouldn't leave and risk falling behind—"

"She didn't have a choice. There's been a tragedy in Loretta's family. I can't tell you any more than that. I'm sure when the family has had suitable time to mourn, Loretta will return to school."

"But she left all her things behind!" *Why would Loretta leave school and not take her books or clothes with her?*

Headmistress West stood up, her skirts sweeping around her ankles as she pointed toward the door. "That is all, Ms. Waite."

"But—"

"I've been kind enough to award you five points for showing concern for a fellow student, but I'll deducting ten points for insubordination," her cheeks flared with scarlet. "If you do not leave my office in the next four seconds, I shall deduct ten more."

I shot the headmistress a filthy look as I stormed out of the office, slamming the door so hard it rattled on its hinges. Who the fuck cared about her stupid point system when Loretta was missing? It was bullshit. Rewarding students for ratting each other out and giving points based on whose family donated the most money rigged the game from the start.

One thing I was damn sure of – Headmistress West had been lying to me. Which meant that she knew where Loretta *really* was. Was it something to do with all this weird stuff that had been going on... the teachers with their black robes and candles heading down to the gymnasium... the students who had unheard-of privileges and license to make their own rules... the fact that Quinn was seriously injured and they refused to call an ambulance.

It was obvious I wouldn't get any information out of Headmistress West. Maybe if I hunted through Loretta's stuff, I'll be able to find some clue as to what was going on. I clattered down the stairs and swung open the door to our room.

My heart flew into my mouth.

All of Loretta's things were gone. Her books, her clothing, the small lamp she'd brought from home. Her bed had been taken away, and mine moved to the center of the room. All that remained of hers was that annoying alarm clock.

It was as if she'd never been there at all.

CHAPTER TWENTY-TWO

"This is weird." Greg whistled through his nose as he surveyed my single room. Andre peered under my bed and lifted up all my books, as if somehow hoping Loretta was hiding somewhere.

"I know, right?" I bounced on the edge of my bed. "The janitors must have snuck in here while I was speaking with the headmistress and cleaned the whole place out. Honestly, I don't know why we even bother locking the door at all, given the number of people that come and go without our knowledge or consent."

"This is scary," Greg peered at the spot near the wall where Loretta's bed used to be. "It's like they've cleared away every trace of her."

"The headmistress said her grandparents picked her up. Did Loretta say anything to you about her family?" I asked them.

Both Greg and Andre shook their heads. "All I know is the gossip I heard," Greg said. "About her mother killing herself and her grandparents being left to raise her. Apparently, they saw Loretta as kind of a demon child infecting their perfect Christian family or something. You?"

"Nope. I'm scared, you guys. Yesterday, Courtney and the monarchs stole a journal Loretta was writing and read it out in front of everyone." I dug my fingers into the mattress as I filled them in on what happened. "It sounded like a suicide note. It was a serious cry for help. I'm worried something's happened to her. I don't trust Headmistress West to tell us the truth."

"How naive is it to believe Loretta's family realized how awful it was to lock away a child just to punish her for the supposed sins of her mother, and took her home to shower her with gifts and get her the specialist help she needs?" Greg suggested.

I shook my head.

"Yeah, I didn't think so." Greg looked stricken. "What do we do?"

I lifted an eyebrow in mock surprise. "Break into the head-mistress' office and look at her student records, of course. Maybe if we call her grandparents we could get some answers."

Andre scribbled a note on his pad and handed it to Greg. "Why is the answer with you always some kind of dangerous stunt?" Greg read the note out with a smile. "Andre does have a point."

"It's worth the risk if Loretta is in trouble. I just have a bad, bad feeling about all this. Too much weird stuff has been going on."

"I'm not saying we *don't* do it, but we can't do anything about this now." Greg slung his bookbag over his shoulder. "We have to get to homeroom."

I swiped my books from the desk and joined the guys in the hall, locking my room behind me. Everything felt wrong without Loretta, like I'd left without my underwear. But Greg was right, we had to keep going like everything was normal, for now at least.

"So what are you going to do about Ayaz?" Greg asked as we headed across the atrium. "Do you have some new revenge in store?"

"No. Who Ayaz chooses to fuck is his own business." My cheeks flushed with the memory of what I'd seen. "Courtney's the one we have to take down."

Everything was off this morning. As we crossed the atrium to head to our first class, students leaped out of our way like we were poisoned. Groups huddled together under the class lists, talking in hushed whispers. Eyes averted from mine wherever I looked.

"What's wrong? Do I have food in my teeth or something?" I gave Greg and Andre a big, toothy grin. They didn't laugh.

"Um, Hazel." Greg tugged on my arm. Andre pointed up to the board where the merit scores were posted, his eyes wide, like he couldn't believe what he was seeing.

He pointed to my name.

Hazel Waite: 934 points.

What?

But how...?

Overnight, I'd somehow gained 500 extra points. I was now firmly in the upper half of the table, nestled in the middle of the rich, mediocre students. *But why... how?*

"That's impossible," I muttered.

"Or not," Greg breathed. "Look at Trey's score."

My eyes flew to the top of the table, where Trey's name had remained ever since the beginning of the school year. It wasn't there. Instead, Ayaz was now leading the school, followed by Courtney. Trey wasn't fourth, or fifth, or even tenth. Where was he?

My heart hammered against my chest as I started from the top of the list and scanned each name. I eventually found Trey, only a few names above me, on 946 points.

I'd gained 500 points, and Trey lost 500.

How is that possible?

A heavy hand fell on my shoulder. "We need to talk," Trey's voice whispered in my ear.

I found myself nodding. Andre's eyes widened, and he made the sign of the cross before hurrying away, dragging a protesting Greg with him. Trey grabbed my arm and dragged me toward the dormitory. "Not here. In my room."

Numb with disbelief, I followed him up another floor and down a corridor even more opulent than the one below. He pushed open a door right at the end and ushered me inside, slamming the door shut behind me.

My breath caught in my throat as I stared around the enormous space. *This isn't a dorm room, it's a* palace.

Trey occupied a suite of rooms at the top of the tower. Tall windows on three sides looked down over the courtyard and fields below. A large black sofa wrapped around a glass-topped coffee table and faced a TV that practically covered an entire wall. Beneath the TV were stacks of DVDs and video games. I guess if you were a rich student, the rules about electronics didn't apply. There was a full kitchen in gleaming black marble and chrome, a bar area, and doors leading off into what I guessed were a bathroom and bedroom. Everything was modern and gleaming – stainless steel and black leather, sharp corners and polished surfaces. It was magnificent – it just wasn't the room I'd pictured Trey living in.

Not that I'd been picturing Trey in a room, in a bed, naked in the shower. *Not at all*.

Quinn lounged on the sofa, flicking through an ancient *Playboy* magazine. It was weird that so much stuff at this school – from the teachers' laptops to the magazines to that condom wrapper someone threw at Greg – was a decade or two out-of-date.

Quinn's eyes were still so swollen he had to hold the magazine practically against his nose. One look at my face and he flashed his lopsided heart-melting smile. "So you've seen, then?"

"Put down your scratch and sniff porn mag and tell me what's going on," I demanded. "Why do I suddenly have 500 extra merit points?"

"Because we gave them to you," Trey said.

Simple. Just like that.

I folded my arms. "Why would you do that?"

Trey's eyes flicked to the door. Quinn suddenly appeared very interested in Paris Hilton's cleavage. *Okay, now we're getting somewhere. They're nervous. The Kings of Derleth are actually nervous around me. But why? Do they think I'm planning another itching powder stunt?*

"Let's wait until Ayaz gets here," Trey said. He moved to the kitchen and opened a large stainless steel fridge that looked more like a food replicator from the starship *Enterprise*. "Want a drink?"

"No thanks. I prefer not to drink anthrax this early in the morning."

Quinn snorted. Trey cocked an eyebrow as he filled the coffee machine with beans. "Suit yourself."

I leaned against the counter, watching the muscles in Trey's shoulders contract as he pulled frozen croissants from the freezer and shoved them in the oven. "So if you won't tell me why you did this, will you at least tell me how?"

"We broke into Hermia's office last night and hacked the list," Quinn said. "Ayaz did the actual programming. He's a whiz with computers. That's why his people man all the call centers."

From behind me, I heard a sigh. "You're thinking of India, bro."

I whirled around. Ayaz leaned against the doorframe, his eyes raking over my body like he was a hunter and I was a tiger ready to pounce. I wondered if he wanted me to pounce.

"India, Turkey, potato, potahto." Quinn flipped a page.

"Name one person who actually says potahto," I said. Quinn grinned.

Ayaz moved into the kitchen and made his own coffee in a tiny cup. When he poured it out, it was so thick and dark, it looked like tar, which reminded me uncomfortably of what Courtney did to my hair. The guys all looked relaxed in this gleaming room, like they hung out here all the time. Which I guessed they did. The place was bigger than any of the other student rooms I'd glimpsed. It dwarfed the entire dining hall.

I glared at Ayaz, still thinking about the tar. "Are you the one who's been breaking into my room and locker?"

He stared at the floor. "I stole your keys from you when I dumped those maggots in your breakfast, made a copy in the art studio, and then returned them to you. Fucking Courtney's got the key now, though, so I'd put something heavy in front of your door before you sleep if I were you."

Great. Yet another thing to worry about. "If you didn't have my key until then, how did you get my journal?"

Ayaz jabbed his thumb in Trey's direction. "Trey paid the maid to bring him anything she found that looked personal."

My face flicked over to Trey, flushed with anger. At least they both had the decency to look sheepish. "Amazing that a Derleth King would resort to petty breaking and entering. So what's this latest torture about?" I demanded. "Let me guess. You're going to tell the headmistress I stole all those points from Trey, and have me kicked out. Fine, whatever. I don't care anymore. I have bigger problems. My roommate is missing."

"Not missing," Trey said. "She's gone."

"What do you mean, gone?"

Trey sipped his coffee. "I mean, that's she's no longer here at Derleth Academy."

"That's what the headmistress said, but I don't believe her." I told them about how Loretta's stuff was in our room one minute, and gone as soon as I returned from speaking with Headmistress West. "She didn't take her things with her."

"Loretta had the lowest score of all the scholarship students at the school. That means she has to leave," Trey explained. "They eliminate one scholarship student each quarter, so at the end of the year, only one of you graduates with the rest of the class. You don't understand just how deep hatred of the scholarship program goes."

"I..." Did they tell me that when I enrolled? I don't remember anything about having to compete to stay at Derleth. I was pretty out-of-it when the scholarship officer visited, but I think it'd remember *that*.

"It's a secret," Ayaz said, his eyes flaring with anger. "You can't let on that you know about it, or they'll send you away, despite your ranking."

"But..." My heart thudded in my chest as I realized what they were saying. "But yesterday, I had the lowest score."

"And now you don't," Ayaz growled.

I stared at the three of them, struggling to form words. "Why would you help me? You hate me."

"That so, Hazy?" Quinn pressed his body against me, his eyes dancing over my neck. God, the way he touched me in the grotto, at the library... I wished then, as I wished every time I laid eyes on him, that I could be loved by a guy like Quinn. I had a feeling that once you cracked him open, a lot of goodness and vulnerability would pour out.

Trey and Ayaz exchanged a look I couldn't read. I shoved Quinn away, gently, and shrugged. "I don't know. I don't understand you guys at all."

"Good," Quinn grinned, then winced as if the action hurt his swollen eyes. "We like being mysterious."

I turned to Trey, trying to focus on the guy who had tried to kill me, not the one who had kissed me like I could cure all his pain. "You're no longer top of the school."

He shrugged. "Some things are more important than that."

"Like keeping me here at Derleth?"

No answer. *Hmmm*.

Above our heads, the bell rang through the intercom system. The guys ignored it. What were three tardy points to them? I guess three points meant little to me now, too. I was safe, for now. I was here at least until next quarter.

But what did that mean? Why would the school force the scholarship students to compete like that? Why would they not even tell us?

I folded my arms across my chest. "I need more than this. I need answers."

"Have a croissant instead." Trey pushed a plate of hot croissants across the table. I hesitated. He laughed, and for the first time, his laugh had none of its usual cruelty. "I promise I haven't spiked them. My Dad's chef has them flown in from Paris. They're amazing. You've never had anything like them."

I took a croissant and nibbled off the tiniest corner. *Omigod, that's divine.* Hot buttery goodness melted on my tongue.

Trey threw his blazer over his shoulder. "We should get going."

The guys scrambled for jackets and ties. "This talk isn't over!" I yelled. No one paid any attention to me. *God, they're so infuriating.*

Trey leaned over and pecked me on the cheek, his lips leaving a red-hot mark. Ayaz glared at me as he followed Trey into the hall, but the glare held an odd kind of possessiveness that made my heart do all sorts of flips in my chest.

"You've got to be careful out there, Hazy," Quinn whispered, draping his arm over my shoulder. His breath caressed my earlobe, and I almost missed what he said.

Almost.

"Careful of what?"

Quinn pointed to the massive television, which nearly covered one whole wall. It displayed the school rankings, with my name highlighted in the middle of the table, sandwiched between two average rich students and miles above my fellow scholarship kids.

And miles above Quinn, I couldn't help but notice.

"So? I'm ahead of you. Get used to it."

"Not that." Quinn pointed to the shield emblem above the boards. "This school... there's something going on that we can't tell you about, but it's some dark shit. We're trying to keep you out of it, but you can't keep getting yourself into trouble and leaping in where you shouldn't be. If you become too troublesome, they won't stick to the protocol. They won't care that they've already taken Loretta this quarter."

"What do you mean, 'taken' Loretta? I thought she got kicked out? What could I do that might be troublesome?"

Trey sighed from the corridor. "Just... keep your head down, do your schoolwork, try not to draw attention to yourself."

I glared between him and Quinn. "Your girlfriends are making that difficult."

"We'll handle Courtney and Tillie," Quinn said, his voice angry. "If they give you any more trouble, let us know."

I rubbed my temple, where a headache was blooming. "I still don't understand why you're suddenly being so nice to me."

The three guys exchanged a glance – long and hard and full of hidden depths. Ayaz stepped forward. He wrapped my hand in his dark, sensuous fingers. When he spoke, his voice was silk and butter. "Because you're a breath of fresh air in this stuffy, hellish place. Because when you're around, you make us all feel alive. Now stop talking so damn much, and get to class before you lose all Trey's points."

CHAPTER TWENTY-THREE

"You're really keeping Trey's points?" Greg leaned against the piano, resting his cheek in his palm. We'd just finished an hour of rehearsal for our main duet in the audition. We sounded fucking *tight*, which meant we could allow ourselves a bit of gossip time.

"Apparently so. Trey's talked Professor Atwood into saying that he converted them to me because he sabotaged my assignment. Even though Courtney was actually the one who did it." I slammed my palm against the keys. The piano emitted a discordant shriek. Greg jumped. "Trey's parents are being notified. His dad is going to be even angrier with him. It's a big fucking deal and I just don't understand why they did it. Why do they care that I'm not the one being kicked out?"

"Because they're hot for you," Greg whistled. "Check you out, winning the heart of the most eligible bachelor at Derleth."

"That's the other thing," I groaned, letting my elbow fall on the keyboard. Greg jumped again at the loud note. "Trey's not even a bachelor. I don't want to steal anyone's guy, not even a bitch like Tillie."

"Didn't you hear? Trey broke up with Tillie at lunch today.

Apparently, he said he didn't care what their families wanted, he was doing his own thing. It's quite the coup."

My stomach flipped. "He... he did?"

"Yup. So your King is a free man."

Trey was single? Butterflies fluttered in my stomach. "I don't care. He tried to kill me."

"Your face says something different."

I slumped over my assignment, placing my chin in my hands. I wanted to tell Greg what I'd discovered about our rankings, and our place at Derleth, but Ayaz's warning held my tongue. *What if the teachers listen in to our conversations through some secret device? What if I get Greg in trouble? I'll tell him later, outside on one of our walks, where no one can overhear.* "This is crazy. Dinner tonight is going to be interesting."

"Sure is." Greg glanced at the clock on the wall. "Speaking of which, we should get going."

I grabbed my bookbag and shoved my books and papers inside. "Yup. Not even a plate full of maggots could keep me away tonight."

Greg winced. "Don't jinx us. I've only just got my appetite back."

We linked arms and headed across the quad to the glowing lights of the dining hall. Heads turned toward me, but this time their whispered conversations didn't bother me. As we entered the hall, my eyes flew to the royals table. Trey, Quinn, and Ayaz sat there, along with a few of their lacrosse buddies. But Courtney and Tillie were nowhere to be seen.

No, wait... there they are. I noticed Tillie's flowing black mane at the end of the table where the scholarship students normally sat. She sat with Courtney and a few other girls, and they'd spread out their bags and purses so Andre was smushed right up into the corner. He couldn't even get out without tripping over the girls' things. *Bitches.*

"Hazel, wait, what are you doing?" Greg fell in step behind me as I stalked over to the table and kicked a large shopping bag out of the way.

The girl sitting across from Courtney whirled around to face me. I opened my mouth to give her what-for, when my words died in my throat.

She looked the same, but different. Instead of being a ball of frizz, her hair sat in stylish curls atop her head, swept off her face with clips studded with what looked suspiciously like real diamonds. Her skirt had risen several inches, and her regulation dress shoes were replaced by a pair of shiny designer booties with a low, sexy heel.

But most different was her face – instead of eyes wracked with nerves or swimming with pain too deep to speak, she looked bright, confident, self-assured. She looked like a *monarch*.

I managed to choke out a single word.

"Loretta?"

My old roommate regarded me with bored indifference from her seat at our table, sweeping a strand of her now perfect hair from her eyes. "Hello, Hazel."

CHAPTER TWENTY-FOUR

"...um, hi." I tried to recover from my surprise. "What are you doing back at school?"

"I go here," she said, rolling her eyes like *I* was the one who was crazy. When she spoke, I noticed her accent had been ironed flat. She didn't sound like Loretta. She sounded... like Courtney or Tillie or one of the Queens.

"Yes, but—" *But the Kings said you'd been 'taken away' because of your low score, so why are you back?* I couldn't say that. I cleared my throat and tried again. "Headmistress West said your grandparents pulled you out of school because of a family tragedy—"

"I'm back now." Loretta turned back to her table, leaning across to whisper something to Courtney. *Okay, so I guess that conversation is over.*

Courtney's eyes flashed at me. "You're still here, gutter whore. You should fix that."

"Can you all move your shit?" I pointed a finger down the table. "We've gotta get down there to our friend, and you're blocking the aisle."

In response, Courtney used the heel of her shoe to move her

bookbag even further into the middle of the narrow aisle. I nudged it back. She slid it out again, glaring at me.

"The mime can sit by himself. Touch my stuff again, and I'll report you for stealing," she hissed.

"Fine." I reached for the empty chair between her and Loretta. "I'll just sit with my old friend Loretta here, because it's a free country."

Courtney's bookbag slammed down on the seat, blocking the space. My tray wobbled in my hands as I steadied myself.

"That seat's taken."

"By your bag? Are you feeding it like a pet?" I reached down to knock it off the table. Courtney glared at me and covered the bag with her arm.

"Don't touch that. I don't want you to contaminate it."

"Then move it. I'm not dextrous enough to eat standing up, balancing a tray on my nose."

"You can't sit here," Loretta said. Every pair of eyes at the table stared at me. The cafeteria grew quiet.

"It's a free country," I shrugged, grabbing a strap of the bag and jerking it onto the floor.

"This is our table now." Loretta gestured to the Queens sitting around her. I noticed as she waved her hand that her nails were covered in pink glitter nail polish, the exact same shade Courtney was wearing.

Loretta never wore nail polish. It was a violation of the rules and an automatic loss of 3 merit points if you got caught. Loretta never did anything that might cost her points.

Okay, I don't get this. I stood with my tray in my hands, turning over what I should do. *Loretta was missing for a day and now suddenly she's friends with Courtney and is talking in this weird robot voice?*

"There a problem here?" Trey appeared at the end of the table, leaning over his muscled arms.

"None of your business," Tillie snapped.

"These ladies won't move their stuff so we can get past," I

said, making another move to slide down the tiny gap between Courtney's chair and the table behind her. Trey reached out and grabbed my wrist.

"Forget it. You're sitting with us now."

What?

"What?" Courtney shrieked.

Trey shrugged as if it was no big deal, as if he asked gutter whores to sit at the monarchs' table all the time. "Yeah. Your friends can come, too. If you'd prefer to sit with Courtney, I completely understand—"

"Nope, we're good." I picked up my tray and followed Trey across the dining hall. The only sound in the hall was the clop of my shoes against the granite tiles as I followed Trey to my new table, and the *whoosh* as the jaws of three-hundred students collectively dropped to the floor. Greg followed and, after some jostling to get over Courtney's bags, Andre appeared beside me as well. After inspecting the seat Trey held out thoroughly for some kind of prank, I set my tray down opposite Quinn and slid my legs under the table.

Greg took the chair beside me, facing Ayaz, and Andre sat beside him. Trey leaned in close, wrapping his arm around me. All along the table, guys and girls studied me as if seeing me for the first time.

"Hazel, I don't think I've introduced you." Trey indicated his friends with a lazy wave of his hand. "This is Barclay, Arthur, Kenneth, Rupert, and Paul. That's Mary, Paul's girlfriend, and Nancy. She's—"

"Head cheerleader and captain of the school debating team," Nancy said, standing up to lean across the table to shake my hand. Her grip was firm and surprisingly warm. "Welcome, Hazel, Greg, Andre."

Greg, Andre, and I exchanged a glance. None of this made any sense, but damned if I wasn't going to enjoy it while it lasted.

I took a huge bite of my omelette, Trey's fingers rubbing warm circles on my back. Beside me, Quinn and Ayaz argued back and forth about some obscure Russian science fiction book they both loved, while Nancy and Mary chatted about the latest collection from some hot designer. Greg chimed in and soon they were chatting like old friends.

Across the room, Loretta was still sitting with Courtney and her cronies. They bent their heads together, occasionally sending a glare in our direction and then laughing – I assumed the laughter was at my expense.

A strange mix of hurt and triumph welled up inside me. I was happy Loretta was back, but that meant Headmistress West had told me the truth. There was no conspiracy. There was no plot by the school to kick out scholarship students.

Or was there?

Why did it take Loretta only a day to get over her family tragedy? A day was barely enough time to even make it down the peninsula on that death road. And why had she come back sounding like a robot and sitting with the Queens? Why wasn't she back in our dorm room? What wasn't Ms. West telling me?

Why did the Kings tell me all that stuff if it wasn't true? Were they trying to scare me again?

I knew I was missing something important. But what? Why did Loretta's sudden transformation and my sudden rise to the top dinner table feel like part of a sinister plot?

CHAPTER TWENTY-FIVE

"So, Hazel, any secrets you'd like to share with the group?" Greg leaned against my locker after the last class of the day, all smiles and sweetness. Behind him, Andre gave me a curious once-over, as if he were seeing me for the first time.

Something fucked up is going on in this school and it centers around the scholaship program.

"Nope." I shoved Greg out of the way and stacked my books on the top shelf.

"Yes, you do. Like, why we're suddenly sitting at the monarchs' table?"

"You'll have to take that up with Trey. He seems to be the authority on seating arrangements."

"Come on, just tell me," Greg begged. "You know I'm a gossip whore. This is the juiciest morsel I've had all year, and you're teasing me with it."

"I really don't know, okay? I think it has something to do with Loretta disappearing and suddenly coming back." I lowered my voice as Loretta and Courtney strode past, arm in arm. Here in the corridor with all the noise, no way would anyone overhear us. "This morning, the Kings told me that there was something sinister happening at this school. They said they'd given me the points so that I wouldn't be sent away. Apparently, the school kicks out the lowest-performing scholarship student every semester, so by the end of the year there's only one left. Because I wasn't the lowest anymore, Loretta was sent in my place."

"What?" Greg gasped. Andre's eyes were wide as saucers. "I was never told that."

Andre shook his head.

"Me neither. It's gross, but fine, okay. It's their school, their scholarship program, their rules. But then why is Loretta back? Whatever they did to her, she's come back completely different."

"I'll say," Greg's eyes followed Loretta as she hitched up her skirt another inch. "Did you hear she got a room in the dormitory wing?"

"What?"

"Yeah. Her own private suite with a four-poster bed and ensuite and everything. Maybe her grandparents inherited a fortune from whatever relative just died."

"Somehow, I don't think that's it. Have either of you managed to talk to Loretta? She's clearly got a bone to pick with me, but she always had time for both of you."

Andre scribbled a note and passed it to me. "I waved to her in physics and she just ignored me," it said.

"Same here." Greg leaned against the lockers. "I know people change when they become popular. I just didn't think it happened overnight."

Greg's eyes swam, and I know he was thinking of something in his past. Loretta wasn't the only one who hadn't divulged many details about their life before Derleth. His eyes followed Loretta as she walked with Courtney toward study hall, her skirt flying up to reveal a pair of lacy black panties. I knew he was wondering what secrets she had sold Courtney in exchange for her friendship.

Truthfully, I wondered, too.

"Should we try to talk to her again?" Greg asked.

"I can't. I have to go back to my room before my study session with Ayaz," I rolled my eyes.

"That project still going on?"

"Yeah. Our final presentation is the first week of the second quarter. We want to make it perfect now so we don't have to work over the holidays." The end of the quarter was only a week away.

"Okay, catch you at dinner tonight. Andre and I are going to shoot some arrows. I was going to see if you wanted to come, but you're just too popular for us." Greg, Andre and I had been heading out for archery every chance we got. Something about the *THWACK* of arrows smacking into a target that I imagined was Courtney's face made heading out in the freezing cold worthwhile.

"I'd hardly call my forced proximity to Ayaz 'popularity', but whatever. You guys have fun. If you go out this weekend, I'll happily join you," I grinned as I headed back toward the dorms. I made my way down the narrow staircase, flicking the light on once I reached the bottom.

A dark shape wearing a black robe – a little like an academic dress – fled across the hallway.

"Loretta?"

It had to be her. The shape and the clip-clop of heels told me it was a woman, and who else would come down here apart from Loretta? *Maybe she came to talk, and I wasn't here.* I leaped down the last three steps. "Hey, Loretta! Stop, please, I just want to talk to you."

Black robes billowed out as the figure disappeared into shadow. The storeroom door slammed on its hinges. I raced down the hall, my shoes echoing on the cold stone floor. I yanked the door open and flicked the light switch.

The dark square of the secret passage gaped back at me. The hidden door was open. Footsteps scrambled up the stairs toward freedom.

"Loretta? Are you up there?" Without a light, I didn't dare move from the door.

Only stony silence answered me.

My heart pounded in my ears. I had no idea Loretta knew about the passage. Quinn knew about it, but none of the other Queens seemed to. It was weird she was using it now, in the middle of the afternoon, when she was supposed to be in class.

I turned around to head back to my room. My body froze as I noticed a box on top of a stack beside the door. It had been slashed open and the contents pulled out and strewn across the floor. I was so preoccupied with Loretta that I hadn't even noticed it.

I bent down and picked up the papers. They were pages and articles cut from newspapers, old and yellowed at the edges. I held up a front page of the *Arkham Gazette* under the light. The date in the corner was November 1st, twenty years ago.

TRAGIC FIRE CLAIMS LIVES OF STUDENTS

A large picture showed a fire blazing from Derleth Academy. Flames billowed from the tower windows, and the stone bridge between the dormitory and the academic wing had collapsed. Smoke obscured the sky, so it was impossible to tell if the image was taken at night or during the day. My fingers flew to the scar on my wrist as I scanned the words of the article.

Firefighters battled all night to halt the blaze at Miskatonic Preparatory School but were unable to save the lives of the 245 students who were trapped inside.

That was weird. The caption called the school a different name, but the building in the picture was Derleth Academy. I recognized the distinctive crenelations on the top of the dormitory tower. In the background, I could just make out the rolling green sports fields. It was *definitely* Derleth.

All those dead students... I thought back to what Quinn had said about that tiny graveyard near the pleasure garden. Were they buried there? How could they just start up the school again like this never happened? The whole thing was all kinds of creepy.

Because it's a school for rich people, of course. If people like Vincent Bloomberg II and Damon Delacorte wanted the school to remain open, then oceans would part to make it happen.

The more pressing question was, why had I never heard about this? You'd think a fire killing 245 teenagers at my school was something that might have come up.

After the scholarship administrator visited me, I did some extensive internet sleuthing about Derleth Academy, trying to find out everything I could. There wasn't much information – a flashy website and some social media profiles of celebrated alumni – prominent sports stars, philanthropists, writers, politicians, and businessmen I'd never heard of. Nothing about a fire that killed 245 kids. If one kid died at school, it was all over the national news. How did they hide this?

Maybe that's why they changed the name – so they could hide the school's past from the media. But how you could conceal that kind of loss of life from prospective students, especially when so many were legacy students, with family attendance at the school going back decades? I bet half the kids at Derleth today had a relative who'd been immolated in the blaze.

Jesus.

I flipped to the next article, expecting to read something about the rebuilding and re-opening of the school, or the change of name policy to distance themselves from the tragedy. Instead, it was an even earlier article from a tabloid about whether or not the school was haunted. Apparently, students had reported odd smells, strange visitations in their beds, and teachers seen walking off through walls and into storage cupboards in the middle of the night. The article was from a tabloid. It linked all the strange happenings to haunting by the school's original architect, Thomas Parris.

The bell rang overhead. *Shit.* I had to book it all the way across campus to get to the library to meet Ayaz. I grabbed a handful of the articles and shoved them under my blazer. I thought about slamming the secret passage shut – it was creeping me out, gaping open like that and sending a crisp chill through the room. But I didn't want to risk locking Loretta out. Especially since she hadn't been carrying a light.

I quickly unlocked my room, grabbed my history books, shoved the clippings inside the cover at the top of the stack, and sprinted back up the staircase and into the dormitory. Courtney and her brood gathered in the middle of the hall, admiring a new necklace her mother sent her. Every time I tried to step around them, one of them would shuffle into my way.

By the time I made it onto the landing in the atrium, the second bell was ringing. Only a couple of students were still out in the halls, and they scampered. I quickly glanced up at the class lists, admiring my beautiful new score, courtesy of Trey. If a teacher caught me in the halls, I'd lose three points, and I didn't want to do that to him after he'd given up his place to me.

Footsteps echoed on the marble. Someone was coming, someone with the power to take away my points. It took a split second to make the decision. I sprinted across the hall and down the darkened wing, swinging my body around the wide metal staircase toward the gymnasium.

I noticed light switches on the walls but didn't dare flick them on, in case the teacher behind me spotted the light and came looking. I knew from seeing a map of the school that the gym was coming up on my left, and if I went directly through it and down another corridor, I'd end up at the back of the library. The teachers had come down here, and none of them wore gas masks, so the contamination couldn't have been *that* bad.

I searched the gloom for obstacles, picking my way carefully down the corridor, using the wall as my guide. My nose itched as a musty, rancid smell wafted over my nostrils. Quinn wasn't kidding about the toxic odor – it really did smell like rotting meat. I ran my hand along the wall, passing a row of lockers and then a wide rolling wooden door.

This is it.

I grabbed the heavy wooden handle and yanked it. The door's wheels creaked, metal scraping against metal as a cloud of dust billowed up to meet me. I rolled the door open just enough to squeeze through, sucked in a breath of rancid air, and slipped inside the gymnasium.

The smell slammed into me, punching through my skin and seeping into my pores. It was a hot, fetid ichor that clung to my body like the embrace of a creepy uncle, tugging my throat closed and shriveling the inside of my nose. I gasped for air, but every breath I took only made my body fight the stench more violently. I staggered across the gymnasium, desperate to reach the other side as quickly as possible and get out of here.

Skylights on the roof cast squares of dull light across the court. My feet zigzagged over painted court lines, kicking up plumes of dust. I clawed at my throat, coughing and retching as I fought for air. *Almost there, almost there, no point turning back.*

One skylight illuminated the central circle, where basketball players met for the toss. My old school had one of the best teams in the state, but somehow I couldn't picture guys like Trey and Ayaz shooting hoops. Foldable tennis nets in front of the bleachers seemed more their style.

The stench enveloped my body in thick, mucus-like air. I swung my arms and legs, but it was as though I was swimming through molasses. Slowly, achingly slowly, I dragged my weeping, protesting body across the court, scanning the darkened bleachers for the exit I knew was there somewhere.

Scritch-scritch.

What's that?

I whirled around, straining my ears to listen for the sound I'd heard behind me.

Scritch-scritch. Scritch-scritch.

Now it was on the other side. I swung my body back around, just in time to see a low shadow dart behind the bleachers.

Someone's here.

I tried to call out, but all I managed was a choking noise. It wasn't a teacher, because they'd step right out and admonish me for being where I wasn't supposed to be. If it was a student, how were they crouching so calmly in the shadows while this infernal odor attacked their nose and lungs?

Scritch-scritch. Scritch-scritch. The sound resolved itself. Tiny rat claws scraped against wood, scrambling for purpose.

It's nothing to be afraid of, just the same rats you hear every night.

Only they sounded closer, their scrambling legs echoing in this cavernous gloom, as if... as if they'd escaped the walls and were coming for me.

Scritch-scritch. Scritch-scriiiiiiiiiiitch.

Something hot brushed against my foot. I wrenched my leg away, my body twisting and toppling to the ground. My knee cracked against the court, and pain shot up my leg.

Get up, get up, before they get you. Dust jammed my nose. My eyes wept. I planted my hands on the ground and shoved myself upright.

Beneath where I'd fallen, a faint light glowed on the floor. At first, I thought it was moonlight shining in from the skylights, it wasn't late enough for the moon to be that high. The light wasn't disturbed by my shadow. It seemed to rise up from the floor itself to cast an eerie glow over the central circle, illuminating lines drawn on the court.

As I watched, gape-mouthed in horror, the light shimmered and drew outward, forming lines that crisscrossed each other to make a five-pointed star and a glowing eye – the same symbol inside the school's crest.

Scritch-scritch-scritch. Behind me, the scratching noises grew louder, trilling in my ears as they rolled down from the tops of the bleachers, hundreds of sharpened claws pounding on wood, scrabbling down metal, tiny teeth gnashing as they prepared for the first real snack they'd had in years...

I strained to see them in the gloom. Shadows crept from beneath the bleachers, stalking on all fours like animals – dogs with twisted limbs and clicking tongues. But these weren't dogs, they couldn't be. They were creatures of dark malevolence that only a diseased mind could conceive.

This can't be happening. I have to be imagining this.

I froze, trapped by the smell and the thick air and the terror of my own mind. Shadows stretched and slithered along the court, and behind them the rats leaped over the bleachers, coming closer, closer...

One of the shadows reached out long claws toward me, scraping my cheek. I swung my fist in a tight uppercut, my fist connecting with hard bone. The creature grunted and lunged for me.

I found my voice. I screamed.

CHAPTER TWENTY-SIX

The cold fingers wrapped around my throat, pressing into my skin, silencing my scream. Air leaked from my lungs, and my oxygen-starved brain swirled, trying to connect the things I'd seen to the very real and very familiar guy who was practically choking me.

"Quiet," Quinn's voice whispered in my ear. "You're attracting them. I'm gonna get you out of here, but you have to stay quiet."

The fingers slipped from my throat, and I could breathe again, not that it was a relief. Thick arms wrapped around my shoulders and behind my knees, hoisting me off the ground.

Scritchscritchscritchscritchscritch.

My body jerked and jostled as Quinn ran across the court. His breath came out in ragged gasps. Shadows danced around us, caressing us with fingers of ice. In the center, the white star glowed bright. The air sucked out of the room, flowing into the star. My lungs burned and I struggled for every breath. Quinn stumbled, but kept fighting, kept walking away.

When we reached the door, Quinn leaned me against the wall. He wrapped his hands around the handle and pulled. "The door's stuck," Quinn groaned, his face straining. "I can't—"

The white star glowed behind my eyes, and the whole room exploded with black fire as the shadows consumed it.

I can't breathe. I can't...

CHAPTER TWENTY-SEVEN

A triumphant cry pulled me from the brink of passing out. Quinn dragged me through the door and slammed it shut behind him, just as something pounded against the wood.

"What are you doing here?" Quinn's voice came out in a ragged gasp. "Come on, we've got to go."

He wrapped an arm around me and helped me to my feet. My legs gave way beneath me, and I slid back to the ground. Pain shot through my arm as my elbow bent at a bad angle.

"Fuck. Hazy, come on." Quinn slipped his hands beneath me again, hoisting me back into his arms. My body lurched as he staggered down a darkened hallway. With the last ounce of strength I possessed, I clung to his cloak.

His black cloak.

Why is Quinn wearing a black cloak? Why is he dressed as a shadow?

Quinn pounded up a staircase to a security door, flicking something at the lock. The door clicked open. He ducked through and kicked it closed behind him, sinking to the ground with me still cradled in his arms. "Shit," he panted, laying me against the wall and rocking back. His face was white as a sheet, his eyes swollen and black and weeping. "I told you to be careful, to lay low. So you immediately go and snoop around in the *one* place where you shouldn't be looking."

I tried to speak, to ask the questions I needed to ask, but Quinn mashed his lips to mine. My body didn't question why a King was voluntarily kissing me again. I melted against him, sucking power and fortitude from the fire he stoked inside me. The moistness of his mouth drove out the foulness of that room, replacing it with something far sweeter, far more intoxicating. Quinn's coconut and sugarcane taste brought up memories of fun and frivolity to push out the darkness. I drew strength from his presence so that I could face the horror I'd just encountered.

This kiss – it wasn't like the others we'd shared, where Quinn had been in control. This was wild, desperate, as if he needed something from me that he could only ask for with his mouth tight against mine.

Well, whatever it was he needed, he wasn't getting it from me until I had answers.

"What... did I see... in there?" I gasped, pulling away. I had so many questions, but my throat wouldn't cooperate.

"I don't know, Hazy. You tell me. I heard you screaming, so I came running after you." Quinn rubbed his jaw. "You've left me smarting from that uppercut of yours. Ever thought about joining a boxing team?"

"You didn't... I screamed after..."

Quinn's face darkened. "Yeah, you got me. I was following you. Okay, up you get."

He rocked forward, swaying as he stood up, and staggered toward the end of the hall, which opened into the library's reading room. Toward light and civilization and books.

"Where are we going?" I gasped.

"I'm taking you to Ayaz. If anyone is going to explain this, it's gonna be him."

The last thing I wanted right now was to look into Ayaz's dark, cruel eyes. "Why him?"

"Because," Quinn's mouth set in a firm line. "He was once one of them."

CHAPTER TWENTY-EIGHT

"You're late—" Ayaz looked up from his cubicle where Quinn entered the reading room. He jumped back as Quinn sat me down on one of the tables. "Fuck! What happened?"

"Hazy here was running late to meet you, so she thought she'd take a shortcut through the gymnasium. Something attacked her and she screamed and punched me in the jaw."

Something that might have been fear flickered through Ayaz's dark eyes. He knelt down in front of me and started to press his fingers all over my body. "Are you hurt? Did you break anything?"

"You're not a doctor yet," I muttered.

"You can have a look at my jaw, though," Quinn complained. "It really fucking hurts."

"Sort yourself out," Ayaz continued his examination, probing my cheeks and running his hands over my neck, where I still had bruises from Trey's attack at the party. Ayaz picked up my arm and pressed his finger to the burn on my wrist. Fire flared through my body, the dangerous heat that came over me whenever I was around the Kings – the kind of fire that could easily rage out of control.

I snatched my hand away. "I'm fine."

I wasn't, but I had more important things to worry about. My elbow still smarted from where I'd wrenched it, and I was afraid my heart would never return to normal. The adrenaline was starting to flee my body, and I shivered. Ayaz shrugged off his blazer and threw it over my shoulders. Despite myself, I sucked in a deep breath of his honey and roses scent, letting this second olfactory sensation scrub the horror from my nostrils.

Quinn left and re-entered the room, Trey baying at his heels. The three of them crowded around me, touching me, stroking me, bombarding me with questions.

"Give me some room," I grumbled. They all stepped back, and I wished they hadn't. My body ached to feel the warmth of them.

Ayaz gripped my shoulders, studying me with his hard, dark eyes. "Listen, it's really important that you tell me exactly what you saw and heard."

"It was so weird." I rubbed my temple, where a headache bloomed. "I think whatever chemical is causing that smell gave me hallucinations."

"Maybe. But I need to know what happened, no matter how weird you think it is."

In between coughing and dry heaving, I related to them every detail I could remember about the gym – the scritching in the walls, the shadowy figures that scuttled under the bleachers on all fours and then crept across the court, the eerie light that seemed to come from beneath the court and formed the five-pointed star and eye of the school's crest.

"You seem positive that the scritching noise was rats," Ayaz said. "But you didn't actually see a rat."

"No, but it was exactly the same as the scritching in the walls. If that's not rats, what could it be?"

Quinn screwed up his face, as if he could think of lots of things it could be. "You've been hearing this scritching noise at night, right?"

"Yeah. Don't you?" Then I shook my head. "Of course you

don't. You sleep in the fancy dorms. It's only us scholarship students who get the basement rat-hole rooms."

"Maybe not for much longer," Trey growled. "That's got to be some kind of health code violation. Maybe we could go to Headmistress West and—"

Ayaz shook his head. "I tried that already."

That was right. I forgot that Ayaz had been a scholarship student. Supposedly, he'd slept in the same room I now occupied. I couldn't picture it. Did his rise to the rank of King in the school have something in common with whatever happened to Loretta?

"Did you get my books when you carried me out?" I asked Quinn. "I had something to show you."

"Nope, sorry. And neither of us are going back to get them, not if there are killer rats."

"Damn. I found something really odd." I scrambled to remember the details of the newspaper clipping. "Did you know there used to be another school here?"

Trey whistled his breath through his teeth. Quinn cocked his head to the side and flashed me a smile that was kind of tight-lipped. "That so?"

"Yeah. I found all these newspaper articles in one of the boxes in the storage room on my floor." I told them about chasing Loretta – or who I thought was Loretta – into the room, and finding them scattered everywhere. "Apparently, this place used to be called Miskatonic Preparatory, and it burned down in a tragic fire twenty years ago. It killed 245 students. Do people not know this or do you just not talk about it?"

"You shouldn't be reading these." Trey looked murderous. "They're not for your kind."

"My *kind?* I may have grown up in the Badlands, but I'm not a simpleton, Trey. So you guys knew about this fire and about Miskatonic Prep?"

"Of course we do. It's not a secret." Trey said, sounding exasperated. "Some of our class has family who died that night. But the school has worked hard to distance itself from what happened, and our reputation is beyond reproach."

I shuddered. "So many people died. How is this place still open?"

"You want to be in business one day?" Ayaz's eyes sharpened. "This school is a valuable lesson for you – behold the power of rebranding. A new name, a new intake of students, a generation of powerful people who wanted to keep their status symbol alive. Miskatonic Prep was erased from history, and Derleth Academy rose from its ashes."

I glared at Quinn. "You said Ayaz would give me an explanation for what happened. I need to know."

The guys exchanged a heated look – some kind of challenge for supremacy. Ayaz lost. He stepped back and shook his head. "Sure, Hazel. It's as you said, the chemical gives students hallucinations. That's why the wing is closed."

"Shouldn't the whole school be closed down? That staircase isn't even closed off. What's stopping any student wandering down there, like I did, like Quinn did, and getting themselves killed?"

"They don't want anyone on the outside to know about it, because the health board would shut the school down and that would be too much scandal for the families, especially after the fire."

"Why would that have anything to do with the fire?"

"Some people – namely some of the families of the victims – feel as though the school was opened too quickly. The alumni want to keep the school open at all costs, but some people in our circles think the place is bad luck, haunted by the ghosts of those dead kids."

"That's why there's this whole mistrust of the scholarship students thing," Quinn added. "Because it means there are students here the alumni don't control. Any wrong move, any scandal, and the school's reputation will be tarnished beyond repair."

"So if I go to the headmistress with this story..." I trailed off. I knew exactly what would happen. *She'd deduct all my merit points for breaking the rules.*

Trey nodded, as if he knew exactly what I was thinking.

"And why are you guys trying to help me?" I demanded. "How did you go from hating me to following me and giving me your merit points?"

Trey grinned. "We just wanted to make this year more interesting."

I didn't buy that, not for a minute. But I could see by the glance they shared that they'd already agreed not to tell me. I tried again. "And Loretta? You said she'd been kicked out. Why has she come back?"

Another pointed glance between them. Quinn shrugged. "Yeah, we don't get that, either. All I know is that Courtney made a case for her to the school board, and she was allowed back."

"Courtney? Why would she..." I rubbed my head. Pain throbbed against my skull. "I think I need to visit the nurse."

"Nope." Trey scooped me into his arms. "We're taking you to Ayaz's room."

'I can't go there. I'm not a monarch..."

But it was too late. My vision swam as weariness and delayed terror washed over me. I sank into Trey's arms. Quinn's eyes widened as he reached out and clasped my hand. "Stay with us, Hazy. We're not going to let them take you."

CHAPTER TWENTY-NINE

Ayaz's room was on a similar scale to Trey's, but it couldn't be more different. The walls were a pale grey, completely devoid of decoration, and the Scandinavian-style furniture was simple and practical. A low bed stood on top of a dais. The stairs around the outside doubled as bookshelves. I longed to scan the titles, suspecting they might hold the only true hint of Ayaz in this room, but no way was I getting down on my hands and knees in front of Ayaz.

Unless he asked me to.

Wheee, where did that thought come from? I rubbed my temple as my mind swam with vague images and sensations. *I think... maybe that smell got to me worse than I thought...*

Trey laid me down on the bed, pulling off my shoes and blazer. He traced his fingers along the inside of my leg, dancing over my skin.

"What are you doing?" I murmured.

"I'm removing your stockings, so Ayaz can make sure you don't have any rat bites on your legs, or... other things."

"Oh, okay." I flopped back on the pillows, my head screaming. My shin sizzled with heat where his fingers trailed.

Trey glanced at Quinn. "No protests? No threats? Dude, I'm seriously worried now. She's given up fighting us."

The room spun. My eyelids fluttered shut. Good, that stopped the spinning.

A warm hand pressed against my chest, over my heart, and I murmured in approval. *That feels nice.*

"Hazel, can you hear me?"

Yes, I can hear you. But I couldn't seem to speak. Or move.

"I think she's out cold." Quinn stroked my cheek. *That feels nice, too.* "Her breathing's ragged, but regular. She doesn't have a fever or anything."

"That's a good sign," Ayaz said. "It means they didn't reach her mind."

What didn't reach my mind? I grasped for consciousness, but it was a losing battle. I faded further into sleep, unable to speak or move, unsure if their words were real or part of a dream.

"We should tell her the truth," Quinn said. "She's tough. She's handled all that shit you bozos did to her. She can handle this."

"Us bozos?" The smirk in Trey's voice was unmistakable. "If I recall, *you* were the one who lured her to that party."

"Don't talk about that party," Quinn growled.

"You think she can handle the truth?" Ayaz muttered, his voice so dark it forced a shiver through my body. "You want to look into the void and claim that?"

"Whoa, cool it, I'm just making a suggestion." I imagined Quinn with his hands up in a gesture of surrender, his eyes with that mischievous glint that said yes, he meant every word. "You'd know better than me, Charity Boy."

"I told you not to call me that," Ayaz growled. "I earned my place here, which is more than you can say."

"Can you both shut the fuck up?" That was Trey. "Of course we're not going to tell her anything. She'll just think we're bull-shitting her and do something even more dangerous."

"Her mother was killed in a fire," Ayaz whispered. "And her best friend, too. Do we think that's a coincidence?"

There was silence for a few moments, and then Trey said, "It doesn't matter. We've seen what they're capable of. And now she's caught their eye, and Courtney's out for her blood. I don't think we'll be able to protect Hazel for much longer, especially not if she goes around telling people about Miskatonic Prep."

"She's good at keeping secrets," Quinn said. "I didn't know about the fire."

"That's because you never read her file."

"Of course I didn't. Reading is for nerds like you."

"Her whole apartment building burned down in suspicious circumstances," Trey said, his voice breathy. "According to the statement she gave police, some kids from a gang were threatening her friend, Homer or Milton or someone. They'd stolen something from him and she got into a brawl with them. The friend ran to Hazel's apartment to tell her mother like a fucking coward. The gang followed him, and someone threw a molotov cocktail that got out of control, and burned the building down."

That's not what happened. That's not—

"She went after a whole *gang?*" Quinn whistled. "That sounds like our Hazy."

"Except it doesn't explain why she had burns all over her hands," Trey said. "As if she was the one who started the fire."

There was a few moments of silence, where I almost drifted away, then Quinn said, "What was she saying about following someone into the storage room?"

"I've looked in all those boxes," Trey said. "There's no newspaper clippings."

"Well, she wasn't lying. How else did she know about Miskatonic?"

"This person she said she saw, they must have planted them there. It's like they led Hazel into that room, like they wanted her to know."

"You know what I'm thinking," Quinn said. "I think it's Zehra—"

"No." Ayaz growled. "It's not."

"But couldn't it—"

"Zehra is *gone*," Ayaz practically whispered, his voice choked with pain. "It's not her."

What are they talking about? Who's Zehra? What... but I couldn't finish the thought before I slipped into darkness.

CHAPTER THIRTY

My eyes flew open. For a moment, all I could see was darkness, and panic rose inside me. But then a row of candles flared to life – a clever magic trick – and I got my first glimpse at my surroundings.

I stood in a wide, dark cavern, lit by the candles standing in niches around the walls and torches placed in a circular structure in the center of the room. The rock was grey with veins of some mineral twisting through it – the mineral glowed an odd color that seemed to disappear as my eyes tried to focus on it. I turned to the center of the cavern, where a wooden platform covered with a scaffold and ropes of different lengths had been erected, almost like a gallows. A shadow slid out from the cavern wall and floated toward the platform.

Something about the place seemed familiar, like I'd been there before. A faint sound reached my ears. Scritch-scritch-scritch. Tiny feet scraping against stone. An unsettling presence hiding in the gloom.

This is the cave from my dream. Only this time, it was lit up.

But why am I here?

As the candlelight flickered around the shadow, I resolved it into a robed figure, head bowed, hands clasped at the waist. I yelped and staggered backward. My arm flew out and brushed another figure who advanced toward the platform. More figures poured out of the shadows. As one they raised their arms, their fingers splayed, and let out a low, guttural sound that chilled my blood.

It wasn't a hum or a chant, more like a dog baying with hunger – the kind of sound no human could make.

The invisible, malevolent force wrapped around me, dragging me toward the platform. I tried to cry out, but my lips froze shut. I scrambled for something to hold, but my hands clasped only air. My feet skidded across bare stone, tripping and kicking as the force dragged me up the wooden stairs.

I stood on the platform, staring down at a metal seal, covered with the same star symbol in the school crest. It looked like a manhole cover, made from whatever mysterious element was veined in the cavern walls, but sewers had nothing on whatever was underneath.

The force that held me... it came from below the platform. Whatever it was, was on the other side of that cover, and it was a thing of such overwhelming vileness that its dark energy could not be contained by any earthly metal.

The baying, keening sound of the robed figures rose higher, jamming my ears. I couldn't move, I couldn't think. The great and terrible hand that was not a hand, the limb made of darkness and terror itself, dragged me closer, held me in place.

The lip opened and fear itself poured out. I stood on the edge, frozen in place, and stared down into a void – so dark that it was no longer darkness, so deep that it pierced space. It was as though all the malignancy in all the universe had been poured into that void, and it now leered back at me, dragging me closer, pulling me down down down...

"Hazel!"

My vision wobbled. The void dragged me forward. My foot

slid across the slippery wood, catching on the edge before my body toppled over the edge. I tore my lips open in a silent scream as the void reached up to swallow me...

"Wake up, Hazy." A sultry voice called me back from the void. "You're having a nightmare."

My body jerked, the hand slithering over my skin as I was torn from its grasp. A room came into focus – not the stone cavern with the veins my eyes couldn't quite see, but grey walls, trendy furniture, and a massive TV and sound system. A shirtless Quinn leaned over the bed, staring at me with wide, curious eyes.

I sat up, rubbing my throbbing head. "It felt so real."

"Dreams usually do. Coffee?" Quinn held up a cup. "Ayaz has a new machine, specially flown in from Europe by Trey's dad. A piece of advice, though – never ask a Turk to make you a coffee. They only like it when it has the taste and texture of dirt."

"Yeah, sure, coffee sounds great." I accepted the cup, flopping back against the pillows and taking a sip. Ah, warm liquid gold. Some of the fear from the dream slid from my shoulders.

Now I was awake, I could figure out what the fuck was going on with my reality.

I peered down at myself under the covers. I wore a large, over-sized t-shirt with some heavy metal band logo on it, and my own underwear. *Where are my clothes?*

Quinn sat on the end of the bed with his own cup, grinning at me. *Shit shit shit. What's going on? What happened last night?*

Snatches came back to me. I took a shortcut through the gymnasium. Something attacked me. Quinn carried me out, and the guys brought me back here. But what did it all mean, and why wasn't I wearing my clothes?

Why can't I remember?

My chest tightened. "Quinn, did we... do anything last night?"

"Nope. Not unless you count drooling all over Ayaz's pillow and Trey kicking me in the face." Quinn pointed to the sofa, which had been folded out into a bed. Trey and Ayaz topped and tailed on it, the sheets thrown over their bodies. There was a third space on the end with an indent of Quinn's body. Muscled limbs poked out in all directions. I swallowed hard.

Have I died and gone to heaven?

And if so, why did my head hurt so much? Was I sick? Surely if God thought I deserved three semi-naked Kings, one of which was bringing me coffee in bed, he also saw fit to ensure I was well enough to enjoy it?

"We thought you wouldn't be comfortable in your uniform," Quinn said. "Ayaz undressed you and he was very gentlemanly. Trey and I didn't look, although it was fucking tempting, let me tell you. I only resisted because I'm basically a saint."

"What's the time?" I muttered, rolling over and searching the nightstand for some kind of clock. There was a huge stack of books – I noticed biographies of famous artists and what looked like poetry books. *Poetry? The mystery of Ayaz deepens.*

Quinn glanced at an expensive gold watch on his wrist. "We've missed breakfast. But that's fine. I'll get Ayaz to make us something when he wakes up. He's a halfway decent cook."

I threw the sheets off, panic rising in my throat. "I can't stay here! What if Courtney sees me? I have to get to rehearsal..."

"Don't worry." Quinn climbed up on the bed beside me. I finished the rest of my coffee. *Oh, god, that's amazing.* "You've got a bit of time before rehearsal, and we've got ways to sneak you around without anyone seeing. How do you feel?"

I rubbed my temple. "Like I was run over by a truck."

"And you haven't even had any alcohol," Quinn grinned. "I wonder what you'd be like with a few drinks in you. I bet you're wild."

"Nope. I fall asleep and then I vomit on your shoes." I remembered a night Dante and I had stolen a bottle of vodka from his foster dad and got drunk in the park together. For once, the memory didn't sting as bad as usual.

"You didn't vomit last night."

"Give me time." I took another sip of coffee. My stomach grumbled.

The pile of hotness on the sofa stirred. Trey raised his arms above his head, stretching his body like a cat. He turned his head toward me and his face lit up in a most un-Treylike smile. God, he was beautiful when he smiled – a whole different person. I could almost imagine him as a kid, running free without a care in the world.

"She's up."

There was a knock on the door. The woman who I'd first encountered the day I arrived at Derleth was on the other side, bearing a pile of fresh laundry. Her eyes flicked over me with suspicion, but she didn't say a word as she slipped out again.

Quinn kicked Ayaz's sleeping figure. "Get up. Hazy needs breakfast. And so do I."

"All right, all right," Ayaz grumbled, tossing his pillow at Quinn. As he lifted his arm, I noticed a tattoo on his wrist. A rune, identical to Quinn's and Trey's. "Hazel, do you like eggs? I'll make you my special *menemen*."

"Take him up on that," Trey said, standing up and buttoning his white uniform shirt. "It's like scrambled eggs on acid."

Okay, now they're making me breakfast. This is insane. I needed to step out of the room for a moment. I needed to think. Also, I needed to pee.

I slid out of bed, tugging the hem of the t-shirt down so it covered my ass. "I need the bathroom."

"It's right through there." Ayaz pointed to a door beside the kitchen.

I shut the door and sat down on the toilet, staring at the crisp marble tiles on the walls and admiring the gleaming shower with its multiple heads. *Don't imagine Ayaz standing in that shower, the jets spraying his body as he lathers up and...*

I groaned and looked away, which was just as well, because I realized there was no toilet paper on the holder. *Boys.* Dante never used to replace it, either. I pulled open the door under the vanity to hunt for more paper. Something large and heavy fell out.

A book.

Curious, I picked it up and slid it onto my lap. The cover was some weird material, like leather, but more irregular and dry. The texture felt familiar, but I couldn't describe it. I flipped open the cover to reveal yellowed pages covered in handwritten text in some weird foreign language, strange symbols, and dark illustrations of skulls and constellations and eviscerated corpses.

As I turned the page, a series of loose papers slid out into my hand. They were files. The first showed a picture of a young girl, about my age, with frizzy brown hair and glasses. *Sadie Lancaster. Scholarship student.* No parental details listed, only the address of a CPS case worker. The file was from nineteen years ago. Sadie's picture had a giant cross slashed through it.

My chest tightened as I flipped to the next file. Another scholarship student, another ugly cross slashed through his face. I scanned his file, recoiling in horror from all the personal information it contained – newspaper clippings about his parents' death, psychiatric reports, his eulogy from their funeral. All over the files, someone had scribbled notes, underlined sections, and made crude drawings – strange symbols, little maps, a hangman's noose.

It was Ayaz's handwriting. I recognized it from our history project. And the drawings bore his distinctive style, too. Frantic now, I flipped page after page – all scholarship students from the last twenty years, all orphans, all with their private files exposed and their faces crossed out.

What is this?

My stomach twisted. Pain slashed at my chest as the full horror of what I held in my hands dawned on me. My hands shook as I flipped through files for Loretta, Andre, Greg, and myself. My vision blurred, and I couldn't focus on the words. I *wouldn't.*

I leaned over and threw up in the sink. My undigested coffee swirled down the plughole.

"Hazy, are you okay?" Quinn banged on the door.

"No." I stared at myself in the mirror. My hair stuck straight up, rumpled from sleep. Ayaz's t-shirt clung to my curves. My eyes were hollow, ringed in red. I looked like shit, like the gutter whore they said I was.

I reached up to touch the bruises on my neck left by Trey, exposing the burn scar on my wrist. As soon as I saw that scar, the reality of my situation came flooding back to me.

One act of kindness and I've forgotten who they are and what they've done to me. My hand gripped the lumpy spine of the book so hard my knuckles turned white. *I'll not forget again.*

I flushed the toilet, yanked the door open, and stormed into the room. Ayaz looked up from the kitchen, where he was stirring a bowl of eggs. "What the—"

I threw the book down on the bench. Ayaz stiffened, his whisk hand frozen. Trey's face darkened, and Quinn... Quinn's lower lip trembled. The Kings stared at the book, then at each other, then finally at me.

I broke the deafening silence. "Well?"

"It's not what it looks like—" Ayaz started.

I held up a hand. "Don't even fucking pull that shit. What I'm looking at here – is it some kind of torture guide passed down from one generation of bullies to the next? I can't even fathom how malicious you have to be in order to pull something like this, year after year after year. So go on, out with it, is this why you were being nice to me? Because you wanted me to find this?"

Quinn beamed, but his smile was all crooked and broken. "I was always nice to you, Hazy."

"No, you weren't!" My voice rose. I was in serious danger of becoming hysterical. "I don't think you did any of the really mean things, like the maggots or tearing up my journal, but you liked making me uncomfortable. Even when you took me to that party, it wasn't you trying to get to know me as a person. You just wanted to be with someone who was unique, a challenge."

Quinn looked hurt. "That wasn't—"

"Yes, it was. But at least you never hated me." I jabbed a finger at Trey's stomach. "*You* wanted me gone from the minute I walked out of the car."

"You don't know the whole story," Trey said, his jaw tightening.

"Yeah? Well, the *Reader's Digest* version you've given me doesn't exactly paint a flattering portrait. And you," I jabbed a finger at the folder, then turned my gaze to Ayaz. "You didn't even *know* me. You saw yourself reflected back at you, and it made you ashamed."

"You think you got us all figured out, Meat," Ayaz hissed. "You have no idea what we've done for you."

I folded my arms. "No offense, but you've done nothing this year that makes me able to trust you. You give me your points, and you take me back here and give me medicine and coffee, and you expect me to believe all this isn't some elaborate prank you're setting up? Forget it. You destroyed the most precious thing I owned, so this psychological game you're playing doesn't even come close to measuring up to that."

"What precious thing?" Quinn looked genuinely confused. "You guys melt down her dead mother's jewelry or something?"

"Dante's journal!" I cried.

"That shitty book of scribbles?" Trey laughed. "If that's your most prized possession, then you really are more pathetic than we thought."

"We can buy a new notebook for you to scribble on," Quinn said. "Headmistress West won't even question it if it came from us."

"You don't understand." My hands balled into fists. I whirled around and stalked out of the room. "You never even tried to understand."

"Well, fuck you very much!" Trey called after me as I slammed the door so hard the wall rattled. In the hallway, students turned in surprise.

What the fuck are you doing in Ayaz's room?" Tillie cried out. I shoved past her without answering, barreling through kids in my desperation to reach the stairs.

No more Kings. No more flirting. No more entertaining the idea that they might be half-decent guys under all that privilege and bullshit. No more hoping that those stolen moments with Quinn and Trey could be more than they were.

I'm done.

CHAPTER THIRTY-ONE

I lay in my bed, staring at the ceiling. Confused thoughts rolled around in my head. All day I'd been avoiding the Kings. I managed to fake a sore throat and was excused from singing at rehearsals, and at breakfast and lunch I grabbed fruit from the bowl and ate it in between classes, which wasn't allowed, but no one stopped me. I managed to completely avoid Greg and Andre. Between activities, I crawled back into my bed with only the company of rats and tried to figure out what the fuck was going on.

The shadows in the gym, the glowing star, the infernal rats in the walls, that horrible, horrible folder of faces, all crossed out...

But I also hadn't mistaken the conversation I'd overheard when they thought I was asleep. All that stuff they talked about, it sounded like some weird secret club. Did it have anything to do with the teachers going down to the gym in their academic gowns? And Loretta's sudden re-appearance?

I know from watching *Gilmore Girls* that the children of privilege loved a good secret society, but was one in force here at Derleth? I was guessing so, based on those tattoos I saw on their wrists. But did it have something to do with the fire that killed all those students?

What sick prank were the Kings and their secret club cooking up next? Why were they so interested in me? Why did they care about what happened to Mom and Dante? Panic circled in my gut as I thought back to the day I'd made that statement to the police, my hands wrapped in bandages, how they'd glared at me with a mixture of horror and suspicion, but didn't have enough evidence to charge me.

There had to be a prank, a design of some sort. Because there was no way those guys were being nice to me out of the goodness of their hearts. Especially not after I said all that stuff... I cringed as I recalled my words, how I'd taken those tiny nuggets of real-ness they'd given me and thrown it back in their faces. They deserved it, but I still didn't feel good about it.

Dante, I wish you were here now. I wish I could curl up in your arms and hear you tell me that everything is going to be okay.

The rats in the walls circled around my head. Above the steady scritch-scritch, I could hear thumps and shouts as the rich students returned to their dorms after dinner. My stomach rumbled. I hoped I didn't miss roast beef. I just couldn't face everyone's eyes on me today, the awkward dance of figuring out where to sit, especially after they'd all seen me coming out of Ayaz's room, my hair all rumpled, wearing his t-shirt.

Footsteps sounded in the hall. "Hazel?" It was Greg. "You missed dinner two nights in a row. Are you okay?"

"I'm fine." I stared at the wardrobe I'd pulled in front of the door to keep out Courtney. "I'm just tired."

"You didn't come back for dinner last night, and you've been avoiding me all day." There was a pause. "I heard you were in Ayaz's dorm. Care to explain?"

"Not really."

"Hazel, can you open the door?" Greg sounded really upset. "I'd really like to talk to you. We could even go for a walk. The teachers are all at a faculty meeting tonight, so the place is pretty quiet."

"Not right now."

Greg stayed outside my door for a couple of minutes, then I heard his footsteps retreating down the hall to his room. The sun dipped below my window. I stared at the books stacked on my desk. I still had to write up the conclusion for the history assignment. Ayaz had given me the job once he acknowledged I was the superior writer. I shuddered at the memory of how my skin glowed from his praise. I was sick, chasing after the approval of those guys who were plotting something so terrible they needed a whole secret society in on the joke.

A fist pounded on my door, startling me from my stupor. I rubbed my eyes. I'd fallen asleep still wearing my skirt and Ayaz's t-shirt. A whiff of his honey and rose scent wafted off it and caught me under the nose, causing an ache to tear through my chest. "Greg, I mean it. What part of 'fuck off' don't you understand?"

"Hazel."

I knew that voice anywhere. *Ayaz.* I sat up, noticing the time on Loretta's ancient alarm clock, which for some reason had remained behind when she moved into her upstairs dorm. 1:22AM. Why would Ayaz be knocking on my door in the middle of the night?

Why would he use my name like that, his voice rising with fear?

I sat up, hugging my knees to my chest. My heart thudded. "What do you want?"

"Open the door. You have to come with me. *Now.*"

"You didn't say please."

"Hazel, this isn't a joke."

"No, it's not. Fuck off, Ayaz. I don't have to do anything with you or for you."

"Just open the door."

The desperation in his voice chilled me. What could make Ayaz lose his cool like that? I had to know, but that didn't mean I was going to trust him. I pulled the piece of glass out from beneath my mattress and held it in my hand as I shoved the wardrobe aside and opened the door a crack.

Ayaz stood in the hall, holding an old-fashioned lantern with a flickering flame inside. He smirked at the glass in my hand. "You going to give me a haircut with that puny thing? Come on."

"I'm not going anywhere with you."

"You will if you want to live through the night."

What?

I reeled at his words. "Is that a threat?"

"Nope. A promise." He held up a lantern, the flames flickering over his muscled torso. "But not from me. We've got to be quick. They're coming for you."

"Ayaz, what's this about? Who's coming for me, Courtney? Is this the big prank you and the guys have been working on, because..."

My words died in my throat as Ayaz lifted the lantern, illuminating his features. Something burned in his eyes that I'd never seen before. *Fear.*

Ayaz, one of the rulers of the school, was truly afraid. Of what, I didn't know. But it sure as fuck wasn't me.

I stepped back and slid the glass into my skirt pocket. I yanked a hoodie off the end of my bed and pulled it over his shirt. "Fine. But one false move from you and I'll cut your pretty face."

"That seems fair." He tapped his foot impatiently while I pulled on leggings and sneakers. I looped my arm in his and he led me down to the storage room, threw open the mirror door, and climbed inside the secret passage. "Come on."

"Is it another party?"

"There is a party, but you're not invited. Come on." He gave my arm an impatient tug, the fear rising in his voice. He wrapped his long body around the wall and shoved me ahead of him, probably to stop me from running back to my room.

"I can't see a thing," I complained.

"Here." Ayaz shoved the lantern into my hands. I held it up, watching the flames dance along the bare stone walls. My ears rang as I remembered flames leaping out of the windows of our apartment building as the heat exploded the glass, licking at the fire escape the way any touch from the Kings sent heat coursing through my veins. Fire destroyed my family. Fire turned this school into a funeral pyre. Fire made me want my bullies. Fire followed me everywhere, burning my life to ashes.

Is that... my gaze flicked to a thin vein running through the stone – an iridescent light my eyes couldn't quite focus on, that was gone as quickly as it appeared. It looked just like the veins in the cavern I saw in my dream.

But that couldn't be possible, because it was a *dream*. That cavern wasn't a real place.

Ayaz nudged me in the back. "Faster. We've got to get out before they know you're missing."

"Who's they? Trey and Quinn?" Was Ayaz trying to rescue me from what the others had planned? That might make sense. After all, he was in my position once, the victim of the games the Kings and Queens liked to play. Maybe he felt they had gone too far. He had given me that warning about Trey at the party, even though it was as good as useless in the end.

"I'll explain it all, I promise. But not now. Go, go!"

I ducked low and scrambled out of the cave. Salty wind blew up from the ocean, biting my face as it roared along the cliffs. I hugged my arms, glad I'd thought to put on the hoodie.

Ayaz pointed down the path. "Go."

I picked my way along the path I'd traveled with Quinn only a few weeks ago, hugging the side of the cliff. After a few minutes, we emerged into the flat terrace where the party had been held. Only this time there was no music or laughter or clinking of glasses, no students making out between the crumbling pillars or bobbing in the steamy grotto. I listened hard, but couldn't even hear an owl or other night creature. Only the steady crash of the waves.

"Quickly. Down here. They're waiting." Ayaz gestured to the edge of the cliff. I was about to tell him to fuck off, I wasn't getting that close to the edge with him, when I noticed the narrow set of steps carved into the rock.

"What's down there?" I demanded.

"Your way out."

My knees locked. *This is it. I'd gone this far trusting Ayaz's vague warnings. If he thinks I'll walk down the precarious steps of doom without answers, he can eat a bag of dicks.*

I backed away from the ledge. "Hell no."

Ayaz must've sensed that I'd come as far as I could, because he grabbed my hand, twisting me so I had to look into his eyes. There was a wildness there, a panic that was so completely out of character it gave me pause. "Look, Hazel. Courtney and Tillie and the others... they're going to do something to you tonight. It's really awful, and we can't stop them. So we're getting you out of here."

He blinked, his eyes darting away. *He's lying to me. Maybe not about the danger, but definitely about where it was coming from.*

"Why should I trust you?" I demanded. "You're lying to me right now."

Ayaz rolled his eyes at the sky, as if begging for strength. When he spoke again, his voice was softer than I'd ever heard it. 'You're right. We've given you absolutely no reason to trust us. You're right about a lot of things, Hazel. We should never have let you leave the way you did. You hit a nerve with those things you said."

"I... did?"

He nodded. "I can't speak for the other two, but you're got me pegged. Judging by the way Trey went all quiet and Quinn was pissed as hell, I think you nailed them, too. So yeah, maybe some poor girl from the gutter knows us better than we know ourselves, and *maybe* that same girl is in some serious danger and we want to help her. Now, will you hurry up and move, because there's a chance they might look for you out here."

Far below, waves smashed against the cliffs. Salt spray misted the steps. I held the lantern out in front of me, using my other arm to steady myself on the cliff, and stepped down.

I moved slowly, because the steps were narrow and slippery from sea spray, and the lantern only illuminated a small circle in front of me. The trees overhead sheltered the staircase from the moon as it curved around the cliff. I peered up, but couldn't see anything through the thick branches.

"Here she comes," a voice called up from the gloom. *Quinn.* My stomach tightened again. I was down here alone with the three Kings. The only thing I had on me for protection was that piece of glass. If they did something to me, no one would find me.

I should have told Greg where I was going. Fuck.

I yelped as something grazed my arm. A warm hand curled around my arm. "Watch out," Trey said. "That last step is a big one."

My foot slipped on wet rock and I fell into Trey's arms. He gathered me up and steadied me while I caught my breath. I held up the lantern and stared into the gloom. "Where are we?"

From what little I could see, we were in a tiny bay, sheltered from the worst of the wind by the protruding cliffs and from above by the thick, bent trees and a rock overhang. Waves crashed against the rocks, soaking my jeans and sneakers. A few feet from Trey stood Quinn, holding a rope that tethered a small rowboat to a thick tree.

Ayaz jumped down beside me. "Are you okay?" he asked. "I heard you cry out."

"I slipped. Trey caught me." I stated those facts like they were nothing, like my body wasn't on fire from being in Trey's arms.

"Okay, good. Get in the boat."

"Huh?"

Ayaz reached behind a rock and pulled out a backpack. He unzipped it and showed me inside. Some sandwiches and chicken from lunch and dinner, a few brownies, all wrapped in pages torn from his exercise books. "There's water in here, as well as a flashlight and a first aid kit. And some money in a waterproof pouch. About five hundred in cash. I just hope it'll be enough until we can get you more."

"Enough for what? What's going on?"

"Put your arms up," Trey commanded. When I didn't comply, he grabbed my wrists and jerked my arms in the air, pulling a wet, cold life jacket over my shoulders and buckling it at the waist.

"Seriously, why am I wearing this?" I growled.

"Because you're getting in that boat and you're rowing as far from Derleth Academy as you can get," Trey said, like I was the one being difficult. "Now, get in."

"Hell no."

"Hazy—"

"Don't 'Hazy' me like I'm being unreasonable," I stepped back. "This is crazy. It's downright ludicrous."

"What's ludicrous is you not following simple instructions."

"Simple, is it? Just casually row my way to shore even though I've never even been on a boat? I'm from Philly, not fucking Martha's Vineyard. The water's rough out there. I'll be dashed against the cliffs in minutes. And you haven't even told me what I'm escaping from."

"From Courtney and the Queens—" Trey started.

"That's bullshit and you know it. What could they possibly be planning that's so bad I have to risk my life in order to avoid it? If it's so awful, why don't you just report it to a teacher? Why all this skullduggery cloak-and-dagger stuff—"

"Because the teachers are part of it," Ayaz growled.

The air left my lungs with a whoosh. I staggered back against the steps.

"I don't believe you," I whispered.

The robes, the shadows, Headmistress West's face as she checked the dormitories before their staff meeting. The glowing star in the gymnasium floor.

"Yes, you do." Trey loomed over me. "Get in the boat, Hazel. It's your only chance."

"Trey will go with you," Quinn added. "He'll do most of the work. He's captain of the rowing team."

"Of course he is," I muttered.

Trey bent down, rolling up the legs of his uniform trousers. He stepped into the water, wincing as the cold slammed into him. He steadied himself on the edge of the boat and swung his leg over. Water lapped against the sides as the boat rocked dangerously.

Turning to face me, Trey held out a hand to me. "I'll help you," he said.

Three faces looked at me in the gloom – desperate, frightened, expectant. And suddenly, the full force of what they were asking me to do slammed into me. Every rotten thing they had done to me slammed against my skull. All the times they'd tried to break me. My hand flew to my throat as I remembered the squeeze of Trey's fingers as he held me out over the cliff.

They were asking me to trust them, but I couldn't. They had already taken so much from me; I wasn't about to let them take my one shot at a better life, too.

I lifted the lantern, spun around, and fled back up the stairs. Tears burned in the corners of my eyes, but I didn't know why I was crying. I scrambled up, up, and away from them as fast as I could.

"No, Hazel. Come back!"

The climb up was faster – I used the steps above me as a hold while I scrambled as fast as I could. My throat burned. My eyes stung with bitter tears. But I didn't turn around, didn't look back.

I reached the top of the staircase and stumbled onto solid ground. Wild with fear, I spun in all directions. Where to go, what to do? At any moment Ayaz would reach the top of the staircase and—

I took a step toward the tunnel, but changed my mind. They'd expect me to go that way. And it would just take me back to the school, where some other horror awaited me. No, I needed to hide out here. If I could wait it out until morning then I could walk down to the village, call the police, tell them that some boys at Derleth Academy tried to kill me. *Let's see their parents cover up the scandal I'm about to unleash.*

I took off in the other direction, sliding over the damp rocks on the edge of the grotto until I dropped down on the narrow path that led down into the trees, down toward the cemetery.

My feet slid out from under me as I scrambled for cover. *Please don't let them see me. Please let them go to the cave so I can get away.*

"Hazel, where are you?"

They were close, too close, walking around by the grotto. I poured on speed, my chest heaving as I entered the trees, my boots crunching in the dead leaves.

"I see her!"

Damn, I was hoping the trees would hide the lantern. I should have thrown it away but... but I couldn't be out here, alone, in the dark. I needed the light. I needed the fire.

They all shouted my name as they scrambled over the grotto. I heard leaves skidding over the ground. Trey cursed. I gulped back my fear and sprinted ahead. In front of me loomed the metal gate of the cemetery. I grabbed the latch and yanked. It lifted surprisingly easily, and I staggered backwards.

"No, Hazel, don't go in there."

I don't have to listen to you, Trey Bloomberg. You may be King of Derleth Academy, but I'm nobody's servant.

I grabbed the gate and pulled, throwing myself through it into the cemetery beyond. Small, crumbling stones rose from piles of dead leaves. There was no path, just lines of graves all facing the ocean, bending around the slope as they followed the contours of the hill.

I skittered across the top, thinking that if I could somehow circle back without the guys noticing me, I would make my way down the road until I got to the town. That was miles and miles of walking in the dark, but I'd rather that then get in that death-boat or face whatever was waiting for me at the school.

"Hazel."

The gates hinges creaked. Shit, they were faster than I thought. The lantern was giving my position away, but if I let go of it, I'd be running blind along these cliffs and that was bound to kill me faster than they would.

Move downhill, through the trees. Get below the cliff and they won't see the lantern. Wait until they leave.

Sucking in a deep breath, I pumped my arms and skidded down the slope, passing through the rows of graves as I plunged toward the treeline. If I could reach it, I could clamber down the rocks and hide under one of the overhangs until the guys got tired of looking for me.

My chest burned as I poured on speed. *Almost there. Almost—*

My foot caught on a low headstone. I fell hard, my knee slamming into the stone. Pain arced up my leg. The lantern fell from my hand and bounced across the ground. The fire inside flickered but didn't go out.

No, no, no…

"Shit. She's down!"

"Hazel, are you okay?" Voices called from the top of the slope. Feet shuffled toward me through the leaves.

I moaned, rolling over and clutching my knee. *Fuck, fuck.* I could hear the guys calling my name. I tried to put weight on my leg, but my knee collapsed.

I crawled through the dead leaves and grabbed the lantern, holding it up so I could see them coming, three shadows looming down on me. "Get away from me!" I screamed, swinging the lantern back. *I'll throw it as soon as they got close.*

Heat rushed down my arm toward the lantern, and the flames flared higher, wrapping around my arm without touching my skin, without burning me.

Whoa, what is that? How did I do that?

The flames seemed to tug at me, pulling my arm around, swinging the beam of the lantern across the graveyard. I squeezed my muscles to stop my arm moving, but it kept going. I wasn't in control any more.

My arm jerked to a stop. The lantern light fell on the gravestone in front of me, dancing over the words carved there.

AYAZ DEMIR.

Huh?

"Hazel!" Quinn's voice drew my attention from the stone.

Don't get distracted by an old grave. It's probably just one of Ayaz's ancestors. Quinn said the graveyard was filled with alumni—

But it can't be. Ayaz was a scholarship student, like me. None of his family attended the school. So how was there a grave here with his name on it?

I swung my lantern around until the beam caught the stone next to it, illuminating a border of four-leaf clovers and a name:

QUINN DELACORTE, BELOVED SON.

My blood froze in my veins as I swung the lantern again. Next to Quinn's stood another stone – this one tall and grand. Thick weeds obscured the writing. I dug the glass sherd from my pocket and hacked them away, revealing an elaborate carving of a winged skeleton over the name of the deceased.

VINCENT FRANCIS BLOOMBERG THE THIRD

(TREY)

A boot slammed down into the dirt, obscuring my view of the grave. Ayaz. The lantern picked up the fire in his eyes. Trey and Quinn pulled up behind him, their mouths open in horror as they saw where I was pointing the lantern.

"You saw," Ayaz growled.

"Saw what?" I cried, cold creeping through my veins. "I don't understand!"

"You saw the stones," he said. "You know that Quinn, Trey and I are dead. We're all dead."

TO BE CONTINUED

Secrets. Lies. Sacrifice. Find out what happens next in book 2 of the Kings of Miskatonic Prep, *Initiated*

Read now:
http://books2read.com/initiated

Or devour the entire Kings of Miskatonic Prep series (with bonus POV scenes) in the boxset:
http://books2read.com/miskatonicbox

Turn the page for a sizzling excerpt.

Get your free copy of *Cabinet of Curiosities*, a Steffanie Holmes compendium of short stories and bonus scenes. To get this collection, all you need to do is sign up for updates with the Steffanie Holmes newsletter.

http://www.steffanieholmes.com/newsletter

FROM THE AUTHOR

She is nine years old. Two girls at her school pretend to be her friends, but mock her and humiliate her behind her back. She confronts them one day, tells them she's sorry if she'd done something to upset them.

"I just want us all to be friends," she says.

Their faces break into smiles. "That's what we want, too!"

One of them says she has something awesome to show the others. "We just found it!" She drags the girl behind the school hall. "You'll love it." She tells the girl to bend down and look under the hall.

As the girl bends over, a hand grabs the back of her neck, forcing her head down. She twists away, but not before her face is pushed into a pile of dog shit.

She stands up and watches her friends double over with laughter, cackling like the witches of Macbeth. She floats outside her body, looking down on herself – this pathetic girl with dog shit all over her face. She runs. She runs from the school, their laughter following her down the road, around the corner, somewhere, anywhere away from them. She doesn't remember how far she runs or how her mum finds her. She just remembers running.

This is a true story. It happened to me.

I have a rare genetic condition called *achromatopsia*. It renders me completely colour-blind and legally blind. I was also a generally imaginative, weird, and introverted child. I was good at art and making up stories and terrible at sports. I wasn't like the other kids, so they ostracized me, called me names, deliberately invented games to humiliate me, locked me in cupboards, told me that I was stupid, useless, pointless, that I should just go away, that I should never have been born.

It took me years to learn to trust people, to let them see the real me. Social situations still make me anxious, and I've struggled with low self-esteem and internalising anger.

In part, this is why I put myself inside Hazel's head to write this book. But it's not the main reason.

I want to tell you a different story.

During my first year at university, I met this girl in my dorm. We bonded over a mutual love of *Stargate SG1* and Terry Pratchett and became fast friends. We moved in together and were flatmates for two years. We had many of the same classes together, we participated in the same clubs and societies, and she inserted herself into my growing circle of friends. She even started dating my BFF.

In my fourth year, the friendship started to unravel. I was doing postgraduate studies in a different subject to her. I'd moved out of our flat. I was making new friends and developing new interests. I started dating a guy she didn't like. She felt like she was losing me – this person who was so important to her life and her sense of self.

She was frightened, I think. And her fear pushed her behaviour to greater extremes. She became obsessive, demanding to know where I was every moment, controlling my life, forbidding me to go out without her. She accused me of lying, of stealing from her. She created elaborate scenarios in her head where I had wronged her and had to make amends. I moved her into my new flat, hoping that some proximity would help her to calm down. Instead, she grew more erratic and obsessive.

My boyfriend at the time saw all this happening. He watched me become fearful of this person who was supposed to be my friend. He noted me trying to appease her, cancelling plans because they'd upset her, choosing her over my schoolwork, retreating into my shell.

He knew I was giving into her because of my past, because I was so grateful to have a friend that I didn't want to lose her. He could see she was taking advantage of my nature to control me.

One day, my friend and I had a particular horrible fight about something. I was staying at his house, and I was terrified to go back to my flat because she was there.

My boyfriend couldn't watch me hurt anymore. He drove me to the flat. He insisted on coming inside with me. Just having him by my side made me feel stronger.

He marched up to her and he told her that she was going to lose me as a friend if she continued what she was doing. He didn't raise his voice. He didn't call her names. He calmly laid out how she was acting and what it was doing to me. He reiterated how much he cared about me and he wouldn't stand by and watch me hurt.

It was the first time in my life I remember someone standing up for me. Listening to him speak to her that day was like hearing him speak to every one of my old bullies.

Reader, I married him.

Time and again in my life my husband has stood up for me, stepping in where I wasn't strong enough. And I've done the same for him – I've been the lighthouse to his ocean when he needed me most. Now, I don't need him to fight for me, because he helped me uncover the strength to fight for myself.

I'm not Hazel, and she isn't me. She's way more badass. She says the things that I think of an hour after a confrontation and *wished* I'd said.

Hazel doesn't need no man to help her find her strength. But I hope as the series progresses, you'll see how Trey, Ayaz, and Quinn can become her lighthouses when she needs them most.

I know this note is insanely long. Bear with me – I just have a few peeps to thank!

To the cantankerous drummer husband, for reading this manuscript in record time and giving me so many ideas to make it better. And for being my lighthouse.

To Kit, Bri, Elaina, Katya, Emma, and Jamie, for all the writerly encouragement and advice. To Meg, for the epically helpful editing job, and to Amanda for the stunning cover. To Sam and Iris, for the daily Facebook shenanigans that help keep me sane while I spend my days stuck at home covered in cats.

To you, the reader, for going on this journey with me, even though it's led to some dark places. Warning: if you thought book 1 was tough, book 2 is a whopper. Get it here – http:// books2read.com/initiated.

If you're enjoying *Kings of Miskatonic Prep* and want to read more from me, check out my dark reverse harem high school romance series, *Stonehurst Prep* – http://books2read.com/ mystolenlife. This series is contemporary romance (no ghosts or vampires), but it's pretty dark and strange and mysterious, with a badass heroine and three guys who will break your heart and melt your panties. You will LOVE it – you'll find a short preview on the next page.

Another series of mine you might enjoy is *Manderley Academy*. Book 1 is *Ghosted* and it's a classic gothic tale of ghosts and betrayal, creepy old houses and three beautifully haunted guys with dark secrets. Plus, a kickass curvy heroine. Check it out: http://books2read.com/manderley1

Every week I send out a newsletter to fans – it features a spooky story about a real-life haunting or strange criminal case that has inspired one of my books, as well as news about upcoming releases and a free book of bonus scenes called *Cabinet of Curiosities*. To get on the mailing list all you gotta do is head to my website: http://www.steffanieholmes.com/newsletter

If you want to hang out and talk about all things *Shunned*, my readers are sharing their theories and discussing the book over in my Facebook group, Books That Bite. Come join the fun.

I'm so happy you enjoyed this story! I'd love it if you wanted to leave a review on Amazon or Goodreads. It will help other readers to find their next read.

Thank you, thank you! I love you heaps! Until next time.

Steff

EXCERPT: INITIATED
Kings of Miskatonic Prep 2

Enjoy this short teaser from book 2, Initiated.

"We've checked the entire eastern wing, Headmistress," Professor Atwood said. "Hazel's not there."

"She can't have gotten far," Headmistress West snapped. Flashlight beams bounced across the grounds. "Alert the maintenance staff. Send them down the peninsula to guard the road. That girl cannot be allowed to leave the grounds alive."

Her words were a shard of ice, thawing the fire inside me.

That girl cannot be allowed to leave the grounds alive.

If I'd wanted evidence, I had it now. But what could I do? Where could I go? For the first time, the helplessness of my situation washed over me. There was no one I could trust at this school. I had no family, no one to call for help. Even if I did make it down to the town of Arkham, what good would it do? The police wouldn't believe anything I told them. "The teachers are trying to kill me, Officer." Yeah, right. I hardly believed it myself.

Something brushed my ankle. I spun around, my heart leaping into my throat. Quinn's face peeked out from between the rocks. He held out a hand to me, fingers reaching, grasping at air.

"Trust me," he mouthed.

Trust me.

Something invisible reached through the air between us – a flare of heat that sizzled against my skin. I flashed back to the gymnasium, where Quinn dragged me to safety before those shadowed things got to me. In a surge of heat, my body remembered the brush of his lips against mine and the times he'd let his guard down around me and had been more than Quinn the tormentor, Quinn the trickster.

The beam of a flashlight flickered across the rocks, just above my head. The voices drew closer. It wouldn't be long until they were right on top of me.

Whatever Trey, Ayaz, and Quinn are involved in, they're trying to help me.

I think.

Maybe.

I hope.

It was all I had to go on. But it was better than being caught by Headmistress West.

I reached out and took Quinn's hand. A pulse of heat flared up my arm. I allowed Quinn to pull me under the ledge. We slithered through a narrow gap and dropped down into a pitch-black cave. My ass cracked against wet rock as I slid and skidded down a steeply sloping rock face. Just as my feet slammed into flat rock and I wrenched myself upright, a flashlight beam passed over the entrance several feet above my head, flickering through the space without penetrating it.

"I've got her," Quinn whispered, one hand circling my wrist, the other resting protectively against my hip, radiating warmth through my clammy skin.

A match struck. A moment later, a lantern burst into flame, illuminating Trey's face. He appeared stricken. Dirt smudged along his cheek, humanizing his too-perfect, too-pretty features.

"Hey, Meat," he said, his voice barely above a whisper. "You've decided to trust us."

"Don't make me regret it," I growled. "Where am I?"

Trey swept the lantern around him, casting the warm glow of the flame against unyielding stone. Unlike the secret tunnel connecting the storage room on my floor to the pleasure garden, this cave was rough – not hollowed out by humans or machines, but formed from water being forced up from somewhere deep underground, reshaping the rock, bedding planes and fractures in the immovable chunks and creating a giant's staircase of abutting shelves leading down into an oppressive black hole. Stalactites hung from the underside of the rock shelf above our heads – a hundred tiny swords of Damocles just waiting to drop on me.

I noticed a row of lanterns and a waterproof box resting on a low shelf behind Trey. A symbol had been scrawled into the wall – the same runic symbol I'd seen tattooed on the guys' wrists. Someone had definitely been hanging out in this cave.

Something slapped against the wet floor. I whirled around and stared at that dark hole. Trey thrust out his arm. The lantern illuminated the muscled slope of Ayaz's shoulders as he straightened up on one of the lower shelves.

"They're heading back to the cavern," he called up to us. "We have to hurry."

"Hurry where?" I demanded.

"To the place where you'll get your answers." Ayaz sounded exasperated, as though this was obvious.

"Why can't I get my answers here?" I wrenched my hip away from Quinn and folded my arms across my chest.

"We can't explain, Hazy. You won't believe us."

"Try me."

"There's no point. The whole thing is so fucking unbelievable, I barely accept it, and I'm living it." There was a hint of a smile in Quinn's voice. He couldn't take *anything* seriously. "Perhaps 'living' is the wrong word."

"Quinn, shut up," Trey snapped. He tried to grab my arm, but I jerked it away. "We have to go."

"I don't see why I should go anywhere with you," I shot back.

"Fine. Go back to school and report us." Trey gestured to the mouth of the cave above our heads. When I didn't budge, he added, "Or, come with us and find out what's actually going on."

The lantern caught a glint in Trey's eye – a hint of his usual arrogance. As much as I hated Trey for all the times he'd burrowed into my weaknesses and exposed them, he *knew* me. We were bitter enemies because something inside us recognized an affinity with the other – an equal capacity for cruelty, a duplicitous desire to control, to know everything. I hated that Trey knew me without my permission, but neither of us could take back what he'd done now.

Trey knew that if he turned away from me and started clambering down into that darkness, toward the answers, I'd follow him.

Damn him, he was right.

TO BE CONTINUED

Secrets. Lies. Sacrifice. Find out what happens next in book 2 of the Kings of Miskatonic Prep, *Initiated*

Read now:
http://books2read.com/initiated

Or devour the entire Kings of Miskatonic Prep series (with bonus POV scenes) in the boxset:
http://books2read.com/miskatonicbox

MORE FROM THE AUTHOR OF SHUNNED

From the author of *Shunned*, the Amazon top-20 bestselling bully romance readers are calling, "The greatest mindf**k of 2019," comes this new dark contemporary high school reverse harem romance.

Psst. I have a secret.

Are you ready?

I'm Mackenzie Malloy, and everyone thinks they know who I am.

Five years ago, I disappeared.

No one has seen me or my family outside the walls of Malloy Manor since.
But now I'm coming to reclaim my throne:
The Ice Queen of Stonehurst Prep is back.

Standing between me and my everything?
Three things can bring me down:
The sweet guy who wants answers from his former friend.
The rock god who wants to f*ck me.
The king who'll crush me before giving up his crown.

They think they can ruin me, wreck it all, but I won't let them.
I'm not the Mackenzie Eli used to know.
Hot boys and rock gods like Gabriel won't win me over.
And just like Noah, I'll kill to keep my crown.

I'm just a poor little rich girl with the stolen life.
I'm here to tear down three princes,
before they destroy me.

Read now:
http://books2read.com/mystolenlife

EXCERPT: MY STOLEN LIFE

Stonehurst Prep

I roll over in bed and slam against a wall.

Huh? Odd.

My bed isn't pushed against a wall. I must've twisted around in my sleep and hit the headboard. I do thrash around a lot, especially when I have bad dreams, and tonights was particularly gruesome. My mind stretches into the silence, searching for the tendrils of my nightmare. *I'm lying in bed and some dark shadow comes and lifts me up, pinning my arms so they hurt. He drags me downstairs to my mother, slumped in her favorite chair. At first, I think she passed out drunk after a night at the club, but then I see the dark pool expanding around her feet, staining the designer rug.*

I see the knife handle sticking out of her neck.

I see her glassy eyes rolled toward the ceiling.

I see the window behind her head, and my own reflection in the glass, my face streaked with blood, my eyes dark voids of pain and hatred.

But it's okay now. It was just a dream. It's—

OW.

I hit the headboard again. I reach down to rub my elbow, and my hand grazes a solid wall of satin. On my other side.

What the hell?

I open my eyes into a darkness that is oppressive and complete, the kind of darkness I'd never see inside my princess bedroom with its flimsy purple curtains letting in the glittering skyline of the city. The kind of darkness that folds in on me, pressing me against the hard, un-bedlike surface I lie on.

Now the panic hits.

I throw out my arms, kick with my legs. I hit walls. Walls all around me, lined with satin, dense with an immense weight pressing from all sides. Walls so close I can't sit up or bend my knees. I scream, and my scream bounces back at me, hollow and weak.

I'm in a coffin. I'm in a motherfucking coffin, and I'm *still alive*.

I scream and scream and scream. The sound fills my head and stabs at my brain. I know all I'm doing is using up my precious oxygen, but I can't make myself stop. In that scream I lose myself, and every memory of who I am dissolves into a puddle of terror.

When I do stop, finally, I gasp and pant, and I taste blood and stale air on my tongue. A cold fear seeps into my bones. Am I dying? My throat crawls with invisible bugs. Is this what it feels like to die?

I hunt around in my pockets, but I'm wearing purple pajamas, and the only thing inside is a bookmark Daddy gave me. I can't see it of course, but I know it has a quote from Julius Caesar on it. *Alea iacta est. The die is cast.*

Like fuck it is.

I think of Daddy, of everything he taught me – memories too dark to be obliterated by fear. Bile rises in my throat. I swallow, choke it back. Daddy always told me our world is forged in blood. I might be only thirteen, but I know who he is, what he's capable of. I've heard the whispers. I've seen the way people hurry to appease him whenever he enters a room. I've had the lessons from Antony in what to do if I find myself alone with one of Daddy's enemies.

Of course, they never taught me what to do if one of those enemies *buries me alive*.

I can't give up.

I claw at the satin on the lid. It tears under my fingers, and I pull out puffs of stuffing to reach the wood beneath. I claw at the surface, digging splinters under my nails. Cramps arc along my arm from the awkward angle. I know it's hopeless; I know I'll never be able to scratch my way through the wood. Even if I can, I *feel* the weight of several feet of dirt above me. I'd be crushed in moments. But I have to try.

I'm my father's daughter, and this is not how I die.

I claw and scratch and tear. I lose track of how much time passes in the tiny space. My ears buzz. My skin weeps with cold sweat.

A noise reaches my ears. A faint shifting. A scuffle. A scrape and thud above my head. Muffled and far away.

Someone piling the dirt in my grave.

Or maybe...

...maybe someone digging it out again.

Fuck, fuck, please.

"Help." My throat is hoarse from screaming. I bang the lid with my fists, not even feeling the splinters piercing my skin. "Help me!"

THUD. Something hits the lid. The coffin groans. My veins burn with fear and hope and terror.

The wood cracks. The lid is flung away. Dirt rains down on me, but I don't care. I suck in lungfuls of fresh, crisp air. A circle of light blinds me. I fling my body up, up into the unknown. Warm arms catch me, hold me close.

"I found you, Claws." Only Antony calls me by that nickname. Of course, it would be my cousin who saves me. Antony drags me over the lip of the grave, *my* grave, and we fall into crackling leaves and damp grass.

I sob into his shoulder. Antony rolls me over, his fingers

pressing all over my body, checking if I'm hurt. He rests my back against cold stone. "I have to take care of this," he says. I watch through tear-filled eyes as he pushes the dirt back into the hole – into what was supposed to be my grave – and brushes dead leaves on top. When he's done, it's impossible to tell the ground's been disturbed at all.

I tremble all over. I can't make myself stop shaking. Antony comes back to me and wraps me in his arms. He staggers to his feet, holding me like I'm weightless. He's only just turned eighteen, but already he's built like a tank.

I let out a terrified sob. Antony glances over his shoulder, and there's panic in his eyes. "You've got to be quiet, Claws," he whispers. "They might be nearby. I'm going to get you out of here."

I can't speak. My voice is gone, left in the coffin with my screams. Antony hoists me up and darts into the shadows. He runs with ease, ducking between rows of crumbling gravestones and beneath bent and gnarled trees. Dimly, I recognize this place – the old Emerald Beach cemetery, on the edge of Beaumont Hills overlooking the bay, where the original families of Emerald Beach buried their dead.

Where someone tried to bury me.

Antony bursts from the trees onto a narrow road. His car is parked in the shadows. He opens the passenger door and settles me inside before diving behind the wheel and gunning the engine.

We tear off down the road. Antony rips around the deadly corners like he's on a racetrack. Steep cliffs and crumbling old mansions pass by in a blur.

"My parents..." I gasp out. "Where are my parents?"

"I'm sorry, Claws. I didn't get to them in time. I only found you."

I wait for this to sink in, for the fact I'm now an orphan to hit me in a rush of grief. But I'm numb. My body won't stop shaking, and I left my brain and my heart buried in the silence of that coffin.

"Who?" I ask, and I fancy I catch a hint of my dad's cold savagery in my voice. "Who did this?"

"I don't know yet, but if I had to guess, it was Brutus. I warned your dad that he was making alliances and building up to a challenge. I think he's just made his move."

I try to digest this information. Brutus – who was once my father's trusted friend, who'd eaten dinner at our house and played Chutes and Ladders with me – killed my parents and buried me alive. But it bounces off the edge of my skull and doesn't stick. The life I had before, my old life, it's gone, and as I twist and grasp for memories, all I grab is stale coffin air.

"What now?" I ask.

Antony tosses his phone into my lap. "Look at the headlines."

I read the news app he's got open, but the words and images blur together. "This... this doesn't make any sense..."

"They think you're dead, Claws," Antony says. "That means you have to *stay* dead until we're strong enough to move against him. Until then, you have to be a ghost. But don't worry, I'll protect you. I've got a plan. We'll hide you where they'll never think to look."

Keep reading:
www.books2read.com/mystolenlife

OTHER BOOKS BY STEFFANIE HOLMES

This list is in recommended reading order, although each couple's story can be enjoyed as a standalone.

Nevermore Bookshop Mysteries

A Dead and Stormy Night

Of Mice and Murder

Pride and Premeditation

How Heathcliff Stole Christmas

Memoirs of a Garroter

Prose and Cons

A Novel Way to Die

Much Ado About Murder

Kings of Miskatonic Prep

Shunned

Initiated

Possessed

Ignited

Stonehurst Prep

My Stolen Life

My Secret Heart

My Broken Crown

My Savage Kingdom

Manderley Academy

Ghosted

Haunted

Spirited

Briarwood Witches

Earth and Embers

Fire and Fable

Water and Woe

Wind and Whispers

Spirit and Sorrow

Crookshollow Gothic Romance

Art of Cunning (Alex & Ryan)

Art of the Hunt (Alex & Ryan)

Art of Temptation (Alex & Ryan)

The Man in Black (Elinor & Eric)

Watcher (Belinda & Cole)

Reaper (Belinda & Cole)

Wolves of Crookshollow

Digging the Wolf (Anna & Luke)

Writing the Wolf (Rosa & Caleb)

Inking the Wolf (Bianca & Robbie)

Wedding the Wolf (Willow & Irvine)

Want to be informed when the next Steffanie Holmes paranormal romance story goes live? Sign up for the newsletter at www.steffanieholmes.com/newsletter to get the scoop, and score a free collection of bonus scenes and stories to enjoy!

ABOUT THE AUTHOR

Steffanie Holmes is the *USA Today* bestselling author of the paranormal, gothic, dark, and fantastical. Her books feature clever, witty heroines, secret societies, creepy old mansions and alpha males who *always* get what they want.

Legally-blind since birth, Steffanie received the 2017 Attitude Award for Artistic Achievement. She was also a finalist for a 2018 Women of Influence award.

Steff is the creator of *Rage Against the Manuscript* – a resource of free content, books, and courses to help writers tell their story, find their readers, and build a badass writing career.

Steffanie lives in New Zealand with her husband, a horde of cantankerous cats, and their medieval sword collection.

STEFFANIE HOLMES NEWSLETTER

Grab a free copy *Cabinet of Curiosities* – a Steffanie Holmes compendium of short stories and bonus scenes – when you sign up for updates with the Steffanie Holmes newsletter.

http://www.steffanieholmes.com/newsletter

Come hang with Steffanie
www.steffanieholmes.com
hello@steffanieholmes.com

Made in the USA
Middletown, DE
30 April 2021